CHRISTMAS AT THE LITTLE WAFFLE SHACK

HELEN ROLFE

Boldwood

First published in Great Britain in 2020.

This paperback edition first published in 2022 by Boldwood Books.

I

Copyright © Helen Rolfe, 2020

Cover Design by CC Book Design

Cover Photography: Shutterstock

A CIP catalogue record for this book is available from the British Library.

Paperback ISBN: 978-1-80483-656-9

Ebook ISBN: 978-1-80415-579-0

Kindle ISBN: 978-1-80415-578-3

Audio CD ISBN: 978-1-80415-570-7

Digital audio download ISBN: 978-1-80415-573-8

Large Print ISBN: 978-1-80415-577-6

Boldwood Books Ltd.

23 Bowerdean Street, London, SW6 3TN

www.boldwoodbooks.com

MIX
Paper from
responsible sources
FSC® C171272

For my readers... thank you for picking up this book and the others I have written along the way. I hope you enjoy reading the stories as much as I love writing them.

1

With only three weeks to go until Christmas day, Lucy couldn't wait for her gorgeous Fraser fir to be delivered from the local farm. She'd selected it herself, which had felt like a fitting way to mark her first official Christmas living here in the village. The months had rolled on since she'd moved here back in the summer and she was slowly beginning to feel a part of life in the Cove.

She pulled the plug in the kitchen sink and let the water drain as Shadow, the slate-grey cat she'd adopted a month ago from a shelter, appeared and stretched languorously, clawing the carpet. 'Hey, use your scratching post,' she suggested, but he took no notice. At least the carpet was old. Maybe when Lucy updated the floor coverings in the compact two-bedroom flat above the Heritage Cove blacksmith's workshop Shadow would be settled as much as she was and more willing to conform. She flopped down on the sofa and Shadow jumped into her lap. At the shelter she'd wanted to take every single cat in there, give them a brighter future, let them grow old and live out life to its full potential, but Shadow had been the first to run to her, the one who wouldn't leave her be, and he'd won her over just like that. She hated to think the other felines might not get such a happy ending but she knew she couldn't save all of them.

Shadow purred away contentedly. It was still dark outside and all the lights in the flat were on. It wasn't a good look for this place, it merely highlighted the fact that the entire flat needed a face lift. The carpets were just the start of it. The cream Formica benchtops in the kitchen were stained, the laminate walnut cupboards had seen better days, and the light fittings throughout wouldn't raise more than a couple of quid in a car-boot sale – and that would only be to someone trying to resurrect a look from the seventies.

In the warmer months ahead Lucy intended to make the flat her focus. She could see a lavender feature wall in the spacious bedroom, gleaming white tiles in the kitchen, a fresh shade of paint in the lounge. Her new home wasn't very big, it didn't need to be, but she could still make it special. The galley kitchen was first port of call when you came in the back entrance from the steps leading up from the workshop, then an archway led to the lounge area where the sofa and an armchair offered comfort, then through on the other side were two bedrooms – one not really big enough for anything more than her surplus belongings – and a bathroom that wasn't completely decrepit but definitely needed bringing into this decade.

A rattle from the pane of glass in the window that looked out onto The Street, the main road running through Heritage Cove lined with shops and small businesses, made her jump. It didn't seem to bother Shadow, whose eyes were closed in pleasure at the comfy spot he'd bagged before the rest of the village even woke up, but Lucy hoped it wasn't as miserable out there as it had been yesterday when it'd poured with rain, a tree had come down blocking the main road into the village, and howling winds coupled with plummeting temperatures had made even a trip to the Copper Plough, the Cove's local pub, traumatic. Wintry weather made Lucy want to hunker down inside, cosy up in her flat and appreciate her independence. Some might think she was lonely, but she was very happy with her own company. Far better to be on your own than with someone who was completely wrong for you. Her friends at the pub last night had tried to get her talking about her love life, looked around at the local talent or anyone who'd come in from afar and might be perfect for Lucy, but with Christmas fast approaching she wasn't interested in getting carried away in the romanticism of it all. She had her own business, a place to live, she had Shadow, and she had Heritage Cove. Right now, there was no place else she'd rather be.

Shadow's purrs of contentment were accompanied by dribble seeping into the arm of the sofa. A gift from Lucy's ex-husband Julian's gran, the sofa and matching armchair were floral efforts with enough bounce to mimic a trampoline, and they were neither attractive nor comfortable. When Lucy had split up with Julian they'd divided the furniture between them and she'd taken this combo because although it was a gift, it was less valuable than either the rosewood dining table that had been in his family for generations or the early-nineteenth-century bookcase Julian had found at an antiques fair in Surrey and brought home thinking she'd fall in love with it. She hadn't. And their finances hadn't either. But it had been typical of Julian to go off and act impulsively without considering the consequences. She'd been glad to walk away from the house they'd shared with all her personal belongings, the spare bed, most of the kitchenware, the vintage storage chest she'd bought on holiday in Scotland, and the sofa and armchair. And although the soft furnishings weren't very attractive or comfortable, at least they fitted in the flat once they were up here. The removal men had had a terrible job getting the sofa through the door though. They'd used the wide staircase that came up from the workshop but the door wasn't the biggest. Still, it was a better option than using the official entrance to the flat, which was at the top of an incredibly narrow flight of concrete steps leading up from the end of the path that went out to The Street. They'd taken one look at that on moving-in day and shaken their heads.

'I hope you're going to behave yourself when my tree arrives later,' Lucy told Shadow, still fussing over him. He was a distraction when she needed to get on with her working day. She'd never been one to sleep in and because her business was right downstairs without a commute, early starts were easy. It also meant she got to finish up at a decent time and have the evenings to herself. 'No playing with the ornaments,' she warned him, already wondering how it was going to go with a Christmas tree and a cat in such a tight space. Her mum had already sent her several GIFs of cats wreaking havoc with Christmas trees, using their paws to swipe anything within reach.

With a final fuss between the ears for Shadow, Lucy turned the heating dial down a little now the flat had warmed up – the decor might be old-school but the heating and water system were not, something she was very grateful for now it was December. She pulled on her Blundstones – hardy footwear was a must when you were working with metals, heat and tools all day long. Her dungarees were a key feature of her blacksmith wardrobe too and she had enough pairs in khaki to last a whole week. It was usually a pair a day, they got so mucky and dusty.

She opened the back door to the flat ready to go down to her workshop. *Her Workshop*. It had a good ring to it. She put the lights on from upstairs and, pulling the door closed behind her, went down to start work.

In the run-up to Christmas her list of bespoke requests had

grown with people wanting gifts made and ready to wrap in time. Today she'd get to work on a trivet commissioned by Barney, a local man who was everyone's favourite. He'd had his fair share of ups and downs and now, at seventy-three years to her thirty, he was the one with another half to buy a gift for this year. The trivet was for Lois, the love of his life, who had a passion for cooking. He'd thought it would be perfect, something hand-crafted by a local, and Lucy had got a little thrill at his use of the word *local*. She was beginning to feel part of the tapestry of Heritage Cove, the little village on a mostly forgotten stretch of the Suffolk coast.

Lucy had first come here to work as a temporary blacksmith for Fred Gilbertson, who'd been taking leave from his job. Her remit was to work on any existing orders for customers and keep the business ticking over. But when she and Fred had danced at the Wedding Dress Ball in the summer – an annual event that was as much a part of the Cove as were the pub, the tea rooms and bakery, the chapel and the little track that led down to the water's edge – he'd told her he was ready to retire for good. It was time someone else took over, he'd told her, and he really wanted that person to be her. Fred, a wonderful, kind man, hadn't dragged his feet with the sale and now the business as well as the flat belonged to Lucy. She'd carried on with the few clients Fred had on his records but, unlike Fred, she wasn't a farrier. Her work instead focused mainly on bespoke items made from forged steel and wrought iron and she'd made everything from garden benches, light fixtures and decorative garden gates to smaller household items including candlestick holders that she'd supplied to Tilly at Tilly's Bits 'n' Pieces, decorative bowls for the table at home, coat hooks, coasters and ornaments.

She heated up the solid fuel forge. She'd got used to using it now and although it wasn't needed as much nowadays in her line of work, it was something passed down to her by Fred. He'd used the same methods for years and part of her wanted to respect that and not completely rip everything apart and get rid of his mark on the place. She knew she could, the business was hers, but this forge felt as much a part of it as she now was. She found it quite fun using it too – loading up the fuel, seeing it glow. Lucy loved her job. She always had. And even though she'd never been encouraged by those around her, she'd known this was what she wanted. Sometimes she felt as if she should pat herself on the back because she'd ignored everyone else's doubts and gone right out there and got what she wanted. Her parents had come around eventually and they saw the joy she got from her work, her determination and now her success. Her ex, Julian, had never quite got it.

She went over to the desk on the side of the workshop that the stairs from her flat came into. This was the side of the workshop she let potential customers linger in rather than the messier, more industrial side with the equipment that would be dangerous in the wrong hands, risky if you weren't careful. Along with the desk was a filing cabinet, a couple of chairs, and shelves displaying some of her work that was available for sale. Usually items were made to order but sometimes she made extras and sold them to people who came in on the off-chance or found buyers via her website. From the desk drawer she took out the ring binder with commissions detailed inside – as a blacksmith she usually had multiple projects on the go; she was sure this was where the phrase 'many irons in the fire' had originated from – and she recapped the details from the sheet of paper on top, the worksheets gradually collecting marks from dust and dirt as she flicked back and forth between projects. It was a 'dirty' job, which Julian had discouraged her progression in, but she'd thought one day she may prove him wrong, he might get over it and see for himself as she succeeded that it was a career path that made her happy. But he'd been blinkered to so many things. And so had she.

Lucy found a playlist on her iPod and set it to blast out through the speakers in her workshop. Loud music on while she worked was a must, it motivated her, and luckily she didn't have to worry about having a neighbour as this whole place was detached. The ice-cream shop was a few metres away on one side and wouldn't be open until much later today, on the other side of her was the bus stop so anyone waiting there would probably enjoy some Christmas music if they could hear it, and beyond that there was nothing but the village field where the big Christmas tree now stood in all its finery and a log cabin had gone up in place of an old beach-supplies shop. Nobody had any idea what the log cabin was going to be either. Word had it that it could potentially be an eatery, but no one knew for sure and speculation as well as excitement were mounting in Heritage Cove.

Lucy couldn't help bopping a bit to the Christmas tunes blaring out. She found a length of metal from one of her collection buckets of materials through on the other side of the workshop and, sure the forge was hot enough, put as much of the length as was needed into the fire. Once it was heated and red-hot she took it over to the anvil and, with the hot end in the pritchel hole, she pulled down on the cool end of the metal to bend it into a curve. She did this with another piece, each time banging the curves a bit more to produce an attractive curly edge. The pieces had to be cooled, measured and marked for their centres to have dents made, then, using another red-hot piece of cylindrical metal through the centre, she banged it into place along with another four cylindrical pieces, one on each corner, to make the feet. She finished by putting the entire trivet into the forge, held by her blacksmith tongs, pulled it out and used a hammer to ensure it was shaped well. The final touch was using a wire brush to smooth it off and she set it onto a rack at the side with other pieces she'd left there waiting for the next step – a wine-bottle holder she wanted to add an engraved shiny metal label to, a four-piece tealight holder that only needed a shine giving to it before it was ready, and the fourth coat hook she would add to three others on a wooden panel.

Time for a break and some very fresh air. She'd struggled in here in the summer, sweating profusely as she worked away, her femininity all but forgotten, and now the forge kept the workshop so warm she needed a breather. She opened the door and despite the frostiness that barrelled towards her on a wind from The Street, she took a minute to appreciate the cool blast.

Leaving the door open to cool the place down a bit, she went back into the workshop and moved on to another so-called 'iron' in her fire – this time a wine rack for Hazel, who ran the riding stables in Heritage Cove. She'd had to inform Hazel that Fred wasn't coming back and so they wouldn't be able to return to using him as their farrier, but there hadn't been any hard feelings. Hazel said they were happy with the alternative farrier they'd been using and she'd welcomed Lucy to the Cove in the same way everyone else had. Hazel's brother had placed the order for this item, getting in early with his Christmas list and keen to avoid a big shopping centre. He'd come in one day and browsed the items Lucy already had made up – a picture frame, a clock, a fancy bowl for chips and dips – but he hadn't been sold and so she'd sketched out a couple of alternatives. It was what she loved about bespoke work – coming up with something a client may not even have thought of. He'd loved one of her ideas in particular – a wine rack of sorts that held a bottle of wine at the bottom on its side, another at a right angle to that one, and above, two glasses could be held upright. The rack would be made by joining horseshoes together, making sure the horseshoes were the correct size so the glasses didn't fall through, so the bottles would slot in just so.

For this project Lucy was going to use her stick welder. She might be called a blacksmith but really that encompassed a multitude of roles – designer, artist, welder, metalworker. The term 'blacksmith' was a little old but with Heritage Cove being quaint and traditional, the name kind of fitted. It was one of the reasons she kept the solid fuel forge going too – when customers visited her premises to collect bespoke items, it felt like part of the magic to have the forge burning away; she'd always make sure it was on, the bright red coals giving the place a glow and the smell of hard work and creativity.

Lucy found her welding hood from the shelf next to her desk and popped it on. The hood was one of the most important pieces of protective equipment and would shield her eyes and skin from the sparks and vision-damaging ultraviolet and infrared rays emitted by the bright electric arc that would be created. The current would come through the arc welding machine and, by means of a metal rod that she would touch to the workpiece in question, it made a closed circuit. When you pulled the rod away the arc was created and it was one of the most efficient ways to fuse two pieces of metal together.

She positioned the horseshoes she'd already shaped in the forge onto the anvil, before flipping the visor of her helmet down. Ready to make a start, she thought she saw something move in the corner of her eye. She flipped her visor back up, holding it this time. It needed tightening so it would stay up on her head when she needed it to and, seeing nothing unusual, assuming she'd imagined the movement, she was about to make the adjustment to her headgear when she got a sickening feeling in the pit of her stomach. The flash of 'something' that she'd seen had been grey, hadn't it? But she'd shut the door upstairs – Shadow couldn't have got out, surely?

She was being daft. The visor had already fallen down again but as she picked up the rod held in the grip of a special clamp attached to the machine, she saw something again, and this time she knew it was Shadow. She put everything down and switched off the machine. No sudden movements as the front door was open and she knew he'd likely dart out of there if he thought this was a game. She'd let him out twice since she'd brought him home. He'd been hesitant both times and was easily spooked, but when she turned now he was eyeing the door as though it led to nirvana.

'Here, Shadow,' she said in a high-pitched voice, the one she used when it was feeding time. But he wasn't stupid, his tummy would already be full from this morning's breakfast and he didn't budge. She took another step forward, repeated her entreaty. But when the wind caught the upstairs door, which she mustn't have shut properly, it made an almighty bang against the wall and the cat scarpered.

Lucy ran out of the workshop after Shadow, who looked like he was in a race he didn't intend to lose. She bolted down the path in the morning that might be creeping into daylight hours but was far from being bright. She held her visor up as she chased Shadow along The Street, looking out for icy patches just in case. Every now and then the cat stopped, turned, and copper eyes filled with mischief looked at her before he carried on running away.

Steel-toe-capped boots weren't the best footwear to be running in either as Lucy legged it behind the bus stop, across the field and past the village Christmas tree, calling Shadow's name. He'd run all the way over to the new log cabin, alongside it and behind. Lucy followed and around the back of the cabin lost sight of him. The brambles were overgrown, the owner obviously had some landscaping to do, but she searched fruitlessly, calling for him.

'Please don't let him be lost,' Lucy muttered to herself. 'Please don't let me be the woman who adopts a pet and sends it to a worse place than it came from.'

Her bare arms began to feel the cold as she tramped back down the other side of the cabin, one hand holding up her visor. She looked in more of the scrub, her visor flopping down yet again, and this time she gave up with it. Face covered, she suspected she looked something like a knight from the Middle Ages with her headgear but all she really cared about now was finding Shadow.

She turned to walk along the front of the log cabin but yelped when she bumped into the solidity of a man she hadn't expected, his chest hard beneath a chunky fisherman's jumper. She took a couple of steps back and so did he. In fact, he went all the way back to the safety of the veranda at the front of the cabin.

'I don't know what you want,' his deep voice rumbled, 'but I don't have anything to steal. And if it's money you're after, you'll have no luck here.'

What on earth was he rambling on about? she wondered. And it was then she spotted Shadow.

The man spotted the cat too when Shadow decided to check out this stranger by jumping onto the railing of the veranda, and Shadow wasted no time being traitorous by sidling up to the man until the stranger scooped him up in one protective arm. 'Please leave,' he demanded as though she were a cat killer looking for her next victim.

'Not without my cat,' she said, forgetting her mask was down. He didn't appear to have heard a word with the wind howling around them yet again. She was starting to feel the cold too – all the more reason to get out of here now before she developed frostbite.

He stood his ground and somehow it amused Lucy. He was clearly wary of her. Perhaps it was the mask that freaked him out; she never usually had this effect on men. In the dim light, all he'd be able to see was a character in dungarees wearing a helmet as though about to go into battle, and thinking she looked kind of threatening gave her a bit of a thrill.

But all of a sudden, she didn't find it quite so funny. He didn't look friendly, he was bigger than her, and here they were at the back of a field that nobody frequented in the winter months unless they were after a good vantage point for the Cove's Christmas tree. He could be a squatter, he could be the one trespassing rather than her. What if he'd followed her around here and wanted her to let her guard down so he could do unspeakable things to her? Her mouth went dry and all she wanted was to get Shadow and be on her way.

But Shadow looked alarmingly comfortable in this man's arms.

And now Lucy had no idea whether she needed to save the cat or save herself.

She tried a different approach, loosened her helmet and pulled it up and off her head, sending straight blonde locks cascading all the way down her back.

Judging by the way he was looking at her now, he hadn't expected that.

2

_____

When the helmeted figure revealed its identity, Daniel tried not to let his jaw drop all the way to the wooden base of the veranda he was standing on. He hadn't expected someone quite so beautiful to be creeping around his waffle shack, and he hadn't expected to be lost for words either. He'd thought it was surely a kid hidden under all that gear and wondered what juvenile delinquent in their right mind got out of bed this early to rob somewhere that hadn't opened to the public yet. There wasn't even much equipment to take unless you were game enough to take on nicking the cooker or the enormous fridge. Not even the waffle makers were inside yet – he had those back at the cottage he was renting so he could try out flavour combinations.

He finally found his tongue when he realised what she was telling him. He looked at the cat in his arms. 'He's yours?'

'He is and he ran off, I had no choice but to chase him in my work gear. Sorry about that, didn't mean to scare you.'

'You didn't.' She had but he wasn't going to admit that. Scared of a girl? Not a chance.

She put her helmet down and gestured for him to hand the

cat over from where it was comfortably snuggled against his chest keeping him warm. He handed the feline to its owner and caught a distinct waft of fresh flowers from her hair that was nothing but feminine and at odds with her dungarees, a T-shirt that had something resembling oil smeared on it and a helmet that he really wanted to point out didn't display her most attractive features nearly enough. She wasn't tall – about a foot less than his six-foot-five by his estimations – and she had rosy cheeks as though she'd done a workout before he'd even dragged himself out of bed this morning.

'I'm Daniel, by the way.' He held out his hand and she managed to pull hers out from beneath the cat's new position against her chest to return the gesture. 'I own this place.'

'I'm Lucy.' It seemed his self-introduction as business owner didn't impress her. She didn't smile; she still seemed wary, especially when he reached out to stroke the cat again.

He picked up her helmet for her and she gestured for him to loop it over the arm she was holding out, her other clutching the cat. He backed off as soon as he'd done it because no matter that she'd apologised for scaring him, it seemed the roles had been reversed. He tried to be a little friendly, he was a local again now after all. 'Does the cat have a name?'

'Shadow.'

He nodded. 'What happened to his ear?' There was a chunk taken out of it, not that it seemed to bother Shadow.

'I'm not sure, I try not to think about it really. I adopted him from the shelter recently and I don't think he had a very happy life before.'

So that was what made her dash over here. He'd thought it a bit of an overreaction when it was a cat. Cats wandered, it was normal, but her concern made sense now. 'So what's with the get-up, Lucy?' He leaned against the western-red-cedar post that stretched from the timber decking on the veranda to the roof of the porch. 'Are you in a medieval play? Should I expect a battle-field scene coming my way?'

She smiled, a sweet smile that grabbed him straight away. She looked about his age and he wondered who she was – he certainly didn't recognise her as anyone living here back when the Cove had been the only home he knew. He'd kept his return on the q.t. so far. He'd bought the old shop knowing exactly where it was, its surrounds and its potential, and after the shop was demolished a project manager had taken care of the planning and construction stages of the cabin. Daniel had been there in the background every step of the way but the project manager had also looked after the interior fit-out so he'd been able to stay away from Heritage Cove until now. When he'd wanted to come and check out progress, he'd done so quickly and discreetly. Otherwise, he suspected, there'd be trouble, and he wanted a chance to get this place ready first. Ready and almost open for business and then there couldn't be any question he was serious about this, that he was a changed man with responsibilities and a business of his own. He was well and truly standing on his own two feet. But not everyone would be happy about his return to the Cove and he knew he couldn't put off making his presence known forever.

'I'm the local blacksmith,' she answered.

He whistled from between his teeth. 'Fred, you've aged well.' He could tell she was hiding a laugh as she pressed a kiss to Shadow's fur. What he'd give to be that feline right now. 'Did he retire?'

'You know Fred?'

'I do. And actually I did send him a commission request.'

'You did? Sorry, what did you say your name was?'

'Daniel.'

'I do recall one request from a Daniel, for a sign, just with sizing, rough idea of materials to use, but no confirmation of the precise design or wording.'

'That'll be me.'

'No contact details either, just "Daniel" and a note that said you'll be in touch. I put it to the back of my work folder but it's still there. What's the sign for?'

'This place.' He looked behind him at the log cabin constructed mainly from Douglas fir, known for its strength, with western red cedar, known for its natural ability to resist decay. The entire log cabin was even more impressive than he'd envisaged and seeing it for the first time had left him feeling proud.

It was time for him to finally come home.

'And what is this place?'

'You're shivering.' He spotted the goose pimples all down her arms; he could see them every time her long locks of hair blew back.

'Funny name for a business,' she grinned. 'But yes, I'm bloody freezing and I can't afford to catch a cold with all the work I have on, so I'd better get going. I guess I'll see you around.'

'I hope so, Lucy.' He smiled after her, reached back for the mug of coffee he'd rested on the window ledge, turned, and leaned against the upright log and watched her go. 'I'll be in touch about the sign,' he called after her. She was definitely an unexpected bonus of being back in the village.

She turned and smiled once and then she was gone, out of sight.

Daniel had always liked Fred – he was a good sort, minded his own business and didn't interfere like some people. But Lucy? She was something else. And now the urgency to get the sign ready was something that would force him to get back into the village epicentre, The Street. He'd put it off long enough.

He swigged the remains of his coffee and headed back inside the log cabin. When the old shop had come up for sale he'd already been toying with the idea of moving back this way and it had been the signal he needed. These days he spoke to his mum, Carol, regularly and he knew she wanted him home even though she never put any pressure on him. But she wasn't the reason he thought twice about returning – it was his older brother, Harvey, who he hadn't spoken to in years and who would probably prefer him to stay away for good.

Daniel wasn't sure when the pivotal moment was that had shifted him and Harvey from brothers and comrades to boys who no longer hung out together and who went their separate ways, but that was what had happened. It seemed the worse things got at home with their father, Donnie, who bullied and belittled all of them, the more Daniel rebelled and got into trouble, and the more he got into trouble, the more Harvey resented him, and their mum didn't know which way to turn. It got to the point where Daniel could only see one solution: to leave. And so that was what he'd done. He'd thought Harvey and his mum would do better without him. And they had for a while. Donnie left and it looked as though it was for good, but when Daniel found out he'd shown up out of the blue one night and Harvey had had to fight him off, leaving him in a whole lot of trouble with the police until the truth surfaced, Daniel had almost fallen apart with guilt. He'd wondered how much Harvey had blamed him, how much he'd resented his brother for not being there to help him that night. When Daniel heard his dad had died suddenly and the family no longer had to worry about him ruining their lives, he had almost wept in relief for Harvey and his mum. But the damage to their family had been done. He'd left, and at the time Daniel couldn't see a way back.

Now, he knew he couldn't turn back the clock but he hoped

that in time Harvey might be able to see things his way too and understand why he'd acted the way he did.

Daniel shut the door to the cabin behind him. Standing outside in the cold with the beautiful Lucy for company and the backdrop of the village Christmas tree with its twinkling lights was one thing, but those charms aside, it was just plain freezing.

The heating in here was working a treat as he'd been assured it would. He didn't want it to be too stifling – he wanted it welcoming, just enough to encourage customers to order from his menu to warm themselves up on a winter's day. He'd always envisaged his business being in this kind of outlet so he'd been glad it was the very old shop that came up for sale rather than a sturdier, heritage listed building like some of the houses and premises were. It meant he'd been able to knock it down and start from scratch in creating a venue with character, a high-street eatery except not on the high street, a woodland escape except near people. All of these phrases and descriptions hadn't gone far to impress the bank's business loans advisor until he'd presented a proper business plan, but he'd got there in the end.

The Little Waffle Shack. That was the dream business Daniel was launching two weeks from now. He'd been advised to publicise but he'd held off for personal reasons, his back-up plan being the festive season that would send people in droves to look at the village Christmas tree, hungry and wanting to spend time outside with friends and neighbours, food bringing everyone together. Apart from that, he knew from his mum that locals were speculating, excitement was building about what this place could be, and that kind of buzz was something that advertised by itself. And before he distributed any flyers announcing the business, inviting everyone to opening night, he knew he'd have to announce his presence in the Cove. All he could do until then was ensure everything would be ready to wow the community, even those against him.

It was almost time for the Little Waffle Shack to be born. The outside was established apart from its sign, the tables and chairs for inside had arrived yesterday after dark and he'd already arranged them into the configuration he wanted. With your back to the door of the cabin, directly in front of you were four small tables each with four chairs, behind that the counter with a glass front to show off toppings and sauces and additions to the waffles on the menu. To the left of the counter a narrow corridor led to the kitchen behind, to the right was a bigger table to seat eight customers, another small table against the wall and then a separated-off smaller corridor leading to the bathrooms. The outside benches would arrive later today and with a metal finish to withstand the seasons; they were earmarked for the grass area out front that was part of Daniel's plot of land, bordering the village field. He could picture customers gathering and eating outside despite the cold, looking over at the big tree, talking about what Christmas would bring for them this year. And in the summer months he was going to get more ice-cream toppings on the menu and the grass area as well as the tables would be filled – at least, that's what he hoped. Or customers could opt for takeaway waffles if they so desired and wander off. Maybe it would be so busy that all tables were occupied and it would be the only option. He could hope, couldn't he?

His mum was coming by this afternoon to see the log cabin in all its glory now furniture had arrived. So far she'd only come over on the odd occasion during the building phase but she hadn't wanted to appear as though she knew more than anyone else or people would ask questions, and she knew Daniel needed his return to be done his way. He'd rewarded her silence with the promise of a sneak peek this afternoon, as well as the heart-shaped waffles he made her yesterday. He'd whipped up choco-late-peppermint batter and when the waffles were done he'd topped them with chocolate curls and a dollop of thick cream on the side. The sweet treats had more than met her approval and as they'd talked at his rented cottage he could tell she was proud, if a little trepidatious, about his homecoming. He also got the impression she was hopeful. Their family had been to hell and back in the past and Daniel knew there was nothing Carol Luddington wanted more than for her sons to make peace.

Daniel picked up the screwdriver now and fixed the last shelf bracket onto the wall behind the counter, then lifted the wooden shelf into place below the one he'd put up just before he'd heard something outside and gone out to the veranda to investigate. The till was already on the counter waiting to be christened, the big fridge in the kitchen was plugged in and ready for supplies to come in the next week or so, his licences had been obtained, safety checks done, kitchenware was all tidied away into the relevant drawers and cupboards with very few accessories still to arrive, and he'd already lined up interviews to take on two other members of staff. He wanted to have someone out front at all times if he was in the kitchen, someone who could go from kitchen to front of house without leaving the counter unmanned. Of course, this was all well and good if it was busy but he might have to reconsider staff on a payroll if it wasn't and manage on his own.

Daniel finished up, locked the cabin, and it was time to head to the supermarket to pick up more supplies. He'd been double-checking menu ideas at home – the waffle machines were working flat out with his experiments – and he only had a few more things to try before he'd bring all the equipment here.

In the car, which already had mud splashed all up its dark grey paintwork, he drove along empty country lanes bordered by fields with trees that bent as far as they could in the wind. On a stiller day he'd bet they'd have a layer of frost. He remembered this sort of drive from his childhood; he'd always sat in the back of the car, face pressed against the window to take in the white story-book setting unfolding in a way it only could in the country. In the towns he'd lived in over the years no festive season had ever come close to the magic created out this way.

As he drove he thought about his visitor this morning. Lucy. 'Lucy the Blacksmith,' he said out loud, smiling at the vision of her letting her hair down when she removed her helmet. It had been the best unveiling of a masked offender he'd ever seen in real life or on the screen, and a vision he wouldn't mind seeing again sometime soon. As much as he liked Fred, he was far more eager to have the sign made now he knew it was Lucy he'd be working with, and it was the perfect excuse to see her again.

And it was certainly a far more attractive prospect than going to Tumbleweed House to announce to his brother that he was back in the village.

* * *

'I still don't know what the log cabin is going to be,' Lucy told Tilly when she delivered the half-dozen candlesticks she'd made for Tilly's Bits 'n' Pieces in the same twisted style that had proven popular so far.

Tilly climbed between items so she was in the bay window at the front of the shop and positioned two of the candlesticks with tall, white candles standing proud to really show them off. 'I'm just glad you found Shadow,' she said, pulling her body back the way she went in, her bright pink Doc Martens clumping onto the wooden floor. She was careful not to knock anything from the dresser lined with colourful candles and glass bowls on one side of her and a freestanding giant glass ball on the other that housed a plant suspended from a wrought-iron hanger. 'It's really overgrown behind that cabin.'

'It needs some work for sure,' Lucy smiled.

Tilly straightened a couple of the Christmas-themed tea towels hanging from a handmade clothes airer. This shop had sold only candles once upon a time and these along with related accessories still made up the bulk of the stock, but other homely gifts were for sale too now and they seemed just as popular. 'I want to know what the place is going to be, I can't believe the owner has kept it so quiet,' she moaned as she wrote prices onto cardboard tags for labelling the rest of the candlesticks.

'You'd think he'd want to advertise.'

'If nobody knows about a business, you've got no hope.' Ever the business woman, Tilly could work and talk at the same time and she tied the price tags around the bases of the candlesticks using the string already attached. Her gold bangles jingled on one arm when she put the candlesticks in a group on the dresser to the other side of the till. Her bohemian dress sense carried from her jewellery to her thick cotton dress and tasselled scarf. 'And wait a minute... how do we know it's a he? It could be a female business owner.'

'Definitely not female.'

That piqued Tilly's interest. 'Tell me more.' Now she'd stopped working, with nothing but a cursory glance at the door to ensure she wasn't ignoring any potential customers.

'It's a guy.'

'I got that much. You've met him? What's he like then, this mysterious man at the log cabin?'

Lucy shrugged. 'Tall, dark—'

'Oh, come on, do not say handsome.'

'Well, he wasn't ugly, put it that way,' Lucy grinned.

'I'm going over at lunchtime to have a nosy for myself, see if I can find out more.'

Lucy divulged that he'd commissioned Fred to make a sign – which meant now it was down to her. 'I'm going to need wording, so we should have the low-down really soon.'

Tilly looked when the bell tinkled above the door, letting in a customer and a bite of cold. 'As soon as you know, tell me,' she winked at Lucy.

Lucy left her to it, crossed the lane, passed the tea rooms on the same side of the road and went into the bakery, where Celeste had just brought out a fresh batch of gingerbread cookies.

Lucy closed her eyes and inhaled the sweet, intoxicating scent. 'They smell divine.' She was met with a smile from Celeste when she looked again.

'They sure do, even though I say so myself.' Celeste laid the cookies in a basket behind the glass counter as her sister, Jade, pushed the till shut having handed a customer his change. 'Interested?' She had the tongs poised and her other hand on a paper bag.

'Always. I'll take one to have after my Christmas bap, please,' said Lucy after checking the menu on the blackboard behind them.

'The Christmas baps are popular – I can do the same filling in a focaccia if you like.'

'No baps left?'

'Afraid not. Focaccia's better though, so much flavour, a great choice.'

The sisters had apparently gone from having a fairly staid menu in their bakery to trying all sorts of things following a trip around Europe. Now they were into experimenting with different flavour combinations and encouraging customers to give them a go. Lucy had no problem with that and her taste buds didn't either. 'One Christmas focaccia to go then, please.'

'Coming right up,' Celeste trilled when Jade said she'd go and decorate the rest of the gingerbread men out in the kitchen. 'And I'll add extra cranberry relish with the brie just the way you like it,' she grinned.

The sisters worked well together bar the odd disagreement. They were as much a part of the village as the bakery itself. Both had porcelain skin they'd inherited from their Irish parents along with their tall, willowy height, apparently, but whereas Celeste had short, pixie-cut, black hair, Jade's hair of the same shade was shaped into a graduated bob, shorter at the back and longer at the front. Their green eyes sparkled in amusement as Jade brought the gingerbread men through and they shared a joke about their competitiveness and whose gingerbread was the best, whose batches of mince pies were going to be the tastiest when they got going with those later.

'Don't all mince pies taste the same?' Lucy teased.

Celeste and Jade looked at one another in mock horror, the freckles that crossed the bridge of each of their noses and peppered their high cheek bones changing shape with their expressions. They said in unison, 'No!'

Lucy laughed. 'I can't wait to try them.'

Jade wrapped her order and sent Lucy on her way with an assurance the mince pies would be ready to compare later if she could make it back today, or throughout the week if she couldn't. Lucy didn't doubt it. This was her first Christmas in the village but she'd come to learn that local businesses thrived and gave the festive season their all. Sometimes it was like stepping into a different world, and a good one at that.

Back in her flat, Lucy was relieved to have Shadow trot towards her in greeting. Guilty she'd let him get out in the first place, she was paranoid he'd now try to escape as though he'd suddenly developed the ability to open doors himself. Since he'd run off this morning she'd been sure to give the door an extra tug to shut it properly. Like everything else in here it needed an overhaul to be in proper working order and she'd add it to the ever-growing list.

Shadow had a sniff of her lunch that she clutched in her hand but the Christmas focaccia aroma obviously didn't appeal and he turned his interest to his scratching post before he crept to the coffee-coloured furry bed she'd bought him and up until now he'd ignored. At last. Maybe his scare earlier on and her coming to rescue him had made him see he finally had a proper home and she wouldn't let anything happen to him.

Her phone rang before she had a chance to eat and it was the delivery guy announcing he was outside with her tree. She told him she'd go down to meet him and she picked up Shadow's bed with him still in it and lifted it into the bedroom. 'Just so you don't run off,' she told him, knowing she'd have to leave the door to the flat open, but he seemed content enough as though her arrival had interrupted his all-important snooze time.

The tree, skinny in netting, was no problem to get up the stairs. All she wished was that she could get on and decorate it right now, but with lunch and work demands she had to settle for putting it into its stand filled with a little water and placed in front of the window that looked out over The Street so everyone would be able to see it when it was all lit up.

She smiled, the tree in position as she hungrily devoured her lunch, and let Shadow out of the bedroom to investigate. The second she finished the Christmas focaccia she grabbed some scissors to remove the netting. Already the smell had filled the room and although the village tree was lovely to see when you were out and about, there was nothing like waking to the scent of fresh pine needles in your own home. She ran the scissors from the bottom of the netting all the way to the top, peeled it off and stood back as the branches gradually unfolded. Shadow looked a bit scared of this moving being in his home and approached cautiously, taking a lap of the tree's base and then back again. He may as well get used to it, she thought, but perhaps this year she'd keep baubles and ornaments away from the lowest branches.

Filled with seasonal joy already, she got on with her day. She met a client early afternoon to discuss a garden gate required for the spring. It was an anniversary gift and the man was getting in early; he was rather impressed at Lucy's portfolio, especially the gates with shaped roses she'd shown him. After that client meeting Lucy shifted to working on the wine rack made from horseshoes, which was already taking shape and would make the most wonderful gift. And when the sky began to change colour, the blueish grey taking on tinges of pale orange as the sun prepared to go down, she turned off the forge so that its glow could gradually fade.

She turned when there was a knock at the open door to the workshop and Daniel leaned his head in. 'Busy?' he asked.

She'd been hoping he'd stop by soon, but she hadn't expected it to be today. Already it felt like a long time since they'd first met when it hadn't even been twelve hours. 'Daniel, come in.' She picked up a rag to wipe her hands on, hoping she didn't sound too thrilled. 'You've come about your sign, I presume – does this mean you're going to reveal what the log cabin will be? We're all desperate to know.'

'I suppose I can't keep it secret forever.' Blue-eyed and tall, he'd had to duck to come through the doorway and he hooked his thumb over his shoulder. 'Mind if I close that, it's freezing out? Not everyone is hardy enough to walk around in short sleeves.'

A memory of their early-morning encounter had her flustered. 'Sure, you can close it. I have it open when the forge is on but it cools down pretty quick in here. Come through, away from the mess.'

He seemed to be checking out the workspace and wasn't in any rush but eventually followed her through and over to the desk.

'Take a seat, let me find my folder, and we'll sort some details.' At least this time she didn't have her helmet on. She looked relatively normal, hair wound up in a pleat and fixed in place with a big clip. She looped a piece that had escaped behind her ear, brought down the folder from the shelf and found a pen in the drawer.

Daniel was looking around the space this side and stood up again to take in the items on the shelf against one wall. 'Did you make all these?' He certainly was exactly as Tilly had proclaimed – handsome, as well as tall and dark. His cropped hair suited him, as did the stubble, kept short, running along his jaw and up over his top lip. She suspected it was more him than the clean-shaven look.

'This is impressive. May I?' He was pointing at a copper tankard.

'You may.' She went over to stand beside him. 'I've made a few of those – slightly different designs each time. I made one for a customer recently to give to her son on his birthday, this one was made on request for an anniversary gift.' The elegant metal had been finished with a shaped handle, she'd made grooves running around the external circumference of the vessel at intervals top and bottom and the copper shone after polishing. All that was needed now was the engraving, but that was intricate work she'd pass to someone else.

He put it back on the shelf. 'Right, shall we get down to business?'

Momentarily embarrassed by his sudden focus back on her, she suggested they sit down and draft some ideas. 'I can't make it too fancy if you need it quickly, but I can make something that does the job and looks good. I'm going to need some wording though.'

'The Little Waffle Shack.' His jaw twitched when he shared it with her.

A smile slowly spread across her face. 'Now we're talking. Waffles are a favourite of mine, I may well end up being a frequent customer.'

'Is that so?'

He was flirting with her, she could tell, and she turned her attention to the form for his commission, where she added the extra detail. 'Locals are going to be thrilled with a waffle shack coming this way.'

He harrumphed. 'I doubt that.' He had a jacket on over the same jumper he'd been wearing earlier, a bottle green that she'd noticed this morning was chunky enough to be warm but not so big it didn't outline a body that was no stranger to hard work. And now he was taking off his jacket to put it on the back of his chair.

'I'm used to the heat,' she smiled, 'I forget not everyone is. It tends to hit you a bit when you come in here.'

He flapped at the neck of his jumper. 'I'll be taking this off next.'

'I can open the door again if you need me to.'

But in one move he pulled his jumper off, for a second revealing a glimpse of his chest.

'The Little Waffle Shack,' she repeated, hoping she could use the heat as an excuse for flushed cheeks. 'I can work with that.'

She took down another ring binder from the shelf above, passing it to him to look through. 'These are some of the signs I've done previously. Have a look, see if there's anything that appeals.'

'I've left it late, I know. I just... well, I didn't want to be wandering around the Cove. I didn't want anyone knowing about the business and coming to snoop before I was ready.'

'You're calling it "the Cove",' she smiled. 'That suggests you're not new to this area.'

'No, I most definitely am not.'

'What did you say your name was?' With an eye roll at his reaction that suggested she had a memory like a sieve, she added, 'I know it's Daniel; what's your surname?' Pen poised, she readied herself to fill in more of his contact details.

'Luddington.'

'Luddington.' She began to write but stopped after the second 'd'. 'Any relation to—'

'Yup, I'm Harvey's little brother.'

Except he wasn't so little. And he wasn't so enthralled at sharing the information either. Should she skim over it, not go down that road, or acknowledge she'd already heard enough about him to know he was going to face a fair bit of conflict when Harvey found out he was here?

'Judging by your silence,' he said, pausing his flip through the images of signs she'd worked on and taking the decision out of her hands, 'you know more about me than I know about you.'

Good looks sure ran in the Luddington family. 'I don't know you,' she assured him. 'So, how about we just start from here? I'm Lucy, you're Daniel, and I'm going to do some work for you. Everything else is your business.'

'I like your approach.' When he smiled she wondered, had

those lips and sparkling eyes got him into plenty of trouble before? She sensed the answer would be yes.

'I don't want to get you offside,' she told him, 'not when waffles are concerned. Because whenever opening day is, I'll be there.'

'Happy to hear I have one fan, at least. What's your favourite topping?'

'Don't make me choose only one,' she groaned.

'The menu should have enough variety for you to come in every day from day one until New Year's Eve without getting bored, put it that way.'

She smiled at him before he turned his attention back to the photographs of her previous work. She talked him through some of them, including those that were so intricate they'd take a while. On her pad she sketched something that was similar to a sign she'd made before – simple enough that she'd have no problem getting it done in the next week or so, professional enough that he'd be happy. 'I can add some decorative scroll-work,' she said, pointing to a photograph to show what she meant. 'It'll complement the hand-cut lettering.'

'And you're sure you can do it by opening night on December eighteenth? It's a big ask, but I'd really appreciate it.'

'I could do something a lot fancier if we had time, but what we've come up with is doable.'

'I don't need fancy. Your design is sophisticated, exactly what I'm after.' He looked around him again, noticing other works propped up nearby, a handful of photographs on a pinboard showing off thank-you notes from clients alongside the items she'd made. 'Did you really make all of those?' He moved closer to the pinboard and pointed to one picture in particular. 'This?'

'That was a commission piece. The family sent me a photograph of the old man and his dog; I traced the image and cut it from the metal.' He was clearly impressed and Lucy didn't mind admitting that the thought pleased her greatly. 'I made a tortoise for the same family – for the son, I think, who was crazy about the animal.'

He'd turned to look at her as though he had something to say but, seeming to remember where he was and who he was with, he just remarked, 'You need a sign for this place, out front.'

She went with the change of subject. 'I know, I've got some ideas I'll work on in the new year.'

'Don't tell me... something fancy?'

She smiled. 'We'll see.' Perhaps less focus on her, more on him, was the way to go. 'I'll make your sign and all you'll have to do is worry about hanging it up. Now, is the sign going to be fixed to the log cabin or hanging independently?'

'I was going to put in a lamp-post out front and hang the sign from two pieces of chain. Would that work?'

'Perfect.' She added detail to the sketch, putting two hooks for the chains onto the existing oval-shaped design with lettering in the middle. She pencilled a bracket design showing what it would look like with chains to hold the sign, scrollwork along its length. And she did her best not to let her hand shake knowing he was watching her as she worked. 'Something like this?' she asked when she was done.

'Exactly like that,' he smiled, his eyes soon leaving the design and finding her. She wished he'd look again at the sketch or her folder of previous work, or at least what she had on the shelves in here.

'It's a great name,' she garbled, 'I love it.'

'Luddington?'

'Very funny, you know exactly what I mean. The Little Waffle Shack – it has a good ring to it,' she blathered on, making a complete fool of herself. At least, that's what it felt like. 'And locals will be thrilled. Despite what you may think, I reckon their stomachs will have the last vote. Just you wait.'

'I admire your faith in human nature, Lucy. And I believe in the business – I wouldn't be starting it otherwise. I just need some of the locals to get over what went on before and we'll be good.'

She wondered, what *had* gone on before? She knew a handful of details from Melissa, Harvey's girlfriend who was a flight attendant and working away at the moment, otherwise she'd be straight on the phone asking for more information. Harvey and Daniel didn't speak, Melissa had tried to tell Harvey that maybe it was time to give his brother another chance but he'd shut down the very idea and that was that.

They worked out the cost of the sign, not dissimilar to Fred's initial prediction, before Daniel pulled his jumper back over his head and shrugged on his jacket. 'Pleasure doing business with you, Lucy.' He held out a hand for her to shake and when she took it she knew he didn't drop it as quickly as one normally would. And she wasn't sorry either.

Daniel Luddington was here in Heritage Cove. And for the first time in a long while her heart skipped a beat at a man who was clearly interested.

Before Lucy relocated to Heritage Cove she'd lived in nearby Southwold – lovely, picturesque and right by the sea. She had once thought she'd never leave, but her move had come at a good time. She'd been divorced for a year but her in-laws as well as her ex, Julian, all still lived in the area and bumping into any of them when she least expected – at the pub, the local shops, even a stroll along the beach – had begun to take its toll. She wanted to cut the ties, she knew it was the best thing, but it was hard to do when you saw them so frequently. And worse still, Lucy had been talked into a crazy plan of Julian's to pretend they were still together for the benefit of his dear gran, Maud.

Lucy loved Maud, who had never been a crotchety old lady who didn't want to know; she'd always had a smile, a good sense of humour and a welcoming demeanour that was hard to resist. And Julian was close to her too. So much so that he hadn't wanted to break her heart by telling her about the divorce. He'd begged Lucy to keep up the pretence that they were still together and it was easily done given Maud had moved from her bungalow into Aubrey House, a residential care home. Lucy had agreed to act as his wife and accompany him on the odd visit to Aubrey House. The problem was, the odd visit had become frequent visits and here she was again on a Sunday morning to meet Julian.

Lucy had had such a good day yesterday, insanely busy with her work, making a start on the sign for Daniel's business after he'd been to see her the day before, and the last thing she needed today was this. But apparently Maud had asked to see them both, citing this Christmas as the one likely to be her last. And Lucy couldn't be angry with her – Maud was too nice for that. It wasn't her fault her grandson had so many issues that put him firmly on the naughty list as far as Lucy was concerned.

'I'm sure it won't be her last Christmas,' said Lucy when she met Julian in the car park. The woman had survived two heart attacks as well as what Maud fondly told them was a baker's dozen of minor medical procedures, including having her tonsils taken out, an appendectomy and the extraction of bothersome wisdom teeth.

He pecked her on the cheek, an unnecessary gesture she wished he'd lose. 'She's almost ninety-one and you know what her health is like.' He looked worried, but he always was concerned about his gran's deteriorating health and memory. She still seemed bright enough to Lucy but she didn't disagree with him. Perhaps he was right, or maybe he was letting his imagination get the better of him. He was good at doing that.

They went through to the communal room, where Maud was holding court with a couple of women her age – but she shooed them away when Julian and Lucy came in. Julian had a hand in the small of Lucy's back, another mannerism she wanted to do away with but she couldn't very well swish him away now, could she?

'How are you, Maud?' Lucy leaned in and kissed her on the cheek and, as she usually did, Maud clasped Lucy's hand in her own. Lucy immediately felt guilt set in at any resentment she'd had over coming here.

They did the usual – talking about the high winds of a few days ago, the tree that had come down in the Cove that the council had taken away quickly, Maud told them the lightning had lit up her bedroom and she'd kept her curtains open to watch. They talked about Christmas, family. Lucy let Maud and Julian talk politics for a while, and after a cup of tea and an obligatory piece of shortbread, they were on their way.

'That wasn't so bad, was it?' Julian asked as they cut through the lobby on their way outside.

'Of course it isn't *bad*, Julian, but we can't keep up the pretence forever. You know that.' He didn't even nod, merely looked at her. 'We need to tell her, in the new year. I can still come and see her – I'd quite like to on the odd occasion – but what we're doing is lying. And you know I have no tolerance for that.'

Julian had always had a look about him. An innocent, boyish look with his blond hair and dimpled cheeks. Looking at him now, dressed in a blue-shaded checked shirt and chinos, she saw the semblance of an honest man who rarely put a foot wrong. Maybe it was because he believed he never did. And that had been the problem all along.

He sucked in his lips as though he might be biting down on them as they crossed the car park. 'I'm not doing anything for the rest of the day, we could head to the pub for Sunday lunch if you like.' And just like that he dismissed what she was saying.

'I need to go home.' She found her keys.

'Come on, you always liked the roast dinners at the pub.'

She spun around before she could get into her jeep. 'We agreed to keep up the pretence for Maud, Julian – other than that our lives are separate now. And besides, I've got to get back. I'm working.'

'It's Sunday.'

'And I run my own business, I've got lots on before Christmas.'

'Right then.'

'And, Julian,' she said as her parting shot, 'think about what I said. We'll tell your gran in the new year. We've been doing this long enough.' And she got into her jeep without giving him a chance to reply.

Her flat was a comfort despite its faults and she got home to the welcoming scent of the tree that stood in the window in all its splendour now it was decorated. She'd had soft white fairy lights on standby for months, ornaments hovering in boxes ready for their big reveal after a year of being hidden away, plus a couple of new items she'd bought from Tilly's Bits 'n' Pieces, the shop Tilly had finally renamed because 'The Candle Shop' wasn't an entirely accurate description any more. Lucy had also carefully unwrapped the special angel before stretching onto tiptoes and putting her proudly on top of the tree. She'd bought it years ago at a Christmas market with her cousin Joanna, who'd bought one just the same to decorate her own tree. Lucy and Joanna had both been only children and, being the same age, they'd grown up practically as sisters right up until the day Joanna died. Lucy missed her all the more at Christmas time and, now, the angel could sit proudly at the top of the gorgeous Fraser fir and offer her some comfort as she remembered how lucky she'd been to have Joanna in her life, if only for a short while.

Lucy changed out of her jeans and ruby, roll-neck jumper and pulled on a work T-shirt and accompanying dungarees. She didn't always work weekends but with Tilly, Celeste and Jade planning a big mulled-wine night at the pub tomorrow, Lucy knew the more she got done now, the less guilty she'd feel about having a sleep-in the morning after if she needed it. One of the perks of running your own business was designing your own schedule to suit you. Some people assumed you did very little if they saw you swanning around during office hours or rejigging your work timetable so that you could have the odd day to yourself here and there. But with your own business, you put in so much more time and energy overall because it was down to you to make it work.

Down in the workshop it was time to make a start on the sign for the Little Waffle Shack. Lucy kept her workspace relatively tidy and well-stocked so there were plenty of materials to use when she got last-minute commissions. Cupboards at one side housed a variety of metals – carbon, steel, brass, copper, aluminium – and the overspill of copper and iron pipes was stacked neatly right in the corner behind a bracket to prevent them rolling out onto the floor and causing an accident. Smaller items were kept either in big buckets against a different wall or in the set of steel drawers.

From her selection she took out a length of wrought iron. She'd use this for the main frame, inside which the lettering would be welded onto either the top, the base or the decorative scrolls she'd have surrounding the words. Sometimes she figured it out as she went along.

A few of the signs she'd worked on previously were really fancy; Daniel was right to notice them and she loved it when a client made the piece so personal it took her a long time to get it right. Their reaction was always worth it. But with limited time and a more basic design, Lucy was confident she'd come up with something that impressed as well as did the job. She measured out the length of wrought iron she'd need, put on her mask to protect herself from flying sparks and cut the surplus with the angle grinder. She heated the metal in the forge until red-hot and in the appropriate places, using the anvil and specially designed holes, she bent it round until the ends met. It took some effort to get the oval shape she wanted, returning the iron to the fire when she needed to, and when at last she was happy with the shape, she set it to cool on the rack. This job she loved was a therapy she needed. The manual labour helped her work out her frustrations with Julian; the heat, the noise, the banging things into the shape they needed to be – it was all a way of dealing with the world around her and its complications.

And now, with Daniel in mind, she hummed away to the Christmas carols playing on the radio station and, at the desk, she stencilled the first of the letters that she'd transfer to the metal ready for cutting out.

* * *

On Monday morning Daniel was up well before the sun. He'd been desperate to go for a run and hadn't for days given how flat out he'd been, but today he had headed down to the cove itself, and despite a group of walkers getting in his way near the big village Christmas tree, his route was deserted and pretty close to perfect. He'd made his way down the track that ran parallel to the chapel. Hedges and brambles lined the way, and the track, to the unknowing, looked as though it led nowhere, but locals knew that the part-sand-covered steps and the wonky, thin path with the dodgy handrail led down to a scene of beauty. And it was one he'd missed. He'd stood at the water's edge letting the freezing cold air awaken his senses, remind him that even though he had challenges ahead, he could rise above them, he could make this work.

He'd returned from his run invigorated and spent the rest of Monday morning shifting the waffle makers to the shack and getting the kitchen straight. He had put the batter he'd made at home into the double-door fridge, as well as a few fresh ingredients, so he could do some cooking here ahead of opening day and get a feel for the place. Earlier, he'd taken delivery from the supplier and now he had the more durable ingredients packed away into cupboards. He had catering-sized containers of flour in different varieties – wholemeal, white, gluten-free – he had caster sugar, icing sugar, salt. He had honey, golden syrup, slabs of high-quality chocolate, and a selection of jams. Other ingredients that didn't have quite the same shelf-life would come to him right before opening day – a selection of fresh fruits, butter, eggs, milk, buttermilk, cheese, vegetables and herbs. And he'd spoken on the phone to Zara who ran the local ice-creamery, a new addition to Heritage Cove since he was last here. She'd told him to find a time slot when he could stop by and have some tasters so he could confirm what he wanted to order, and that she was more than happy to supply him anytime. He suspected whatever he tried now, he'd be back in the summertime to ask for lots more of when the season changed his customers' tastes from warm to cooler concoctions, and the thought of still running this place come the summer sent a thrill of excitement through him but one that lulled to a sense of dread in case this business didn't take off the way he hoped it would.

Daniel had come into this business venture knowledgeable, organised and well-financed. Over the years, as he'd got himself straight he'd managed to find his dream, and that was catering. Part of him wished he'd realised it sooner but there'd been too many distractions – namely, his father – when he was in Heritage Cove, and it had taken leaving, going to rock bottom and finally a jolt of realisation that nobody but he could sort his life out to knock some sense into him. He'd got himself onto a hospitality course, worked shifts in a café, he'd done a stint as a kitchen hand and he'd waited tables in a restaurant. And then, after a brief weekend trip to Europe, where he'd visited the beautiful city of

Bruges and attended what was called a waffle workshop as part of a joint hen and stag do with friends, as well as coming away with the biggest hangover known to man, he'd begun to think about where he wanted to go from here. At first he'd thought about a greasy spoon with perhaps a few sweet treats on the side, then he'd considered a sandwich shop, or maybe a food truck, but none of those ideas grabbed him the way his enthusiasm had when he thought about opening a waffle place. He began to envisage a log cabin like you saw in a snowy ski resort, selling waffles with all kinds of toppings to local customers, and the only drawback was that where he lived at the time was urban and already surrounded by a plethora of eateries.

It was during a conversation on the phone with his mum one night earlier this year, when she mentioned the old beach shop was closing down and the owners were moving on, that Daniel began to wonder about the possibility of returning to Heritage Cove. Carol had been chatting away about the previous owner's plans but his mind had already gone someplace else wondering whether this was the push he needed, a sign of sorts. He'd tuned back in to the conversation, his mum chirpy enough now she knew he was okay. Their phone calls always worked that way. He'd initially left it a very long time to get in touch, his life such a mess he truly believed she was better off without him, so, since then, when she first heard his voice there was always an unspoken relief in hers – one he noticed every time – that then moved on in a way that said now she knew he was still breathing, still alive, she could lapse into a normal way of talking like other people did. She'd always insisted she wanted him to be happy wherever he was, but after he'd hit his thirtieth birthday and realised changes in his life could only happen if he instigated them, something had changed in him. And when he mentioned his idea about returning to his mum, she'd been unable to hide the fact she was crying. 'Early days,' he'd told her when he shared his business concept. 'Don't get your hopes up,' he'd said more than once.

The business venture was made possible in a number of ways. Years ago, Carol had sold the family home, Tumbleweed House, to Harvey. She'd inherited the house from her own parents so owed nothing on it and when Harvey bought her out, she spent some of the money on a small cottage for herself and split the remainder between the boys. Daniel had left his in a high-interest account and never touched it after he found out about it, but it was exactly the boost he needed. And so, with the shop in the Cove officially up for sale and his plans exciting him all the more, he was straight on the phone to the bank to talk about a small-business loan for the extra he needed, and then to the agent selling the shop.

Now, at the cabin that was real rather than in its conceptual stage, Daniel took a call from the company designing the flyers he'd ordered. They were ready for collection and so he shrugged on his coat, locked up the cabin and set off to pick them up. But when he looked over at the Christmas tree he saw someone he recognised. He was far away enough, across the grass, that most people wouldn't identify him unless they came closer but he was near enough that he could make out the figure, and when the man turned and started walking his way, Daniel began to smile.

'Hey, stranger,' said Benjamin, getting closer. He extended a hand to shake. Benjamin, like Fred, had withheld judgement when it came to Daniel and he was thankful for another ally.

'Hey, yourself. You were on my list of people to go and see.' He laughed. 'Honestly, I mean it. I've just been lying low for a while. You and I always got on.'

'We sure did.'

'What are you up to now?' He hadn't changed – apart from

tinges of grey in his long mousy hair that Daniel wondered if he'd even cut since he left.

'Besides looking at the village tree?' he smiled, the same cheeky grin Daniel remembered in place. 'Which I blame on my girlfriend, Zoe, who's taking way too long looking around Tilly's shop. I'm the chef at the pub.'

Daniel whistled between his teeth. 'The Copper Plough. Best food in Suffolk.'

'Well, it is now,' he grinned.

When Daniel had left, Benjamin was already at college doing a hospitality course so it wasn't a total surprise he was the local pub's chef. 'You've done well, I'm pleased for you.'

Benjamin looked over his shoulder. 'And it looks like you're doing all right. What's it going to be?'

'The secret is almost out,' said Daniel as he turned to look the same way at the cabin that would prove him a success or not, depending on how things went as of opening day. Lucy must've been too busy with her own job to go gossiping about his, or maybe she'd left the privilege down to him, and he felt a pang of gratitude that she was so willing to give him a chance when she clearly knew a few things about him he'd rather she didn't. 'That there,' he announced proudly, 'is The Little Waffle Shack.'

'Nice one,' Benjamin approved, pulling on a beanie that had been stuffed in his pocket as the wind snapped around them. 'My other half will be pleased.'

'You guys been together long?'

'We've known each other since school. Friends first, then we went to the same college and eventually became a couple.'

Friends often turned into more, and some relationships started off with heat but faded to a friendship that they should've been all along. Daniel knew all about that. 'Well, let her know I'll be opening on the eighteenth, I'm off to get the flyers now so word should soon spread.'

'I'll let her know.' He sniffed, the cold making his nose run. 'I saw Harvey early this morning, he didn't mention you were back.'

Daniel's breath came out in white puffs against the cold air and he rubbed his hands together briskly before blowing into them to warm them up. It was toasty inside the shack but out here it was impossible to forget what month it was. 'That's because he doesn't know.'

Benjamin whistled from between his teeth, eyebrows raised at the same time. 'Playing with fire, man.'

'I know.'

Benjamin patted him on the shoulder. 'I'd better go, but take it from me, might be best to let him know you're back in the village before opening night. He'll be in the pub tonight – it's quiz night.'

'I'm not sure turning up when the pub is packed is the way to go.'

'Or it could mean he's less likely to kill you.'

Daniel had to laugh. 'Safety in numbers, eh?'

'Think about it.' He shook his head. 'First Melissa coming back after years away, and now you.' And with a wave over his shoulder, off he went to meet his girlfriend.

Daniel walked back alongside the shack, down a path leading to a country lane with a generous lay-by, and jumped into his car to go off and collect the flyers. Less than two weeks to go until opening day, and as much as Benjamin's suggestion of turning up at quiz night had sounded the craziest thing to do, somehow it would be like ripping off a plaster – and at least he'd face his brother and anyone else who might remember him in one fell swoop.

* * *

Daniel replied to yet another text message from his mum, who told him to be brave, that he couldn't hide forever. And he had to admit that going between the log cabin, his rented cottage and Lucy's blacksmith workshop had been limiting enough that he needed to get out and about more, if only for his own sanity. Although Lucy's place did hold a welcome all of its own. One he thought he might be able to get by with if he couldn't show his face anywhere else.

But now, he was walking up the path between the iron lamp-posts at the front of the grass area outside the Copper Plough, the four-hundred-year-old pub that held inside a hum of voices falling over him with every step, suggesting it was going to be standing room only tonight.

He pushed open the door, relieved it wasn't one of those pubs that only had a handful of people in it who all fell silent if anyone from out of area dared to cross the threshold. In fact, he didn't recognise any faces and was about to confidently step towards the bar and grab a pint for courage when he spotted a couple of familiar villagers. One was Nola, who he knew was the landlady here now, and she didn't look too different from how he remembered her. The other was Etna from the tea rooms. He'd know her anywhere, with her grey hair in the same crop it had always been in – that, and the fact he'd been on the receiving end of a fury nobody would expect from a woman who usually spoke in the gentlest of voices. He and a couple of mates had broken into the tea rooms one night. They hadn't stolen anything, they'd taken the absolute mickey by sitting down and pouring cups of tea into the delicate china that really was only for display purposes, which they proceeded to drink from with pinkie fingers sticking out. They hadn't found it quite so funny when Etna and the police showed up. She'd been more scary than the long arm of the law, but she'd chosen not to press charges seeing as all they'd done was make drinks and sit around. All she insisted upon was that they washed up every single thing they'd used, put them all back in their rightful places and paid to have the door fixed after they'd used a crowbar to prise it open and damaged the wood.

Daniel knew he'd got off lightly with Etna and hadn't had a conversation with her since. Perhaps he'd go into the tea rooms and apologise one day, maybe offer her a month's supply of free waffles as a sweetener. He stepped closer to the bar again and pulled out his wallet the moment Etna moved away with her drink and Nola turned to serve another customer. But a voice stopped him and this time it was Barney. He supposed it was only a matter of time before they came face to face – himself and the man who was the local favourite and who had been in his brother's life more than he had. Barney must be in his seventies now by Daniel's estimation, was of average height, with silver, almost white, hair. Daniel only hoped the colour in the cheeks of his fair skin had more to do with the warm temperature inside the pub than frustration at seeing a blast from the past.

'I didn't know you were back in town, Daniel.' Barney put down his pint and shook hands with him. It was a good start. 'Welcome home.' He was a man who everyone knew and who knew everyone, and Daniel had history with him. A history he wasn't proud of. One year he and a mate had gone to linger outside the big barn at Barney's property where the Wedding Dress Ball was held every summer and as guests arrived they'd hurled abuse at them for no other reason than that they could. Barney had cautioned them to move on and in the end they got bored and did just that. But Daniel had always been embarrassed at how much of an idiot he'd been to do it in the first place.

'Thanks, Barney. And look, before we say anything else, I

want to apologise to you for the way I behaved at the ball.' No need to pinpoint exactly what year he was talking about.

'All forgotten about, lad.'

'I can assure you I come in peace,' Daniel smiled, with a hand on his chest to show his honour. 'I'm not in any trouble these days.'

'Glad to hear it.'

Harvey had often scooted off to Barney's place. Daniel got it, their dad was an arsehole, but when Harvey started spending his time over at the big barn on Barney's property, Daniel had hated being the only one at home to keep his mum company. Before too long he'd found his own ways to amuse himself, which unfortunately meant getting into trouble, and that had seemed to have a cumulative effect until it got to breaking point.

'Your mum never mentioned you being back in the village,' said Barney.

As usual, the man didn't miss a trick. Not that he was a gossip – Daniel had the good sense to realise that – he was just a man who liked to keep the community well-oiled and ticking over by keeping people talking, knowing what was what. 'I've not been back long. And she was sworn to secrecy, I wanted to deal with things in my own time.'

'I understand that, believe me.' He took out his wallet but Daniel refused his generosity and insisted he buy Barney a pint rather than the other way around.

'Cheers.' Daniel raised his glass and clinked it gently to Barney's once the amber liquid was poured. Neither of them carried on their conversation while the barmaid was close by.

'So, you're home for Christmas,' said Barney when she moved along to another customer.

'I'm back for good, actually. And Harvey doesn't know yet,' he added, leaning an arm on the bar, both of them facing the wall lined with optics, the shelves below stuffed full with a selection of snacks from salty or dry roasted peanuts to pork scratchings and good old Walkers Crisps.

'Ah.'

'That's one word for it.'

'And you're making your big reveal tonight?'

'It was Benjamin's idea,' he said a bit louder as Benjamin brought a couple of limes out to the bar and left them on the chopping board for the staff.

Benjamin turned, grinned and waved. 'Good to see you again, mate.'

Daniel explained their earlier reunion by the village Christmas tree. 'I suppose tonight is as good a time as any,' he told Barney. 'I didn't have the guts to do it before, and perhaps part of me hopes Harvey will be more likely to go easy on me in front of a crowd.'

'He's here already, you know.'

Daniel's insides plummeted. Even though he'd had a suspicion Harvey would show, knowing it for sure was another thing entirely. 'The quiz was always his thing.' He could remember Harvey heading out from the family home to meet Melissa, or coming back afterwards and telling their mum how he and Melissa had won yet again.

'And Melissa's.' Talk turned to Melissa's own return to the Cove. Barney told Daniel all about it, even though he'd heard most of it from his mum, now and then checking behind them to see if they had company but the only folks flocking nearby were business owners Daniel recognised vaguely and, adjusting his position, he stayed out of sight of those.

'I always liked her,' he told Barney. 'I'm glad they got back together.'

'That makes two of us. Took them a while, let me tell you.'

'Both as stubborn as each other, eh?'

'You're not wrong there. How about you? Are you with anyone?'

'Just myself, Barney. I'm enough to contend with,' he smiled.

'And what are you up to these days?'

'As I said, nothing illegal,' he winked, making Barney chuckle. 'I'm all above board these days, starting my own business.' He recapped on the handyman jobs he'd done over the years once he'd picked himself up, hauled himself away from rock bottom and got on with his life. But he didn't share the negative part, only the positive. 'And then I got into cooking – took a couple of courses, worked in catering for a time – and now I'm launching my own business here in the Cove.'

'You're the owner of the log cabin,' he said, piecing it together.

'I'm surprised you haven't been over, snooping around, Barney.' He grinned from behind his pint. 'Thought you'd be first in line to find out who was trying to muscle in on the Heritage Cove way of life.'

'I did have a nosy now and then but I've been busy with my other half, Lois. You'll meet her later tonight if you hang around, she's coming to the Cove for Christmas. Her flight already landed, she'll be in a taxi soon.'

'You look happy.'

'I am,' Barney smiled contentedly.

'I'm sorry for your loss. Mum keeps me filled in on the comings and goings in the Cove, whether I want her to or not, and she told me everything that happened.'

'I appreciate the condolences. I'm only glad I found her again after all this time.'

They drank their drinks in a moment of contemplation, appreciation at what had gone before, what life still had on offer. This man had been through the pain of losing a child all those years ago and had faced an agony Daniel couldn't imagine. It was bad enough putting his own mum through the stresses he had without leaving this earth completely. He lifted his new pint to Barney's almost empty one. 'To you and Lois, may you be very happy indeed.'

'And to you, Daniel, may you also find happiness.'

'Not sure Harvey would appreciate that toast.'

Barney dismissed the doubt with a wave of the hand through the air as an announcement came over the micro-phone that the quiz was about to start. Barney asked if he'd like to go and sit down but Daniel declined, knowing how close he'd be to Harvey, and as the quiz got under way, an awareness that his brother was somewhere in the rabble was enough for now.

With faces focused on the quiz master or pieces of paper at the tables and crowds surrounding anyone taking part, Daniel turned and enjoyed his pint while leaning back against the brass rail that ran around the bar. The beams in here spoke of a pub steeped in tradition. They ran across the ceiling, some up from the floor, others against the wall, with the same dark, almost black, timber that framed the windows on the exterior of the Copper Plough. Soft lighting typical of a pub showed off the twinkly lights interspersed with red baubles that lined the perimeter beams; some of the lower beams of the ceiling that Daniel had had to duck under so as not to bang his head on the way over to the bar had sprigs of mistletoe for hopeful punters. A dog twitched its lips during a dream as it sprawled out on the rug in front of the open fire burning away in the hearth, the maroon leather chairs positioned at the edges taken by two men laughing about something or other.

Daniel lifted his pint ready to down it and either get another or run for the door and face Harvey alone another day, when in the corner of his eye he caught a streak of golden hair – and as far as he knew, there was only one local who had hair like that.

And when Lucy turned, saw him and beamed a smile his way, his feet stayed rooted to the spot. He wasn't going anywhere. Never mind the consequences, she was impossible to walk away from and his eyes held hers as she came towards him in a figure-hugging dress he fully appreciated.

4

Lucy was late for the quiz and although she couldn't see any of her friends through the crowds, she didn't mind too much when Daniel was the alternative. Did this mean he'd already seen Harvey and made peace with him?

'Not quite,' he admitted when she posed the question. 'Let me buy you a drink. It's the least I can do when you've taken on such a last-minute commission this close to Christmas.'

'I told you it's no bother, but if you're offering...'

'What's it to be?'

'I'll have a mulled wine, please.' She was meeting the girls for their planned mulled-wine night so she may as well start as she meant to go on.

'Good choice, I'll join you.' He ordered two and the bartender ladled out a serving each for them into glass mugs.

Lucy took hers between both hands and inhaled the aroma of Christmas. She'd watched Daniel while he was talking to the bartender. He looked even better than he had the other day. Clocking his dark, well-fitted jeans and a light-grey casual shirt with a cutaway collar, she found it hard to take her eyes away from any part of exposed skin. He'd rolled the sleeves up to his elbows and strong forearms showed off tendons every time he moved, pulling out his wallet, picking up the mugs, handing one to Lucy. There was a teasing patch of skin exposed at the neck of his shirt, leaving her to wonder what was beneath the rest of the fabric.

Lucy drank the wine. Probably the safest option unless she wanted him to know the effect he'd had on her. 'Thank you, this is good.' She held the mug aloft. 'And I love the design of these. So pretty.'

'The copper mugs in your workshop are equally impressive,' he countered.

'The ones in the box at the edge of the desk?' He really had taken in all the details. 'They're a gift for Barney from Lois,' she said softly, leaning closer so they weren't overheard. 'They've both come to me to make gifts for the other one this Christmas, but I don't think either of them has any idea what the other is up to.'

'I've seen Barney already and he certainly seems happy enough.'

'I haven't known him long but he and Lois definitely seem made for each other.'

'They'll love the mugs, I'm sure.'

'Fingers crossed. Lois gave me the go-ahead for whatever I deemed suitable. All I need to do is find the right-sized box for them and hand them over when she comes to the village.' They were still close together, talking in hushed tones, as though he was a magnet she couldn't resist. And by the way he smiled at her, he'd noticed too.

'I don't ever remember Fred being this popular at Christmas,' he said as she sipped her wine. 'Certainly not when it came to making gifts.'

'His talents are way more extensive than mine but in a

different realm.' She told him how she wasn't a farrier as many assumed a blacksmith should be. 'Taking over for him temporarily was really to keep up with the commissions he had on the go – the riding stables knew they'd have to find another option while Fred wasn't around – but I'm glad I came here. Running Fred's business gave me a chance to show the skills I did have rather than focus on what I lacked.'

'Here's to that,' he said, tilting his glass towards hers so he could make a toast. 'People need to see what's in front of them rather than focus on the negative.'

'Why do I get the impression we're talking about you now?' When he grinned she added, 'Surely Harvey must've got wind you're over here. It's not that big a pub.' And she was well aware that if any of her friends looked over she'd surely give the game away, unable to hide her attraction from them when they seemed to have made it their personal project to take charge of her love life whenever they were in here.

'If my brother is anything like I remember he'll be into quiz mode right now, so I'm safe for a bit. I've kept my head down in this corner and with it so busy I haven't yet been spotted by many people who would recognise me. I've been away for a while, remember.'

They talked between themselves, Lucy glad she'd seen him before anyone else. They shared experiences of what it was like to start a business from scratch, the pitfalls and the benefits, and when the quiz questions were called out he whispered a few of the answers in her ear. She wouldn't have known them because they were based on local history that he knew, but she was hardly likely to learn anything because every time his arm brushed hers when he got closer and she felt his warm breath against her ear it made her think that even though her friends were around somewhere, part of her was longing to be holed up in a cosy nook of the Copper Plough with Daniel Luddington all night.

The door opened again and in from the cold came someone who Daniel clearly knew because his face fell and he turned away.

Lucy looked around to see Melissa and smiled across at her but Melissa put a finger to her lips.

'I'm not supposed to be home for a few days,' Melissa told Lucy the second she'd squeezed over to stand beside her. 'I'm here to surprise Harvey.' She worked away a lot of the time but her base was here with Harvey at Tumbleweed House these days.

'Get in line,' said Lucy, and hooking an arm behind her, pulled on Daniel's arm until he turned round.

Melissa's jaw dropped but a smile soon formed, she stepped forwards and threw her arms around Daniel, hugging him tight. 'I can't believe you're here. It's been years.'

'Too many,' he confirmed, still seemingly unsure of her reaction.

She soon put him straight. 'Well, it's lovely to see you, it really is. Merry Christmas.'

'Merry Christmas, Melissa.' He smiled down at her as she unbuttoned her coat and laid it across the end of the bar with Lucy's.

'Harvey didn't mention you were coming back to the Cove,' she said, but it didn't take more than a second for her to add, '... oh, he doesn't know, does he?' Daniel shook his head. 'Then this should be interesting. Are you home to spend Christmas with your mum?'

'Something like that.'

Melissa was about to carry on the conversation when a voice behind them all let out a roar. It was Harvey. 'You're here, you're home!' He wrapped his arms around Melissa's waist and lifted her up into the air and Melissa laughed, one hand over her head to mind out for beams.

'Thought I'd surprise you,' she told him when he set her down.

Harvey, blue-eyed and with a stubbled jaw much like his brother's, had his dark brown hair cropped short and, all his attention on his girlfriend, he pulled Melissa up close and kissed her full on the lips. 'You've no idea how good it is to see you.' But he must have noticed her smile wavering and Lucy knew it was only a matter of time before he came face to face with Daniel. He only had to take a couple of steps to the left and turn around, and all Daniel had to do was face the pub again rather than the optics.

'There's someone else who wanted to surprise you,' said Lucy and stood back to nudge Daniel, who slowly turned again as though he needed her to be his puppet master tonight. She figured this had to be hard and so she had no problem helping him get it over and done with, although she wished their chat could've lasted all night.

'And who's that?' Harvey smiled, ever friendly and approachable. But his demeanour totally changed when he clapped eyes on Daniel. 'What the hell are you doing here?'

Daniel bristled, stood a foot taller, and all he said was, 'Outside.'

As both men left the cosy confines of the Copper Plough and Lucy and Melissa in their wake, Lucy looked to Melissa. 'Well, that went well.'

'Didn't it just.' Melissa picked up on the sarcasm straight away. 'I mean, it's great to see him, but whatever made him think turning up at the pub was a good idea?'

'My fault,' Benjamin declared, coming back to the bar to lift the hatch at the other end and take out empty bowls with smeared bits of ketchup on, the only leftover part of the portions of fat chips he'd served to hungry quiz goers. He leaned in and said to Melissa, 'He's facing the same as you did, go easy on him.'

Melissa turned to Lucy when Benjamin left them to it. 'I know exactly what it's like, it's scary. But I wasn't moaning at Daniel, I'm just worried.'

'About Harvey's reaction?'

'Put it this way, it takes a lot for Harvey to miss the second half of the quiz,' she said as the quiz master announced the break was over.

'What even happened between those two?'

'It's a long, long story,' said Melissa. 'I'm going to need a drink.'

'Mulled wine?' Lucy offered as she spotted her other friends and waved over to them. They were talking to a group of lads – that should keep them occupied for a while and give her the chance to find out more.

'Perfect.'

And well before Harvey came back into the pub, Melissa had told Lucy some more of the details. She told her how Daniel had been in trouble with the police as a teenager and brought a lot of upset the family's way, how Harvey resented his fleeing the village to leave him to handle Donnie and watch out for his mum. 'Harvey forgave me for leaving the Cove,' Melissa said quickly when they saw Harvey come through the door and head back their way. 'Let's hope Daniel showing up in the season of goodwill makes a difference and Harvey can give his brother another chance.'

Harvey ordered a pint, gulped back a good portion of it and shook his head at Melissa's suggestion he carry on with the quiz. 'I'm not in the mood.' Lucy was about to leave them to it when he said, 'He told me you were first to spot him in the village.'

'Guilty as charged,' Lucy admitted. 'I'm sorry, Harvey. At first I had no idea he was your brother, then, when I knew, I thought it best to leave you two to your own business without me interfering.'

He was fuming, she could tell, but not at her. 'I suppose I should be grateful it appears he's made something of himself,' he said. Lucy wasn't sure whether she should agree or just keep quiet.

Melissa's confusion had Lucy telling her all about the Little Waffle Shack. Daniel must have broken the news to Harvey that not only was he here for Christmas, he was here permanently with a business to run. 'I'm busy making the sign, it opens December eighteenth.'

'It's good he's sorted himself out.' Melissa linked her arm through Harvey's in a move to perhaps try to calm him down.

'It would appear that way, wouldn't it?' Harvey looked into his pint, his mood more melancholy than Lucy had seen in her whole time living in the Cove. He'd always been upbeat, chatty, good company, but his brother's reappearance seemed to come with demons he wasn't ready or willing to confront.

'You're doubting him?' Melissa probed as Lucy became an observer in the conversation rather than a participant.

'Of course I am. When has he ever been anything but trouble?'

'Harvey—'

'I'm going home,' he interrupted before Melissa could say anything else. He downed the rest of the pint that hadn't lasted any time at all. 'I'll see you there.'

'I'll find Tilly and the others,' Lucy assured them. 'You both go, have a good evening.' Although she doubted it would be quite the relaxed, romantic affair Melissa had had in mind when she surprised Harvey by showing up here tonight.

Lucy joined her friends, who had finally broken away from

the group of lads. She couldn't help on many questions in the quiz given her lack of local knowledge and when someone remarked on Harvey's disappearance midway through, she didn't pass comment.

'Your dress is gorgeous, Lucy.' The quiz over, Tilly admired the figure-hugging, navy, woollen dress she wore tonight. She'd almost put it on for the visit to see Julian's gran but at the last minute remembered Julian had always loved it when she wore a dress, said it was feminine, which she'd taken to mean her work attire really wasn't. In protest, she'd worn jeans to visit Maud yesterday instead.

'I got it from a little shop in Southwold,' she told Tilly. 'And they have other colours if you're interested.'

'I'm more into loose-fitting garments, I don't have a figure good enough for a dress like that.'

Lucy was about to protest but Tilly was already onto another topic. 'I saw you yesterday morning, waved but you drove past with a right frown on your face.'

'Sorry, I would've waved if I'd seen you. I was distracted.'

Tilly got it. 'Meeting up with the ex again?'

'Unfortunately.'

'When are you going to put a stop to that?' She shuffled out of the way of others who hadn't been sitting down for the quiz vying for seats now they were vacant. It was like watching the Changing of the Guard – everyone who'd been sitting down wanted to stand and all those on their feet were desperate to be on their bottoms.

They ordered another couple of mulled wines and stayed by the bar. 'I've told Julian it has to stop in the new year,' Lucy recounted. 'I'll let Maud go into Christmas happy but after that she deserves the truth.'

'Will you stop seeing her?'

'I'd like to keep visiting, but alone. It's Julian I have an issue with, not her.'

'What did happen between you? You never really explained, just that the love fizzled out.'

'I was fobbing you off saying that.'

Tilly pretended to be shocked but then grinned. 'You don't say.'

With the scent of mulled wine snaking through the air and classic Christmas tunes she'd heard over the years giving the pub a lively atmosphere, she told Tilly, 'Julian liked to live a bit in his own world. I think he ended up telling so many lies that half the time he didn't know what to believe himself.'

'That doesn't sound like a healthy relationship.'

'It wasn't. I had to get out and I have never once regretted doing so. His family were all local too so when this job and the flat came up as an opportunity it was the best thing that could've happened.'

'What did he lie about?' Tilly asked, but they were joined by a rowdy Celeste and Jade, who'd been enjoying the mulled wine all evening, and Lucy didn't really want the whole village knowing her business. And anyway, she didn't want to talk about Julian tonight so a change of topic was welcome.

Once Celeste and Jade had talked about their mince-pie battle, citing key ingredients and pastry techniques, and Lucy and Tilly had assured them both that they were on hand to do tastings whenever it was required, Lucy left them to it. There was something comforting about leaving a pub that was still going strong, its punters taking it long into the evening with a hum of merrymaking despite the gradual thinning of the crowd, and, pulling her scarf tight and buttoning up her coat, she set off for home. The weather forecast hadn't suggested snow but it certainly felt cold enough tonight as she made her way along The Street.

The main road in the Cove was decorated for Christmas in true village style. Strung between the lamp-posts on either side of the street, along its entire length, were coloured lights illuminating the way. The air around her was mostly still except for the gentle breeze making itself known every time there was a gap between buildings or houses. The chapel had a nativity scene out front and she paused to admire it. Made in a hutch at the front of the grass area, the figures were lit up from behind so you could see the nativity day and night. Baby Jesus was tucked up in his manger with the angels keeping watch from above, three wise men held their treasures in their hands and Mary and Joseph knelt beside their infant. She continued along, past the track that led down to the water's edge, the beautiful sand at the wine-glass-shaped bay of water that gave Heritage Cove its name. She'd been on a couple of bracing walks down there last week; she needed to go again but work had picked up so much she wasn't sure when she'd get a chance.

As she reached her workshop she wondered whether Daniel had gone home after the confrontation with his brother. Or was he at the shack now? Her feet almost took her there to find out, but did she really know enough about Daniel to disregard all of Harvey's doubts? She was all for giving someone a second chance but Daniel's presence had evoked such a strong reaction from his brother, it did make her wonder whether he really was the kind, genuine person she'd met and been drawn to.

She went up the steps and let herself into her flat, Shadow trotting towards her the second she got in and before she'd had a chance to take off her coat. She popped the Christmas-tree lights on and congratulated him for not destroying the tree after she'd been out for hours. She scooped him up into her arms as she squeezed behind the tree to look out of the window and across to the left. She could just about make out the top of the log cabin from here, but there was no sign of light. Daniel must've gone back to his own house – at least, she hoped he had and that he was staying out of trouble after the confrontation at the pub. And more than that, she hoped the brothers would sort their differences out. Looking to the top of her Christmas tree, she thought of her cousin Joanna and the silly fight they'd had over some boy the week before she died. They'd both been keen on him, they'd argued over who'd seen him first – a stupid, petty bickering they'd never sorted out. Lucy would forever be sorry they hadn't got over themselves and realised how crazy they'd been to let it come between them. Life really was too short to fight with someone so special in your life. She knew that only too well.

5

Daniel had left the flyers in a huge pile at the waffle shack after collecting them before he'd braved the pub last night. The last thing he'd wanted was for Harvey to see him for the first time in years delivering them through people's doors. That would really upset his brother. And although not convinced the pub had been the best place to turn up, Daniel had realised on his way there last night that there wasn't a single place better than any other.

This morning began bright and sunny and, with the encounter out of the way, it was time to get advertising his business. He delivered the flyers to as many houses in the Cove as he could, starting with the area past the riding stables and around his rented cottage. He delivered more and more leaflets to surrounding properties and he'd already decided to avoid Tumbleweed House at all costs. It wasn't necessary to rub salt into the wound now, was it? Harvey would need some time to come to terms with his return if the reception he'd got last night was anything to go by. Still, it had been good to talk to Barney, catch up with Melissa and, best of all, meet up with Lucy before he and his brother had finally seen one another, taken their differences outside the Copper Plough and hurled abuse into the night. Their slanging match had culminated in Harvey storming back into the pub and Daniel stalking off home to his cottage, where he'd slumped on the sofa still in his coat and wondered whether they would ever be brothers in arms. He supposed they had been a long time ago, when Donnie had them running scared as young lads, but that camaraderie hadn't lasted when Harvey found an escape route and then, years later, Daniel found his own when he left the village.

Daniel moved from the surrounding houses in the village back to The Street and made a stop at the ice-creamery for his pre-arranged tasting session, which went well. The owner didn't know him, which helped, and he told her he'd have a think about the flavours and quantities he'd need and get back to her as soon as he could. Pumped full of ice-cream, he continued to post flyers through the doors of businesses along The Street, including the tea rooms, the bakery and the convenience store. He'd saved the last few for the other side of the road, put one under the door to the chapel – he wasn't sure whether that was frowned upon or not – and then delivered one to Lucy's workshop.

He had to knock a few times on the closed door before she came, the last knock more of a thump.

She had her headgear on again, the khaki dungarees and a T-shirt, and she'd flipped her visor up. With a smile she asked, 'Have you been standing there a long time?'

'Not too long and sorry about banging the hell out of your door, you wouldn't have heard me otherwise.'

'You should've rung the bell,' she said.

'I did but figured it wasn't working.'

She put an arm out of the door and reached around, pressing the bell a few times. 'Not again.' She pulled off her headgear and this time her blonde hair stayed in its low ponytail. 'I've bought another one, I just need time to replace it.'

'Do you know if it's the button or the bell?'

Her look suggested she had no clue. 'No idea, I just bought a new one.'

'And, don't tell me, you've been too busy to look at it any further because you keep getting commissions from businessmen who like to leave things until the last minute.'

She grinned. 'Something like that. But there's only one businessman. Is that a flyer?' She saw what was in his hand as he stepped inside, out of the cold. She nodded approvingly at the pictures of the waffle shack, another he'd taken of waffles drizzled with chocolate sauce and a side of whipped cream. 'If these don't get people's taste buds going, I don't know what will. I assume the whole village gets a flyer.'

'If you're asking whether I've been hiding away from my brother or at last venturing out in the Cove to put them through doors, it's the latter. The pub was phase one of me showing my face around here, the flyer drop was phase two.'

'And what's phase three?'

He pulled a face. 'Not sure yet. Coming here seemed a safe option, though.' He returned her smile. 'Let me fix the doorbell for you.'

'Don't be daft, it's probably a two-minute job.'

'That you haven't done yet.'

'Good point.' She went to retrieve the new bell from one of the metal drawers and handed him a screwdriver so he could first remove the faulty one. 'I appreciate it. I'm usually in the zone when I work and making a lot of noise – I'd hate to ignore a customer.'

He went back outside and unscrewed the existing doorbell and button from the wall. He touched the two wires together and when they made the bell inside chime, he told her, 'It's only the button, easiest problem of the lot.' And after she unwrapped the new bell and handed it to him, he soon had it fixed in place.

'Thank you for doing that,' she smiled. 'Unfortunately, Fred hasn't modernised anything around here in years, including the flat, so the doorbell joined a long list of things that are on their last legs.'

'Oh dear, that doesn't sound good.'

'Most things in the workshop are fine but the flat's another matter. And don't get me started on the kitchen.'

'That bad?'

'Cupboard doors falling off, wobbly shelves, tatty, and not enough bench space.' With a grin she added, 'Sorry, I told you not to get me started, didn't I? Come and see the sign so far.' She took the empty packaging for the bell from him and dumped it in a recycling container. 'I've made good progress.'

He went over to the work table, still in the part of the workshop that saw all the action. The forge wasn't on yet so it was a much better temperature and he felt privileged to get such an insight into the intricate work she did. He expected most customers were shunted through to the more comfy area with the desk and furniture.

The oval wrought iron of the sign was on the table and she'd begun to cut out letters she'd stencilled onto the metal pieces that would make up the wording of his business in the centre of the sign. 'You'd want to be able to spell doing this,' he said, lifting up the letter 'T' she'd cut out. 'Imagine if you made a mistake, fixed it all together and then realised.'

'I've done it and, believe me, it's beyond frustrating.'

He reached out without thinking and touched a hand to her arm. 'You've burnt yourself.' His fingers hovered near a pink patch of skin that had almost healed.

She looked at his hand for a moment and, keeping her gaze on her skin, told him, 'Not my first time and unlikely to be my last either.'

He took his hand away, albeit reluctantly. He wondered if she'd felt the same connection he had. 'I suppose it's a hazard of the job. My only likely hazard is putting on a few stone from eating too many waffles.'

She laughed at that. 'At least you're tall, you could probably get away with a few waffles before you had a problem.'

'It won't be so lethal when the place opens up but for the last few weeks I've been experimenting with flavours, which has meant a lot of eating.' He shrugged when she rolled her eyes. 'Yeah, yeah, I know, it's a tough job but someone's got to do it.' He patted his stomach, which, thankfully, with all the physical labour of getting organised at the Little Waffle Shack, still felt as taut as it had when he'd been hitting the spit-and-sawdust local gym every morning. It had been part of him getting back on track, using excess energy by pushing himself to his limit, showing he could do whatever it took and face whatever life chose to throw at him from then on.

'Did you sort out the lamp-post for the sign?' she asked him.

'It's being delivered in the morning and they'll put it up, set the base in concrete and we'll be good to go.'

'Have you tackled the mess at the back of the cabin yet?'

'You really want me to work, don't you?' He smiled at her reference to the morning they'd met. 'As a matter of fact, I have. I'm hoping to get it all cleared by the summer so I can have more seating out there. Unfortunately, those persistent plants and this-tles are a bugger to get rid of – I expect it'll take a bulldozer rather than the trusty spade I bought from the garden centre.'

'You're not wrong there. I'm surprised Shadow didn't get caught up in them when he went walkabout the other day.' She toyed with the pencil she'd used to draw the letters before putting the outline onto metal. 'Are you nervous about opening night?'

'No.' He shook his head. But a grin followed right after. 'Yes.'

'Do you think Harvey will show up?' When he said nothing, she asked, 'What happened when you guys went outside the pub?'

He shrugged. 'I'm still alive, aren't I?'

There was another knock at the door and this time Lucy opened it to take in the post.

'Popular lady,' Daniel remarked on seeing a good collection of envelopes that most likely contained Christmas cards judging by their festive red and green colours. 'And look how many you already have.' He moved to look at those that were placed on the top of a counter she used to stack paper and pots of pens. 'Nice photo.' He peered at the card that had a photo on it of her standing next to a blond-haired guy inside one of those plastic pretend snow globes you find in shopping centres. 'Boyfriend?' He really hoped not.

'Ex-husband,' she said, coming closer.

'And he still sends out a Christmas card with a photo of you together?'

'Kind of... He sent me that one to get my approval before he sent a copy to his gran. I know what you're thinking, it is odd, but it's for her and her only. His gran, Maud, lives in a residential home and Julian, my ex, has always been really close to her. I agreed – probably stupidly – to keep up the pretence that we're still together so as not to upset her. She's what you might call traditional. You should've heard her reaction when we said we weren't getting married in a church... she didn't like it one bit. We ended up changing all our plans and having the wedding in the church where all her grandchildren were christened just because it would make her happy. So now, every week or so I go along to the home to see her and we pretend nothing has changed.'

'I'm not sure I'd want to do that if I were you.' Something in the way she looked at him suggested she didn't like it much either.

'I won't be for much longer, believe me. In the new year I'll put a stop to it.'

'Sounds like a good idea, it'll be easier to move on then.'

'I have moved on.'

He put up both hands. 'I'm not disputing that.'

'Come on, then, I've talked enough about me, what about you? What really happened with Harvey last night?'

Over time he'd got used to talking about his feelings more, sharing his problems before they drove him to do stupid things. And Lucy, well, she was one of the kindest, easiest-to-talk-to people so it all came flooding out. He wondered if this would be the start of sharing just a little bit about himself, and then a little bit more, until it was all laid out on the table – the good, the bad and the downright terrible. 'I was convinced he was going to punch me,' he said wryly.

'He wouldn't, would he? He's never come across as anything other than a big softie – kind, understanding.'

'Are we talking about the same guy?' He shook his head. 'I guess he's always going to be different with me. But I doubt he'd have punched me really. It was just, the way he looked at me... there was so much anger. Sometimes, I think it actually would be better if we fought properly, got all the aggression out – then perhaps we'd rid ourselves of enough frustration to sit down and talk properly.'

She leaned her back against the work table next to where he was standing. 'I don't know either of you very well but I can imagine there's a whole lot of love deep down. When something's happened to push you apart it's easy to focus on that rather than anything else. And there wouldn't be anger and resentment if you didn't both care about the other.'

He smiled at her. 'You sound so wise. You're saying I need to give it time?'

'I really think you do.' Her hand had drifted to his and although their fingers weren't touching they almost were, before she asked if he'd like to see some of the scrollwork she envisaged putting on the sign for his business.

He followed her into the other section of the workshop, with the sofa, and she picked up a sign waiting for collection. 'What do you think of the scrollwork on this? It's a bit like what I drew on the design when you were here last.'

He looked at the curves of wrought iron, thick at one end, tapered at the other, the way the scrolls intersected with the lettering and held it all together. 'I'll be more than happy with something like this.'

'Great.' He must've still been frowning after bringing up the topic of himself and Harvey because she told him, 'Stop worrying, it's almost Christmas.'

'My first back here.'

'My first here full stop,' she said. 'And, listen, I'm new to the village, I arrived in the summer, but I was around when Melissa came back and I know it wasn't easy. Word has it she and Harvey were both so headstrong that Barney had to engineer them both working on running the Wedding Dress Ball to get them talking again.'

'You want me and Harvey to put on a dance for the village?'

She nudged him and chuckled. 'No, but remember he might take a while to be willing to hear what you have to say.' She sat down at the desk, he on the sofa. 'Maybe give him a chance to get over the shock and then try talking to him again.'

His fingers drummed on the fabric of the sofa. 'He always was stubborn.'

'And it doesn't run in the family?'

'I'm a lot more compliant. I am,' he laughed when she looked doubtful. 'I've made mistakes but I'm more the type to get things out in the open rather than brood and make it ten times worse. I wouldn't be back here now otherwise, trying to talk to my brother. And I've got better at believing in myself too. I don't want to sound like a total arse,' he added before she could, 'but from the time Harvey and I were young lads our father didn't do much of a job helping us grow up to be men. Harvey got there on his own and with Barney; I kind of drifted, got lost along the way and didn't take charge of my own life.'

'Don't be too hard on yourself.'

'Harvey managed it, so I should've too,' he insisted. 'I wanted all the bad stuff to go away, it was as though I was expecting a miracle to come along. And when it didn't, I acted up. I don't know if deep down it was to get attention – Harvey was off doing his thing, Mum was trying to hold everything together and keep Dad from blowing his top – I'm no psychologist, but the way I handled it? It definitely didn't set me up with skills for life. Harvey and I drifted apart further and further, I got into trouble and home life became stifling. It didn't matter that Mum had my back, that she wanted me there, my father had done enough damage. People around here knew I was trouble and one day, when I was eighteen, I couldn't take it any more and I figured Mum and Harvey would do better without me. So I packed a bag and I left.'

Seeing the shock on her face, he realised he'd shared a great deal more than he'd intended to. He put his hands on his thighs. 'And now I've bored you with details and I need to get on. I've got a delivery of crockery coming later and before that I'm off to see

Etna and face up to my sins.' She looked confused. 'Don't worry, not a recent sin, but back in the day I may have been part of a group who broke into the tea rooms.' If he sounded flippant it wasn't because he meant to; he was dreading this. 'It's time for me to apologise.'

'Good for you.' And something in the way she smiled suggested she believed he was a changed man. He picked up the remaining few flyers from where he'd left them when he came in. 'Wish me luck.'

'Let me know how it goes.'

'Will do.' Was she inviting him back? He hoped so. She'd been an unexpected perk of coming back here and he liked it.

Daniel stepped out into the cold and buttoned up his coat. He hadn't been back here for thirteen years but already he was appreciating the reminders of what Christmas in Heritage Cove was like. The decorations lined the main road running through the village and businesses on The Street had put up their own festive cheer. He'd passed Tilly's Bits 'n' Pieces on the way home from the pub last night and seen a small tree in the bay window of the shop as well as a four-foot snowman with a black hat and pink dotted cheeks beside the front entrance. He'd crossed over the road to see the nativity display out front of the chapel too. It was still in the same position as it had been every year when he was a kid. One of the wise men still even had a crack in his crown, indicating that although time had moved on here, some things stayed the same. Heritage Cove was still a village people moved to but rarely left. Unless you were running away, of course, like he had.

Leaving Lucy's now, he passed the ice-creamery, which still had its blackboard sign out front. Weighted down so any winter winds didn't carry it away and with tinsel around the edge, it prominently listed winter flavours of Christmas-cake crunch, apple cinnamon, cranberry, and Christmas pudding. He could vouch for the Christmas-cake crunch – one flavour that would definitely make his final cut.

He crossed the road and passed the bakery that was a winter wonderland with its criss-cross glass windows edged with fake snow, the Tudor-style exterior exhibiting a green garland with twinkling white lights looped across the top of the window frame and another around its doorway. A Santa pulling a sleigh full of presents sat behind the glass along with plated displays of gingerbread men with colourful coat buttons, mince pies, meringue snowmen and decadent chocolate yule logs.

Daniel walked past the archway that separated the bakery from the tea rooms and stopped outside. He might be a lot older than when he'd got caught red-handed by Etna, but that didn't make him any less petrified about doing this.

Etna hadn't held back on the decorations at the tea rooms. There was a garland on the front door festooned with gold, velvet ribbon amongst the greenery and tied at the top, and when Daniel pushed open the dark wooden door to the interior it was as inviting and cosy as he remembered, with a small tree in one corner. Each table had a bowl in the centre with red, green, gold and silver pieces that looked like dried petals. A string of lights hung around the front of the counter, framing the menu. It was the way it had always been, and when Etna came out from the back concentrating on carrying two mugs brimming with hot drinks topped with cream she didn't see him at first.

'Merry Christmas,' she greeted, walking back to him and around the other side of the counter. 'Now, what can I get for you?' Her smile wavered when she lifted her eyes to his. 'I heard you were back in the village,' she said after a pause.

'Etna, Merry Christmas to you too.'

'To what do I owe this pleasure?' she carried on formally,

brushing her hands on the green apron that had a big reindeer emblazoned on the front.

'I'm here to finally say I'm sorry.'

She was trying not to grin, or at least he hoped he'd read her reaction correctly. 'You're sorry for what?'

'Come on, Etna, you know what I'm sorry for.'

'I want you to say it.'

'Stop teasing him,' came a voice and he turned to see Barney sitting with a woman who had to be Lois. 'He's apologising. Let him get on with it.'

Etna smiled at last. 'I'm winding him up. If I can't have a little fun at Christmas then when can I? Don't you agree, Lois?' she called over to the woman with Barney.

With delicate features and around Barney's age, Lois sent a smile of reassurance in Daniel's direction. One hand on her mulberry silk neck scarf to stop it trailing in her drink, she shook her head. 'Don't get me involved, I'm just trying to enjoy my hot chocolate.'

Etna picked up her pad of paper and pencil. 'Well, seeing as it's Christmas, Daniel, you're of course forgiven. But only if you buy something and sit down for a while to tell me all about what you've been doing for the last... what is it? Twelve, thirteen years?'

'Thirteen. And you're on. I'll take a mochaccino seeing as you've gone all new age with the fancy machine.' He nodded towards an impressive coffee machine he thought he'd never see in Heritage Cove. And he had enough time before the delivery to take the proverbial olive branch Etna was offering. 'In fact, I'll take a farmhouse breakfast too, if I may.' Apart from a rushed bowl of cereal really early on and a whole heap of ice-cream, he hadn't had much to eat at all, so if he was going to get on with unpacking his delivery later he'd need a bit of sustainable energy rather than a sugar rush, and what better way to get it than with fried egg, a couple of bacon rashers, grilled tomato, baked beans and hot buttered toast?

'Coming right up,' she told him, tearing off the order and heading out back to hand it to whoever was the cook these days.

Daniel spoke briefly to Barney while he waited at a table to one side of the room. He found out Lois was here from Ireland for Christmas and New Year, and Barney was already talking about his next visit over to the Emerald Isle. It seemed this pair had at last found their happy ending and it couldn't happen to a nicer bloke.

Etna took care of a handful of customers Daniel didn't recognise and after she'd called someone through to take over for a while, she brought him his breakfast and his coffee. She was a bit like a mother hen as she sat watching him eat as though it had been days since his last meal, and she got him talking about what he'd been up to. She was thrilled about the new business, said it was good to bring it to Heritage Cove where locals prided themselves on their sense of community. She'd even said that with a straight face and, given his history, he hadn't expected it. She'd told him how sisters Celeste and Jade, who ran the bakery, had come back from a trip around Europe and started introducing locals to different coffees until she had a word in their ear.

When Daniel complimented her on one of the best mochaccinos he'd ever had, she told him, 'Coffees are what we do in here, they were stepping on my toes.'

'So you bought the machine to get one up on them?'

'Of course not. We sat down and had a talk and they agreed they wouldn't have coffees or hot drinks on their menu. That was my domain. But because they'd offered such a variety and people were taken by them, I had no choice but to invest in the beast of a machine you can see from here. Between you and me, Daniel, I've never looked back,' she added conspiratorially.

'Glad to hear it. And even more glad to know where I can get a decent coffee. But I do have to ask, will I be stepping on any toes by having hot drinks on my menu?'

She swished a hand through the air dismissively. 'I never expect to have total authority over food and beverage outlets in the Cove. Some things will overlap – the bakery and I both do sandwiches, and I do have one waffle dessert already – but it's when the business is right next door that it's a problem.'

'To be honest, the main thing with my new place is obviously going to be the waffles, the drinks are an aside.'

'I'm sure between us we can coexist quite happily.' She patted his hand and he felt forever grateful she didn't hold a grudge.

Etna left him to finish his coffee and when the tea rooms began to get busier, Daniel was about to leave and free up his table when the latest customer held his interest. Her name was Lottie and by his reckoning she'd be well into her twenties by now. Even so, he'd recognise her anywhere with her tight-ringleted chestnut hair and dimples that hadn't changed a bit after so many years.

Lottie did a double take when she saw Daniel as though she thought she knew this stranger but wasn't overly sure, and all he kept thinking about was the time he'd defaced the posters she'd carefully drawn and written on and put up around the village when her cat went missing. She was a teenager at the time, must've been about thirteen then, and he'd drawn a giant dog on all of the pictures with its jaws open, suggesting the fate the cat had probably succumbed to. He had no idea why he'd even done it – boredom and the need to cause a stir, most probably – but on the way home from school when he'd seen her sobbing at the edge of the road he'd felt terrible. She was distraught and so he'd dumped his bag at home and, still in school uniform, shirt hanging out and not giving a toss that it was pouring with rain and lightning threatened every corner of the cove, he'd scoured the streets and knocked on doors asking people to check their sheds for the missing cat. He'd about given up when he passed the florist and mentioned the search to the woman inside who was busy arranging a giant bouquet. She'd checked the sheds at the back of the shop and, lo and behold, there was the cat. The woman had helped him coax Lottie's cat into a carrier she had for her own feline, which wasn't an easy task at all, and Daniel had taken the cat straight over to Lottie's family home. She'd flung her arms around him on the doorstep as though he'd been a big brother saving the day, not that it had given him an ounce of pride – shame, more like it, for how mean he'd been to her by defacing her posters.

Maybe it was about time he told her the full truth. 'Lottie,' he called over from where he was sitting when she removed her gloves and sat at the table Barney and Lois had by now vacated.

'I'm sorry, do I know you? I do, don't I?' She was peering across the tea rooms at him, trying to work it out. 'I apologise, I can't place you.'

He smiled, got up and went over to her table. 'I'm Daniel.'

'Yes, that's it. Harvey's brother,' she smiled, satisfied the puzzle was solved at long last. 'Welcome back. It's been a while. And listen,' she added, looping her scarf from around her neck and putting it on the back of her chair along with her coat, 'I know some people judged you when you lived here but, for me, I was never in any doubt you were a good person. You found my cat and brought her home, and that meant the world to me. Not many young lads would've done that.'

He took a deep breath. 'Not many lads would deface a poster either.'

'What are you on about?' She thanked Etna when she

brought over a latte with a couple of gingernut biscuits on the side.

'It was me, I drew the picture of the giant dog looking as though it was going to eat your cat.'

Her biscuit didn't make it all the way to her mouth and she stared back at him in disbelief before she burst out laughing.

'You're not angry.'

'You were quite the artist. I'd forgotten all about that until you reminded me just now.' She was laughing so much she had tears in her eyes. 'I remember asking my dad if there was a giant dog in the Cove.'

He managed a laugh himself. 'Well, for what it's worth, I'm very sorry. It was mean and I'm not even sure why I did it really.'

Enjoying her biscuit, she was still amused. 'So, what is all this, Daniel? Are you making amends with everyone now you're back?'

'Yep. Apologised to Barney, Etna and now you. Few more to go.' He pulled the few flyers out from the back pocket of his jeans. 'This is what I'm doing now, if you're interested.'

She covered her mouth as she finished the biscuit and then told him, 'I saw the leaflet this morning in the convenience store – I own the place and run it now – this is great, I'll be there on opening night for sure. It's nice to welcome a new business to the Cove.'

'And Etna and I have spoken about hot beverages,' he whispered to her amusement. 'I intend to stay on the right side of her from now on.'

By the time Daniel made his way back to the waffle shack for the delivery that afternoon, pleased he'd cleared the air with two more of the Cove's residents, he wondered if he was right to feel so comfortable here in the village already.

He had a horrible feeling Harvey might be the one to make things so difficult for him he'd wish he'd never come back.

6

Lucy dried her eyes and made her way to the front of the chapel and the row of candles lined up before the altar. She lifted a long match, used an already burning flame to light it and held it on the wick of a fresh candle. For Joanna. It was something she always did at this time of the year, bittersweet as she remembered the good times they'd had, the closeness they'd shared. Joanna had always loved to sing carols, attend a Christmas service, and so since then Lucy had made sure she did the same.

Lucy sat down again to enjoy the choir's practice. It was less than two weeks to go until Christmas and this sound was a magical part of December in the village Lucy had all but fallen in love with. A choirmaster stood in front of the group conducting some twenty singers and as their sounds, accompanied by the organist, filled the small space, the sopranos' voices rang out with 'O Holy Night'. It was one of Lucy's favourite carols – as though they'd specially chosen it for her. The next, a tune she wasn't quite so familiar with that was delivered in a rich baritone, fell over her like velvet. She'd always found the magic of Christmas multiplied tenfold with a choir and tonight this local group of singers had well and truly lived up to expectations, and when they began to sing 'Silent Night' she had to cover her mouth to stop laughter from escaping at the memory of Joanna lying at the end of her bed after they'd been out to a pub on Christmas Eve, belting out the song at the top of her voice while all Lucy wanted to do was go to sleep. Her cousin had eventually crept back to her own room under the wine-fuelled impression she may have sung Lucy to sleep, and Lucy had got her own back by flinging open Joanna's door the next morning and belting out her own rendition of 'We Wish You a Merry Christmas'.

As the choir voices filled the chapel and wrapped around her, Lucy thought back to how supportive Joanna had been of her dream to become a female blacksmith. The teachers had looked at her as though she was loopy, her parents' frowns suggested maybe she ought to think of something different, but Joanna had insisted she never give up on the idea. She'd be so happy if she could see her now, see the work she did with her own business, and Lucy knew she'd have backed her cousin all the way in her quest to become a singer. She had talent for sure and although she'd not shared her dreams with many, Lucy knew them. She wanted to take singing lessons, audition for the West End, travel the world.

But she hadn't got to do any of that. All Joanna had got was twenty years – twenty birthdays, twenty Christmases, twenty New Year's Eves – before she was cruelly taken away.

Lucy pushed her tissue back into her pocket after blowing her nose and nodded a thank you to the choirmaster when he spotted her get up to leave. She buttoned her coat and stepped out of the chapel into the freezing, wintry air. There'd been hailstones this morning; Lucy had been woken by them and watched out of the window as they bounced off the tarmac of The Street, pelted the roof of the inn on the corner as you arrived in the Cove from one direction, danced on the pavements outside the tea rooms and the bakery. They were mesmerising to watch, but by mid-morning the hail had given way to shivering rain and bleak skies and now only a gentle wind and the winter cold remained.

Lucy wished it would snow. Tracy, who ran the Heritage Inn, had lived here all her life and when Lucy went to one of her book-club meetings Tracy had shown her photographs of Heritage Cove blanketed in white like a perfect scene from a winter jigsaw. Snow, inches thick, lined the tops of houses, covered the roofs of the bakery, the tea rooms and the pub. It ran up the sides of the bus stop in curved drifts, blended the road into the pavements so you could no longer see the divide. English winters didn't always bring snow, especially at Christmas time, but maybe this year it would grace them with its presence for Lucy's first festive season living in Heritage Cove.

'Lucy...' a voice called out to her as a figure crossed The Street towards her.

Daniel. Her heart skipped a beat as it usually did when he came near and having not seen him since they'd talked in her workshop, it felt good to be back in his company. She only hoped her nose wasn't red from blowing it before. She tried to summon some festive cheer. 'You missed the choir practice, but if you hurry you might be able to try out for a solo.' She laughed at his reaction of abject horror. 'I'm teasing.'

'Thank goodness.' His breath mingled with hers in the cold air beneath the lamplight. 'I thought you were serious and I'd feel obliged to join in. I don't think the Cove is quite ready for my singing yet. Or make that ever. Are you in the choir?'

'No, I'm not sure the Cove is ready for mine yet either.'

He returned her smile but he was pretty switched on and asked, 'You okay?'

They walked on in the direction of her flat and the waffle

shack beyond. 'I always go into a church or a chapel around Christmas to remember my cousin Joanna. I like to light a candle, I think about her, and I let myself have a bit of a cry. Silly, I know. She's been gone ten years, nothing will bring her back.'

His hand came to her shoulder and she stopped walking. 'Grief doesn't have an ending; it'll always be with you. Don't ever apologise for being sad and paying your respects.'

'Life can be cruel,' she said. 'We were like sisters, you know.'

'You grew up together?'

'We were inseparable. We went through childhood together, got into the odd scrape, had adventures as teenagers, annoyed each other sometimes like siblings do. But we laughed a lot too... in fact we laughed all the time, sometimes at nothing much at all.'

'I get it,' he said. 'Harvey and I may not be close now but once upon a time we were. If I dig way deep into my memory bank, I have a lot of happy times to recall.'

'Name one,' she grinned.

He puffed out his cheeks, eyes rolling as though deep in thought. 'The time we built a fort in the garden. Dad was away, it was one of those boiling-hot summer days, Mum sat on a deck chair and we dragged over every bit of wood we could find and constructed what we thought was the best fort in history. It wasn't so big we could stand up in it but it was big enough to get inside, and we even made sure we had a window to wave through to Mum. We took all our toy cars in there too, used our hands to dig the dirt and build ramps.'

'That's a lovely memory.'

'I understand why you're sad, Lucy. You feel a part of you is missing.'

He'd got it in one and she wondered, was that how he felt about Harvey even though his brother was still alive, still here, just not in his life the way he was supposed to be?

'You know, Joanna was a great singer. She'd fit in well with the rest of the choir,' she said tilting her head in the direction of the chapel, where sounds still rang out into the evening air, faint but audible. 'They're all professional and I bet if Joanna was in there she'd be bossing them about.' She found she was smiling as they began to walk on from the chapel and past the top of the track that led down to the cove. 'So, what are you doing out and about tonight?' she asked. 'Been to the pub?'

'I've been for a walk and I'm due at the ice-creamery to collect supplies now I've finally chosen the flavours I want to sell.'

She shivered involuntarily. 'The thought of ice-cream makes me cold.'

'It might work to cheer you up,' he suggested. 'Why don't you come with me? We'll collect the supplies and then what do you say to hot waffles and ice-cream?'

'Your place isn't open yet.'

'No, but I need a guinea pig.' He blundered over his words. 'Not that I'm calling you a pig... I just...'

'Daniel, I'd love to come and try out some flavours.' And just like that she'd gone from sad and thinking she'd have a good cry when she got home to feeling a whole lot better.

They made their way behind the trees and over to the ice-creamery, a modern sea-blue, white-shuttered venue with a big ice-cream cone painted on the outside wall. It was way too cold tonight for anyone to be sitting outside on the picnic bench, and its cherry-red umbrella that came out in summertime was nowhere to be seen. They talked about the flavours on offer and Lucy had to admit that while thinking about cold desserts made her feel the winter even more, the prospect of enjoying the ice-creamery's adventurous festive flavours with hot waffles in Daniel's company had never been more appealing, especially when she saw a teenager inside tucking into what looked to be a small tub of the chunky Christmas-cake crunch with hot sauce drizzled across it.

They carried the tubs of ice-cream between them all the way back to the shack, where Lucy admired the lamp-post now concreted in its base outside and all ready for her sign to be hung on it to give this place a name. With the frontage looking so beautiful and from the veranda a view of grassed area and the giant village Christmas tree, this place was already something special and it wasn't even opening night.

Daniel let them inside and flipped on one set of lights to give the shack a soft glow. 'Low lights tonight,' he explained, leading her through the main seating area to the kitchen at the back kitted out with stainless-steel appliances and a row of waffle makers along a benchtop. 'I don't want people to think I'm open for business.'

'Me neither. I want to be first in line for these waffles.'

He loaded his ice-creams into the freezer and took the stack she had in her arms to slot them in too. 'Let me take your coat. It's warm enough inside, I've been here most of the day washing crockery, stacking it away, doing paperwork. And I'll put the heater back on for us.'

'Can I have a tour?' He was standing close to her in the narrow kitchen, so close she'd brushed her arm against his body when he took her coat.

'A tour? It's pretty much what you see is what you get, but come on.' He grinned. 'This is the kitchen.'

'Funny.' She swatted him with her hand. The flirting between them came naturally from both sides and she wasn't wary of him at all. Even going by past reputation, some of which wasn't good, he was nothing like the man some people would have you believe Daniel Luddington to be.

He took her back through to show her the main area with its

wooden walls and roof, the cosy tables for four and a couple of bigger tables for families covered in wipe-clean gingham table-cloths. There was a serving counter ready for action and at the back through another couple of doors she got to see the bath-rooms, which were on the small side as expected. What wasn't expected was how close she'd have to squeeze against his body to get in there to see for herself.

'I'm thinking it's one at a time to use the bathroom.' The corners of his mouth twitched as he looked down at her, their bodies pressed together. 'Otherwise you'll find yourself in this situation with a total stranger.' She felt her hair shift beneath his breath before she passed back through into the main area of the shack.

He clasped strong hands together as though he didn't trust himself not to reach out and touch her. 'Waffle time?'

She smiled and followed him back into the kitchen. He handed her one of two aprons from the hook at the end of the room. They had a logo with 'the Little Waffle Shack' written in loopy white letters and a print of a couple of waffles beneath the wording. Lucy hitched one over her head, wrapped the belt around twice and tied it in a bow at the back.

Between them they cracked eggs, weighed dry ingredients and whisked batter until it was ready to use in the heart-shaped waffle iron Lucy selected for use.

'Typical girl,' said Daniel with a grin after he switched it on to heat up.

'I've never had heart-shaped waffles, I want to know what they taste like.'

'They taste the same as... oh, you're winding me up.' She was laughing as he poured batter into the centre of the waffle plate and closed the top. 'Get ready for the perfect waffle, coming right up. I'll keep it simple first – plain, with a bit of ice-cream on the side. Sure to be a crowd-pleaser. And, thankfully, I've been for a run and a walk today so I can get away with eating plenty.'

When the waffles were ready, golden and thick and easy to slide off the heated plates, Daniel put them onto a white plate from the stack in the cupboard, dusted the top with a little icing sugar and added a scoop of Christmas-pudding ice-cream while Lucy added a scoop of the cinnamon variety. She put her scoop right on top of the golden waffles to let it melt onto the warm surface.

'Dig in,' he said, handing her a fork.

They demolished the light, sweet waffles between them. 'This one gets my seal of approval,' she told him when there was nothing left on the plate apart from a smear where the ice-cream had once been.

'The ice-cream is good.'

'I was talking about the waffle,' she smiled. 'Take the compliment.' When he nodded she realised he wasn't used to doing that, and that in itself was endearing.

'I'll be adding a Christmas-gingerbread waffle to the menu ready for opening.'

She sucked in air. 'Now, that sounds divine. What's the recipe?'

'Key ingredients will be cinnamon, ginger and nutmeg and I'll serve it with maple syrup drizzled across.'

'People around here are going to love you.' Awkward she'd spoken out loud when those words possibly sounded a lot better in her head, she asked, 'Any more festive recipes?'

He described a couple of the others, one with pumpkin spices, another red velvet – the perfect colour for Christmas. 'So, what would you like to try next?' he asked.

'What? You can't be serious.' She put a hand against her stomach. 'That's quite enough for one night.'

'Oh no, you committed to tasting, you're not leaving until all that batter is finished.'

Her face fell.

'I'm kidding,' he laughed. 'You're off the hook. For now.'

She bit down on her lip, wondering if she was imagining his teasing, the suggestion behind his words.

'I'll put the batter in the fridge, we'll take a break. How does that sound?'

'Perfect. And maybe we can try smaller samples next.' They'd gone a bit crazy with the ice-cream scoops and, with lots of combinations still to try, the only way she'd get through it was if they went a lot smaller.

He offered her a drink from the fully stocked fridge and with a bottle of water each they went to sit at the table right at the back, where they would be almost hidden if someone were to peer in through the window.

'So, what happened to your fort?' she asked him. 'I assume it's not still in the garden at Tumbleweed House.'

He laughed. 'No, didn't last long. A storm blew it down that night, but it did us a favour. We knew we'd have to clear it away before Dad came home from his business trip.'

'He doesn't sound a very nice man, if you don't mind me saying.'

'He wasn't, and I don't.'

'I hate thinking of you and Harvey growing up that way.'

With a sigh he said, 'It wasn't so bad. We had good times – as I've proven, we've got some good memories.'

'I'm pleased your fort wasn't torn down,' she smiled when he didn't volunteer anything else. 'What is it? I can tell you've got another story to tell. Please let it be a good one.'

His face said it wasn't. 'The fort was gone but my dad found another way to get to me. Now, don't laugh but I once had a tortoise...'

'How is that funny?'

'...called Speedy.' He smiled when she covered her mouth to stifle a giggle. 'Not sure why I named him that. But anyway. I'd had Speedy a long while; he lived in an outdoor shelter in our garden. It was the week after the fort blew down and Dad came home. He had the ride-on mower ready to go and I was yelling at him that he had to move Speedy, who'd gone walkabout away from his little house. Dad dismissed me and so I was running around the garden trying to find Speedy before the lawnmower did.'

'Oh, God, please tell me you found him before he mowed the lawn.'

'Dad did.' His face said this wasn't a good thing at all, in fact quite the opposite. 'But he picked Speedy up and threw him to me.'

'You didn't catch him?'

'I caught him. But tortoises can die from stress – honestly, they really can. Loud noises, being handled too much, certainly being lobbed across a garden. I did my best to take care of him after that but he still died.'

'I'm sorry.' Lucy couldn't imagine a parent being so cruel. And she suddenly remembered the first time Daniel had come into the workshop and his reaction when she mentioned making a tortoise for a boy who was crazy about them. Now she realised why he'd looked as though he had something else to say.

'Yeah, not as sorry as I was, or Speedy for that matter.' He blew out from between his lips. 'Anyway, enough talking about my dad. How's the lead-up to Christmas going?'

She readily accepted a change of subject. 'Busy. Lots of commissions so I'm working longer hours but at least it's the season for it. Inside the workshop with the forge going is a lot nicer in the winter than the summer. I'll take a break once the rush dies down and then it'll be on again in the new year.'

He asked her more about the work she did and she told him about things she made for people's homes, both outside and in – wine racks, shelf brackets, ornaments for the kitchen; benches, gates and garden accessories for the outside. 'I have a trellis to make for the Copper Plough's beer garden that they want come spring.'

'And did you always want to be a blacksmith? If that's what you still call yourself.'

'The job title could be artist, metalworker, welder, blacksmith. There are so many facets of the job – one of the things I most enjoy – but I call myself a blacksmith for the business. It fits, especially somewhere like Heritage Cove.'

'It's a unique village, steeped with character.'

'You sound like Etna now. But I agree, it really is. And to answer your other question, yes, I always wanted to be a blacksmith. I was arty at school, loved any design classes, especially when we got to do a bit of metalwork, and I loved nothing more than getting my hands dirty. On a school trip one year we saw horseshoes being made and it got me all the more interested in making shapes out of metal. I was amazed at what could be done. I was fascinated that you could take an ugly lump of metal or a big long stick of it and turn it into something pretty, something that didn't belong in a junkyard but could have pride of place in your home.' He gulped down more of his water as she asked, 'How about you? Did you always know you wanted to make waffles?'

He laughed. 'Not exactly.' His whole face took on the look of a kid getting up to mischief when he was relaxed and happy. 'I bummed around for a while after I left the Cove and then I found work as a maintenance guy. I worked for a company who did refits of warehouses, offices and showrooms. I enjoyed the labouring, working with my hands, but it was all about earning a wage, I didn't ever have a yearning to do it.'

'So how did you go from that to someone who makes waffles?'

Blue eyes, betraying a hint of mistrust, held a wariness as he looked across the table at her and Lucy sensed she wasn't going to get the whole story from Daniel. At least not yet. 'I was always interested in cooking but I suppose I'd forgotten about it somewhere along the line.' His words suggested there was more to it than that but Lucy let him carry on without interrupting. 'I eventually progressed from maintenance man to studying hospitality before I found a job waiting tables, then another as a kitchen hand. And when I say kitchen hand, it was the drudgery all chefs have to go through and work their way up from. Kind of like a rite of passage.'

'So, why waffle maker and not a chef?' she asked, her drink all but gone.

'I'd already heard about a course that offered the basic knowhow of setting up your own business. With nothing on the work horizon to pull me out of my job as a kitchen hand and send me onto the next level up, I thought, why not do it? I knew it wouldn't be a waste of time, so I put my head down and did the work, I learned about writing a business plan, managing finances, competitors, research and marketing. What I wasn't overly sure about was that I wanted to work towards owning a restaurant. I'd been in the environment, seen the stress, and I wasn't convinced I was cut out for it. It seemed one giant leap too far.'

She listened as he told her all about a joint hen and stag do in Bruges that had been a whole lot of fun but had also made him start to wonder about the alternatives to becoming a chef and having a restaurant.

'I began to think smaller – greasy spoon, a sandwich shop, even a food truck, which appealed because of the freedom of going around festivals or funfairs. But I kept thinking about the waffles and the workshop I'd taken part in when we were in Bruges and that was the idea that really struck a chord with me.

'And now you have the Little Waffle Shack.' She smiled, looking around. 'The idea went from a boozy weekend to all of this. You must be thrilled with the way it's looking.'

'I sure am. And I've gone into this prepared – with my eyes wide open, if you like.'

'The only way to be in business.'

'Cheers to that.' He lifted his empty bottle to hers. 'Wine would be better for a toast but these will have to do for now.'

Lucy was about to ask him more about the life he'd had away from Heritage Cove, see if their friendship was already as solid as she felt it was, when there was a knock at the door to the shack.

Daniel groaned but not when he saw his mum peering in through the window. 'Only she can get away with being so nosy,' he grinned to Lucy. 'Anyone else and I'd tell them to bugger off,' he added before he went to answer the door.

Lucy wondered whether he meant he'd get rid of other people because the business wasn't open or because he wanted to spend time with just her. She really hoped it was the latter. And it gave her even more impetus to end this sham with Julian in the new year. It wasn't right and it kept her tethered to him indefinitely, which wasn't exactly the clean break she'd been looking for.

'What are you doing wandering around in the dark?' Daniel asked Carol after he ushered her inside, out of the cold.

'I've come to see the tree, of course. You know I like to see it lots in December, to be out with other people in the village getting excited about Christmas coming.' She leaned around his form to see he had company. 'Hello, Lucy, good to see you.'

'Good to see you too,' she smiled, leaving the table and coming over to chat. 'The tree is beautiful, isn't it?' she confirmed, both of them looking out of the window, across the green space to the impressive marking of another Christmas in Heritage Cove.

'Do I smell waffles?' Carol asked.

Daniel winked at Lucy. 'Your cold has obviously gone, Mum. And, yes, you do. Lucy has been helping me test out some flavour combinations.'

'Rather you than me, Lucy. Who knows what he's already done to my waistline? Thank goodness he's found someone else to taste-test.'

'Did you see the light on?' Daniel asked.

'Of course I did – I don't often lurk around empty shacks. And I'd knocked on the door to your place; you weren't there so it was either the pub or here.'

Lucy took her coat from the back of a chair and pulled it on, dismissing Carol's concerns she'd interrupted. 'No, it's fine. I should be off home. I still haven't written my Christmas cards and it's on my to-do list for tonight. Every year I try to do them on December 1st and I don't think I've ever succeeded. Thanks for the waffles,' she smiled over at Daniel.

He towered over his mum and when his gaze met hers, told her, 'Anytime.'

She left them to it. As well as Daniel being cautious over sharing too much about himself with anyone else, she knew family tension for the Luddingtons ran high and she didn't much fancy getting in the middle of it, especially when she saw Harvey by the tree. Something told her that Carol may well have engineered this meeting of the brothers and she had to hand it to the woman for her bravery. Perhaps if she'd seen the way they'd looked at each other in the pub the other night or heard about their confrontation outside she might have thought twice about this.

Lucy waved over to Melissa, who was chatting with another couple, and then headed back to her flat. She had twenty-six cards to write and she wanted to do them all tonight, post them in the morning and then she could relax. All her gifts were bought, not yet wrapped, and so she was slowly getting ready for Christmas. And when she finished work she intended to take a long-awaited break and hibernate. Although whether she'd hide away when waffles and Daniel's company were on offer she wasn't sure.

She was about to go through the little gate and up her path when she saw a young woman loitering on the other side of the road near the bend and the guesthouse. Talking into a mobile phone, she was looking around her as though she was lost. Her winter coat flapped open to reveal a decent-sized baby bump and she had long, dark hair with a thick-cut fringe and the sort of European skin that was likely the same nutty brown all year round – she was beautiful. But before Lucy could offer her help or some directions, the woman must have realised she wasn't in the right village at all because she got into her car on Lucy's side of the road and drove away.

Lucy, still full from the waffles, got straight on with the cards as soon as she'd hung up her coat, fed Shadow and turned on the tree lights. She started with her parents, selecting a traditional design of a village scene from days gone by, complete with red phone box and a classic car you didn't see much of these days. She sent similar designs to other relatives and when she'd finally addressed all the envelopes, restless and eager to move, probably because she'd eaten so much, she changed into her dungarees and headed down into her workshop. She had an idea and wanted to work on it right now.

She flipped through the photographs of some of her projects

that she kept in case clients needed inspiration and found the picture of the tortoise she'd made for the little boy. When Daniel had told her the story of Speedy tonight he'd tried to act as though it was all ancient history but she had a picture of him in her mind's eye as a little boy, distraught at how his dad had brutally treated the pet he loved.

Now, with a design in mind, she knew what she was going to do. She was going to make a tortoise for Daniel. He could keep it at home on the window sill or at the waffle shack, or wherever he liked – he could keep it outside if he preferred. All she wanted was for him to have a special something and she hoped it might help in some way.

And as she worked with the metal her mind drifted as much as her concentration would allow, wondering how Daniel was going to react when he saw that it wasn't only his mum out to see the tree tonight but his estranged brother too.

Carol's stunt could only spell trouble, and, deep down, Lucy knew she was already invested in Daniel being a part of Heritage Cove again. She liked it even more here now he'd come back for good.

7

'Mulled wine?' Carol asked her son as they walked from the Little Waffle Shack across to the big village tree, passing the cart run by the pub on the way.

Daniel knew it was likely to be Benjamin's recipe so he wasn't going to say no to that. 'Let me get them.' He asked for two and both he and Carol took a polystyrene cup between their hands as they went over to the giant Norway spruce decorated with hundreds of coloured lights.

'Are you going to put a small tree in your waffle shack?' his mum asked after an approving sip of the warming wine mixture.

'I think I will. There's a Christmas tree farm just past the florist, isn't there?'

'There is, and I know they deliver.'

It was only as they got closer to the village tree and Daniel could see faces lit up in the glow of the lights that he spotted Harvey. 'Mum, what are you playing at?' he groaned. 'This is such a bad idea.'

'He's your brother,' was all she said, and when Harvey's eyes came Daniel's way it was clear he hadn't been in on this little plan of hers either. 'Your dad took enough away from us all,' she lectured. 'Don't let him take away your relationship too.'

But sometimes Daniel wondered whether they were too late to save it. And maybe he did have the Luddington stubborn streak after all, because he wasn't about to suck up to his brother if Harvey couldn't be man enough to accept he'd changed and was back here with good intentions. And if Daniel didn't cave, Harvey was unlikely to, and so they were at an impasse. An impasse not even the thrill of the Christmas season with all its twinkling decorations could push through.

Melissa came over with Harvey in tow and said an awkward hello but Daniel stepped forwards and hugged her. It wasn't Melissa he had an issue with, after all. 'Good to see you again – didn't get much of a chance to talk in the pub the other night. How's work been? I hear you're in cabin crew now.' He was rambling, but it was either that or the strong, silent treatment and something about his mum's presence, knowing she'd been through a lot of shit with his dad and then with him going AWOL for so long, made him at least make an attempt to be civil.

Daniel sensed that his good mood after Lucy's close company at the waffle shack was about to disappear when his mum went off chatting with Melissa, leaving the boys alone.

'I didn't know she was going to do this,' he said to Harvey without looking at his brother. Both stood there, a couple of metres between them, as though their attention was solely on a tree.

'What are you really doing back in the village, Daniel?'

'What kind of a question is that?' He turned and gestured to the shack behind them. 'I think the shack kind of speaks for itself.'

'But why here?'

'This was my home as much as yours – you don't own the

Cove.'

'Never said I did,' Harvey huffed. 'But wherever you go you bring trouble.'

With a sigh he admitted, 'Once upon a time you would've been right.'

'So, you've changed all of a sudden?'

'Why is that so hard for you to accept?'

'Experience.'

'Your experience of me was a long time ago and even then we didn't hang around with each other a whole lot, not in the end. You barely knew me before I left.'

Harvey's voice went up an octave. 'You're right, I didn't know you, you made it hard to do that.' He reined it in when a couple next to them looked their way. 'But I knew the things you did, the people you upset, including our own mother.'

'Mum knows I made mistakes and yet she is giving me the benefit of the doubt. Not that she needs to, she can see I'm different to who I was back then. You know, sometimes it's as though you had to endure our dad and I didn't, as though you were the only one suffering.'

Harvey pushed his hands into his pockets when blowing on them seemed to do no good in holding off the December chill. 'I never thought that.'

'Maybe not.' He crumpled the polystyrene cup when he'd finished his mulled wine but it wasn't nearly as satisfying as he'd hoped it might be. 'But you think I'm just like him, don't you?'

'Dad?' Harvey shook his head. 'I hope to God you're not.'

'I don't bully women and kids so there's no comparison.'

'I know.' Harvey's admission startled Daniel into silence. 'I don't think you're like him at all, but he brought trouble and then you did. I suppose that's where the comparison lies for me.'

'Yeah, well, thanks to friends I've made along the way, I pulled myself out of a pretty dismal existence and I think I'm of good character now. But I don't suppose you're interested in hearing about any of that.' Harvey seemed stunned at his claims. His mum knew what Daniel had been through, how he'd got from there to here, but he'd asked her not to share it with anyone, including his brother. He wanted to make peace on his own terms, not for Harvey to feel sorry for him and that be the measure by which he was judged for who he was now.

Daniel waited to see if his brother would ask more but when he didn't, he walked away. The silence was even worse than the slanging match outside the pub the other night.

He left the festive cheer behind and headed home to his cottage, scuffing the ground in the field he crossed part of the way with the toe of his boot, some satisfaction drawn at churning up the mud loosened by the hail that had left it sodden.

Once inside the cottage he kicked off his boots, yanked open the fridge, pulled out a beer and sat on the kitchen chair. He didn't even bother to turn the lights on – the glow from a lamp outside was enough.

Even after all these years Harvey still had the ability to get right under his skin. Harvey thought he had a monopoly on being wronged by a shitty father and a brother who abandoned him, and he was right to think that. But what Harvey failed to see was that along the way, Daniel had taken his fair share of life's crap too. And he'd had nobody to pick him up from his failures, his mistakes or his actions, he'd had to do it himself, and it was the hardest thing he'd ever had to do.

* * *

For the next few days Daniel threw himself into getting ready for opening night at the Little Waffle Shack. He didn't see Lucy –

even when he purposely went on a run past her place he didn't bump into her – but every time he stopped for a break and let his mind wander he was right back there opposite her at the table in the shack, her easiness to talk to and her openness just two of the qualities he knew had him hook, line and sinker. He wanted to turn up at the workshop and carry on their conversation, he wanted to share more about himself and hope she did the same. But, for now, he had a business to focus on. The kitchen at the shack was completely stocked with two days to go until opening. The cupboards and the corner pantry were filled with dry ingredients, the fridge shelf space brimmed with everything that needed to be chilled, he'd tested and retested all the equipment – waffle makers, cooker, the sink, the dishwasher all worked – and now he was up to the stage where he could display the finalised menus in their little stands at the tables.

Daniel had devised his menu so that it offered a whole range, from sweet waffles with fruit or ice-cream toppings or sauces in all sorts of flavours – blueberry, butterscotch, chocolate – to savoury waffles with ham, cheese and button mushrooms mixed into batter ready for pressing into the waffle maker, or parmesan and bacon, or a plain waffle with herbs, or one with cheddar and rosemary. There were Christmassy shaped and themed waffles for kids and adults alike. He could make gluten-free, sugar-free, dairy-free if the customer required, with separate equipment for each to avoid contamination.

And now, with menus standing proudly at the centre of tables, others slotted into a wooden wall shelf beside the entrance for arriving customers to pluck and browse from, he locked up the shack and it was time for a well-earned drink at the Copper Plough. Up until the run-in with Harvey the other night he'd been nervous about bumping into his sibling when he was out and about, but not any more. Harvey could go and take a running jump if he thought he was going to make Daniel feel unwelcome in the village he'd grown up in. He had just as much right to be here as his brother did. And he'd been apologising to even more people he'd wronged along the way and none of them had had a problem with him. He'd given an envelope to Mrs Filligree with a couple of hundred pounds inside to cover the amount she surely must have had to fork out on her garden fence after he'd once fallen into it when larking about and had never admitted to doing. He'd gone to see Kenneth Soames, who still had the same allotment he'd had back when Daniel was sixteen and thought it funny to steal lettuces and carrots from, leading Kenneth to take up a twenty-four-hour watch until the shenanigans stopped. He'd also found Patricia, who turned out to be working in the tea rooms with Etna, and apologised for breaking into her garden shed once. She'd asked him why he'd done it, told him there wasn't anything missing when she saw him leave, and he'd admitted he'd been hiding from his dad until he realised he had to go home eventually and face the consequences of a bad school report. Patricia had taken pity on him at his admission the other day and promptly made him a bacon butty to eat as he walked back to the waffle shack.

Daniel had a list of tame misdemeanours but he also had a more shameful list of worse crimes. He'd broken into a couple of houses; he couldn't claim it was others who'd made him do it, and he knew he'd got off lightly with community service when those he'd picked on hadn't wanted to throw the book at him – maybe out of respect for his mum and the rest of his family. He'd tried to go to those houses and apologise too but neither owner lived there any more. Part of him had been relieved because he was ashamed of the things he'd done and wasn't sure he'd get a very warm welcome. But it wasn't those acts that kept him up at night, it was the other brush with the law after leaving Heritage Cove that sometimes gave him nightmares of being trapped in a cell unable to get out, of Harvey telling him he got what he deserved.

Benjamin was on a rare night off from chef duty at the pub and already waiting on the customer-side of the bar when Daniel walked in, and when they'd had a quick catch-up about getting ready for opening day, Daniel recounted some of his tales of making amends.

'It's like completing one of the twelve steps alcoholics have to deal with,' said Benjamin.

'Yeah, well, I'm glad not everyone is holding a grudge.'

'Is anyone at all?' He thanked the barmaid for the pints of Guinness she settled on the bar top.

'Only one person.'

'Don't tell me' – Benjamin licked away the creamy froth that clung to his top lip after his first sip – 'your brother.'

'Got it in one.'

'He's a good guy, I don't get it. Did you take all his toys when you were little? Blame everything on him? Steal his girlfriend? What?'

'None of the above. I left.'

'That's it? You left?'

Daniel sipped his pint. When the going got tough he'd got going, he would never dispute that, but Harvey had done the same without realising. And he'd done it a long time before Daniel. The only difference was he'd stayed physically in the same place. Harvey had sought solace at Barney's and he'd had Melissa, and his escape route was shockingly similar as far as Daniel was concerned. Harvey just couldn't see it.

'Talking of stealing girlfriends,' Benjamin went on, perhaps sensing a deep-and-meaningful wasn't really on the cards, 'not that it's stealing because she's single... I dated her a while back...'

'Get to the point, mate.'

'How about I set you up on a blind date?'

'Not a chance,' he said swiftly. 'Not interested but thanks for the offer. And besides, I'm way too busy with starting my own business to think about women for a while.' Unless it was a certain blonde who went by the name of Lucy. 'Come on, I'll give you a game of darts.' The board at the back of the pub where the quiz was always held had become vacant.

'You're on. But I warn you, I practise when it's quiet in here.'

'Don't worry. I had a dartboard as a kid.' He'd used it to vent his frustration many a time.

Daniel and Benjamin got through several games before turning their attention to the pool table until they finally took up their stations back at the bar. Benjamin ordered another round and Daniel checked his phone when it vibrated in his pocket.

Lucy. She must've got his number from his contact sheet and was texting to say the sign was ready. He messaged her back. 'Photo?' And her reply came straight away to say there wasn't a chance of her sending one, he'd need to see it in person and could come over whenever he liked.

Shame they'd just got another round in. Because this was an offer he didn't want to refuse.

'What's the smile for?' Benjamin quizzed, pocketing his change.

Daniel pushed his phone into his back pocket. 'No reason.'

'Come on, nobody looks that happy just because they won a few games of darts.'

'And three games of pool, don't forget.'

'I think we should avoid talking about it, don't you?' Benjamin protested.

Talk turned to work in the hospitality sphere, their hopes and dreams and how they'd both started out. They shared anecdotes of the terrible jobs they'd both had as kitchen hands, although

Benjamin's sounded worse than his. He'd worked a stint in a restaurant on the Norfolk coast where the owner had served a good Sunday roast. Unfortunately, as waiting staff brought plates from the restaurant into the kitchen for washing up, Benjamin had been instructed that any roast potatoes left on the plates – whole ones, obviously – could be scraped into an awaiting bowl and reused on the next roast dinner to go out to customers.

'He used to offer me a roast dinner on the house at the end of my shift,' Benjamin laughed into his pint. 'Funnily enough, I'd always tell him I had one waiting for me at home.'

'Don't know how he got away with it. The hygiene courses and certifications now are lengthy and I don't think any business owner can afford to risk their customers' health like that. I can't imagine keeping an uneaten portion of waffle and slapping it onto someone else's plate. And I hope you didn't bring any of those practices here to the pub.'

'He'd better not have done.' Terry, the landlord, had over-heard their conversation as he strode across the pub collecting glasses, ducking each beam. Terry had been one of those to treat Daniel no differently than before, to not even bat an eyelid that he was back, and it was good to be able to sit in here without judgement. Daniel would be forever grateful he'd never wronged Heritage Cove's publican because not having a watering hole didn't bear thinking about when the next nearest pub was at least four miles away.

When Benjamin's girlfriend Zoe arrived, Daniel left them to it and set off along The Street hoping Lucy would still be awake and ready for a visitor. And when he saw a light coming from the door to the workshop, he knew his luck was in and headed on down the path.

There was no need to ring the new doorbell – the door was ajar – and when he peeked in, Lucy was using a tool that produced a lot of sparks as well as noise. She had the same helmet on that she'd been wearing the first day they met and he hovered as she worked so he didn't frighten her.

At last she spotted him, turned off the machine and set down the tool she was handling. She lifted off her helmet and, just like the first time, her hair tumbled down across her shoulders, except rather than being straight, this time it was wavy.

'You're curly,' he said, pointing to her hair when she set her helmet down, removed a thick glove and came on over.

She put a hand to her hair. 'I wound it into plaits last night, I'm experimenting for Christmas-party season, you know what it's like. Or maybe not,' she smiled coyly.

'It suits you.' He had a feeling anything would. And he kind of liked it that he'd caught her off guard. It showed a different Lucy to the confident one he'd become used to, or the sad one he'd seen when they met outside the chapel after she'd been listening to carols.

'Thanks. Right, the sign.' She led him through to the more comfortable side of the workshop. 'Here it is.'

Beside the desk the sign and its bracket sat proudly and a smile broke across his face. 'It's amazing. I'm more than happy with it, you've done a brilliant job.' The lettering was held together in a way that flowed, the scrolling details every bit as expert as he'd come to realise Lucy could deliver. 'The Little Waffle Shack,' he recited, because seeing it on the sign was a confirmation of the business he would make a success of, no matter what his brother thought. He'd opted not to paint wording on the shack itself, preferring to leave it as a log cabin, traditional and welcoming without looking commercialised. Instead, he'd have this wrought-iron sign hanging on his new lamp-post out front and he'd already got approval from the council to put a sign by the bus stop to direct people up to the cabin from The Street.

'I'm glad you're pleased with it,' she smiled. 'You need to hang it.' She picked up her keys. 'Come on, no time like the present.'

He laughed. 'Now? Are you serious? It's dark out there. And cold.'

'Don't be such a wuss,' she called back from the workshop, where she was already ensuring the machine was definitely switched off, her equipment safely stowed away. 'I want to see it in all its glory.'

'Well, I suppose you did fit me in last minute, in time for opening night.'

'Exactly. I'll just go and grab my scarf and I'll be right back with you.' She'd already picked up a different coat, presumably so her grubby dungarees didn't ruin her best one, and when she came back from upstairs, she picked up the bracket, he took the sign, and together they made their way to the waffle shack.

Lucy held the torch and Daniel positioned the stepladder he'd got from inside. He'd put it there yesterday in anticipation of this moment because the lamp wasn't going to be switched on until opening night. With screwdriver in hand he climbed up and took the bracket from Lucy. He fixed it onto the pole of the lamp-post he'd had installed and when it was done she handed him the sign. 'This is it,' he said, almost to himself.

'A moment not to be missed,' she prompted, holding the torch in one hand and her phone in her other to record his moment of glory with a picture.

He slipped the holes in the two chains through the hooks on the bracket and let the sign hang down. 'It looks even better out here than it did in the workshop.' He turned around with a big smile. It wasn't hard – he was completely over the moon.

'I'll send you the photos,' Lucy grinned, flipping through those she'd taken on her phone. 'You can put them on your social media.'

'Thanks, appreciate it. A selfie never would've been the same and to be honest I wouldn't have thought to take one. But I'm glad you captured it.'

'It's a proud moment, one you'll want to remember. And it's a moment that calls for a toast.'

'I could get us some water,' he suggested.

She had him hold the torch. 'No need.' And from the enormous pocket on a coat that could've been picked up in a jumble sale but didn't detract from her beauty or her warm smile in the slightest, she pulled out a miniature bottle of sparkling wine.

'Do you always carry beverages around with you?' he laughed as she pulled a face opening the top. When it popped they both let out a cheer as a little bit of gas snaked into the air.

'Of course not, but I grabbed this earlier when I went up to get my scarf. It's nothing fancy, I had it in the fridge left over from when I had the girls round recently.'

'I'll get some glasses from the shack.'

'Don't worry about it,' she shrugged. 'More fun this way.' She indicated she was about to take a swig. 'I don't mind sharing if you don't.'

'Go ahead.' She did just that and with a smile handed him the bottle.

The bubbles went right up his nose. 'Not used to fizzy stuff,' he spluttered. 'Thanks, Lucy. You've done me proud.' This was a moment he'd treasure forever because of the significance, because of the company.

'It's my absolute pleasure. Would you mind if I included one of the photos on my website? Either with or without you in it, of course, whatever you'd prefer.'

'Happy to be in it if you are.'

'Of course.'

She set down the bottle and Daniel positioned the stepladder.

He put the torch on the ground so its beam highlighted the sign. They each climbed up one side of the ladder, heads together, the phone on a timer on top, and posed for another picture – one Daniel knew he'd choose as the best one.

Photo shoot done, Lucy picked up the bottle again and insisted he have the last swig because it was his business they were celebrating.

He finished it off, set the bottle and ladder on the veranda and pushed his hands back into his pockets. He didn't want tonight to be over. 'It's getting colder, wonder if it'll snow.'

'Hey, you could get snow for opening night.'

'I doubt that. Maybe for Christmas if we're lucky.'

'Christmas,' she smiled. 'My first one in Heritage Cove.'

He was close enough to notice the tiny beauty spot she had above her top lip, to see the way naturally shaped eyebrows arched over cornflower-blue eyes. And he knew it wasn't the moment or the season making him want her all the more. She was single, he was single. He was going to ask her out, it had taken all his willpower not to do it from the first time he saw her. He'd honestly never known anyone to look this good in dungarees and a coat three sizes too big with a grease stain on its sleeve and a torn collar. 'Lucy, I was wondering...' But her gaze was dragged away at that second and she didn't look too pleased with what it found. 'Lucy?'

Lucy still didn't look impressed. And there was a guy walking towards them. It was only as he got closer that Daniel recognised him as the man in the photograph on the holiday card, the man in the fake snow globe with her. His blond hair was the same, cut uniformly, and he was wearing one of those long coats businessmen favoured. This wasn't a man who ever got his hands dirty, he was someone whose entire wardrobe likely featured items with dry-clean-only labels. And next to Daniel, in jeans, sweater and a puffy jacket, the two men were a total contrast. But Daniel knew clothing choices didn't mean a thing. His dad had insisted on wearing pristine suits to work, he'd pretended to be a charming businessman with the reputation for getting things done, when in truth he'd been a bully whose family feared him.

The man extended a hand Daniel's way. 'Julian,' he said, seemingly less than happy to find another guy with Lucy.

Daniel had no choice but to introduce himself and return the gesture. But it was already blatantly obvious that the pretence Julian had Lucy going along with wasn't only for his gran's benefit. He wanted Lucy back, it was evident from the way he looked at her, and that was why he was here now. Daniel took an instant disliking to the man who reminded him of his old boss when he'd done a factory fit-out. He'd had the same air of one-upmanship about him that instantly made you wary.

'Julian, what are you doing here?' Lucy said when the tension between the two men took the place of any conversation. 'And how did you know where to find me?' She wasn't backward in coming forward and it was definitely one of the things Daniel admired about her. But it didn't mean he wanted to be caught up in whatever this was.

'I'm sorry,' said Julian, disregarding Lucy completely and honing in on Daniel, 'and you are?'

'Daniel,' he repeated. He wanted to add 'I already told you that' but didn't for Lucy's sake.

'I mean what are you to Lucy?'

'If you must know, he's my boyfriend,' Lucy said, taking them both by surprise.

Daniel wished he could take out his phone and get a snapshot of the guy's reaction, because he wasn't happy. Daniel didn't mind one bit, especially when Lucy stepped closer and took his hand.

'Can I speak to you, please, Lucy?' Julian, jaw tense above the upturned collar and what looked like an expensive scarf warming his neck, cocked his head towards the village Christmas tree, expecting her to follow.

Daniel felt Lucy's grip tighten. 'You can say whatever you need to in front of Daniel.' She put her hands on Daniel's upper arm and leaned into him, the scent from her hair enveloping him the closer she got. 'And, again, how did you know where to find me?'

'It's hardly the city of London, it's a small village. And you weren't at home, I asked someone on The Street and they said they'd seen you coming up this way.'

'Right,' she bristled. 'And why are you even here in the Cove?'

'I was passing through on my way home from seeing Gran so I thought I'd pop in and invite you to a family gathering she's requested. Maud would love us both to be there. It'll be her Christmas meal, given she won't be at the family lunch on the day.'

Lucy appeared to soften. Daniel had to hand it to the guy, Maud was obviously Lucy's Achilles heel and he knew it. 'Let me know the details and I'm sure I'll be there.' Lucy's grip on Daniel didn't lessen in the slightest.

To wind Julian up Daniel almost suggested he go along too, just for a laugh. Or he could give Lucy a kiss – what he'd give to do that – but perhaps not. Lucy clearly wasn't amused by this whole situation. Daniel wondered whether her determination to put an end to the pretence of still being married to this idiot had even registered with this bloke, given the way he'd shown up rather than sending a simple text message or using the phone, and it was clear he assumed she'd jump whenever he clicked his fingers.

'It's in two days' time,' Julian told her. 'Wednesday, five o'clock sharp.'

Daniel's heart sank and he knew Lucy felt it too. This jerk had picked the very evening the Little Waffle Shack was opening.

'I have some other commitments that day, Julian. And it's really short notice.'

'You've said it yourself, Lucy, you're your own boss,' Julian tried. 'Surely that means you can fit us in. It's Maud, after all. You know how special you are to her.' Clearly unimpressed but with his sights firmly set on achieving his goal, his shoulders jutted out in the long woollen coat he clearly thought made everyone pay attention to him and take him at his word.

'Leave it with me,' Lucy capitulated. 'I'll see what I can do.' And just like that a flicker over Julian's face told Daniel he'd known he'd get his way in the end.

When it became clear to Julian that Lucy wasn't interested in spending any more time with him this evening, he told her, 'I'll be off then. But let me know for definite whether you're coming to Aubrey House. I need to ensure numbers for catering are correct.'

After he left, Lucy seemed to forget for a moment that she was holding onto Daniel's arm and they stood there. He was more than happy to do it for as long as she liked but when the wind whistled past them she snapped out of it and he offered to walk her home.

They made their way past the village tree and along to the front of the workshop but all the joy of the moment had evaporated.

'Thanks again for the sign,' he said when it seemed Julian's appearance had well and truly ruined the celebratory mood they'd both been in before – the mood they'd been in when Daniel was about to get on with it and ask her out. Perhaps it was just as well because if she agreed he knew he'd have to come completely clean about everything in his past. He hadn't dated much over the last couple of years but he'd always known that if he did and it got serious, he'd never be less than honest.

'I had fun tonight,' she said when she found out her keys ready to go back through the workshop, presumably to clear up for the night.

'Me too, and the sign is wonderful.' He didn't mention the moment they both knew the fun had stopped. 'Let me know if you can make it to opening night. It'll be a shame not to see you.'

She put her hands back into her pockets. 'I'm sorry the Christmas celebration with Maud falls on the same day. And I'm sorry I dragged you into all that back there by pretending we were together. I'm not some crazy bunny boiler, you know. I thought it might put him off coming back again, make it easier to tell him we need to stop pretending.'

'Hey.' He couldn't help it. She looked so sad he reached out and, placing his fingers beneath her chin, tilted her face to look at him. 'I don't mind you using me, you're welcome to do it if it helps. And dinner or whatever it is Julian has arranged won't take forever. I'm hoping to be making waffles long into the evening with plenty of crowds for company. Come afterwards?'

She smiled, seemingly glad of his touch. 'I will.'

'Goodnight, Lucy.' He took his hand away, unsure where they went from here.

'Goodnight, Daniel.'

Back at the Little Waffle Shack he pushed his hands into his pockets to keep them warm and sat on the step of the veranda looking over at the sign Lucy had so carefully crafted for him. He'd wanted so much to kiss her tonight, but was he good enough for her? He came with a whole lot of baggage, after all, and not the sort that was neat and tidy either.

Maybe if she came to opening night he might just get carried away in the moment and tell her exactly how he felt.

8

Lucy opened the bottle of prosecco and topped up everyone's glass and then poured a sparkling mineral water for Lois, who'd come along to the book club but claimed she and Barney liked to enjoy a nightcap together and so she'd save herself for that. She'd been thrilled with the copper mugs she'd had Lucy make for Barney's Christmas gift and stowed them in their cardboard box safely in her bag for wrapping later. Lucy had already passed the crafted trivet to Barney so he could gift-wrap and put it beneath his tree for Lois. Lucy wondered how much they'd laugh when they realised they'd both sourced their presents from the local blacksmith. It showed how made for each other they were, anyway, and they'd have a wonderful Christmas, the two of them.

'I'm afraid I haven't had a chance to read anything,' Tilly confessed when Melissa asked who'd read the novel they'd selected months ago. 'The shop is busier than it's been any other year and I can't knock it, long may it last.'

'The inn is the same, Christmas is as busy as the summer season for me,' said Tracy, tucking into a mince pie and enjoying a couple of hours off.

Celeste and Jade apologised that they hadn't read the book either and Melissa asked Lucy whether she'd had a chance.

Lucy shook her head. 'I've been flat out with work too.' That and thinking about Daniel, not to mention working on the tortoise design to give him for Christmas. After the run-in with Julian that had interrupted the special moment she'd shared with Daniel as they hung his new sign in place and took photographs, Lucy had come inside, restless, and being unable to sleep, she'd gone down to the workshop and got on with the gift she was sure he was going to love. It was the same size as the tortoise she'd made for a family previously, and should Daniel want to keep it outside she could easily apply a protective coating later. She'd added a grey tinge to the iron to make it more realistic and had even worked a small compartment into the bottom so he could use it to hide a spare key.

Lucy brought herself back to the conversation. It was Etna's turn to defend her lack of reading this month. It seemed they all had manic lives.

'My tea rooms have been the busiest they've ever been in December,' Etna shared. 'I'm looking forward to palming off some customers to Daniel's new waffle shack, let me tell you. I'm too old to be working this hard.'

Patricia laughed. 'Don't say that, I'll be out of a job if you send people away.'

'Never,' said Etna. 'I'll put my feet up a bit and you can still be busy.'

Lois recalled her first visit to the tea rooms, how they'd stayed in there for hours and commented on what a welcoming place it was. 'For a small village, Heritage Cove does well. The Street has businesses I hope stick around forever.'

Lucy wondered what it would take for Lois to stick around forever instead of going back and forth to Ireland.

'We're small enough that we've got character,' Melissa put in, 'but I agree, we want businesses to stay here for the duration. And I get the feeling Daniel's will.'

'Cheers to that,' said Lucy, raising her glass to each of them.

'Cheers to the businesses staying, or cheers to Daniel?' Tilly teased and Lucy shot her a look. She might be keen on the guy but she was nowhere near ready to share that with anyone else.

'Cheers to Heritage Cove,' Lucy said to distract everyone. A sure way to do that was to bring the attention back to the village and it worked, as Celeste and Jade shared their recipes for mince pies with Tracy and Lucy, and Etna and Tilly lapsed into a conversation about Christmas decorations on The Street and in the shop windows and how snowfall would make everything extra perfect if it happened this year.

'Are you sure you won't have a glass of bubbly?' Patricia said to Lois yet again as she took a turn to top up glasses. 'This is the last book club before Christmas.'

'A fine book club it is when nobody reads the book,' Melissa laughed. 'I was the only one this time. I guess being cabin crew and having stopovers has its perks – I fit in a lot of reading.'

'No bubbly for me,' Lois said again. Patricia had had a few and as a result was rather persistent. 'I'll have a nightcap with Barney but that's all. You know, that man is wearing me out, it's a rest to come here. These days I fall asleep the second my head hits the pillow.'

'Hey, some of us aren't getting any sex,' said Tilly. 'The less we have to hear about yours the better.'

Raucous laughter at Lois's blushes and denial ensured they wouldn't be talking much about any book tonight so instead they carried on gossiping, and when everyone else headed home to their beds Lucy was left alone with Tilly, who pushed a stopper into the unfinished bottle and slotted it into Lucy's fridge.

'We'll have to hold the club somewhere else next time,' said Lucy. 'It's not fair if I get all the leftover booze.'

'Good point. Mine next time, save me stocking up if I get leftovers. Cup of tea?'

'I don't want to sound old or boring, but that would be lovely.'

When the tea was made Tilly said, 'You look worn out. Work crazy busy still?'

'And then some,' said Lucy, opening her eyes as she nursed her tea. 'Rather that than the other way around but just when I get on top of things I get another order.' Or she made something on a whim for a certain man up the road.

'No more business signs for eligible bachelors?' Tilly smirked behind her mug of tea.

'Very funny. But no, no more of those.'

'The sign is brilliant, by the way. And I can't wait for opening night tomorrow. I may well turn into a waffle – I intend to eat loads, just so you know.'

'I'll remember to look out for a waffle-shaped Tilly after Christmas, shall I? And I'll let Daniel know you'll be a regular – it's great for business.'

'*You'll* let Daniel know.'

'Or you can,' she said, her turn to hide behind her cup.

'I saw you with him last night when you took the sign over to the shack.' That explained the teasing earlier, then. It seemed Lucy hadn't hidden her emotions quite as well as she'd thought. 'You both looked in cahoots so I didn't interrupt.'

Lucy put two and two together. 'I don't suppose you told Julian where to find me?'

'I assume Julian was the man I bumped into who asked after you,' Tilly nodded, it all coming together in her mind. 'Wasn't I supposed to? I know you guys have history and are keeping it together for his gran. I thought I was helping – he seemed anxious to find you so I told him you'd gone up to the new waffle shack with the owner.'

Lucy set her mug on the coffee table beside her and unfurled her legs from beneath her when she got a cramp. Anxious to find her wasn't what she wanted from him at all, it wasn't the way it should be when they were divorced and had gone their separate ways. But Julian never had been very good at accepting a decision that hadn't been made by him. 'Honestly, Tilly, don't worry about it. And Julian and I are not keeping it together, we're pretending – it's all a lie. A lie that will be ending very soon, believe me.'

'You sound angry.'

'I'm not,' she bristled. 'Well, maybe I am, but not at you for pointing him in my direction. At him, for coming to the Cove, for hanging around when we're over, for keeping me in his life in a way I didn't see coming so went along with it. Now it's Maud who'd be hurt if I stopped. It's going to be horrible to tell her. She'll realise there won't be the grandkids he led her to believe we were almost at the point of having either, and I can't bear the thought of upsetting her.'

'Sometimes you have to be cruel to be kind. He can't keep lying forever.'

Actually, if anyone could, it was Julian. He had form and he was good at it.

'If you ask me,' said Tilly, 'Julian wants you back. He even asked what you were doing at the waffle shack. I said you'd made the sign for the place and he asked when it was opening. He's taking a lot of interest in anything that's going on in your life for someone who's supposed to be moving on.'

'I know.' And she was tired of pretending.

Shadow had taken a liking to Tilly and it wasn't easy to convince him it was time to get off her lap when she finally decided to go home. 'I'd take him with me if I could,' Tilly admitted when Lucy showed her out the front door, the skin on her arms breaking out in goose pimples at the cold. 'Stick to your guns with Julian,' she told Lucy as she hugged her goodbye. 'He doesn't look as though he likes to hear no for an answer.'

Tilly had got it in one.

With Tilly gone, Lucy washed up the glasses and swept the crumbs from the mince pies they'd shared round tonight. Celeste and Jade were competitive in their nature, but after tasters when Lucy collected a couple of boxes from the bakery this afternoon, she'd told them to muddle them up in her cardboard containers. She wasn't interested in picking sides and so all the mince pies had been bundled into the boxes together and, tonight, nobody had been able to tell the difference.

Another knock at the door had Lucy assuming one of her friends had forgotten something but she couldn't see a pair of gloves or a scarf or anything else lying around the lounge.

'Harvey,' she smiled when she opened the door. 'Melissa just left, she'll be home by now.' She could tell he'd come from the pub; it was happy hour tonight and not many locals missed that. He must've come to walk his other half home.

'I came to see you.' He steadied his footing on the top step. It seemed he'd made the most of cheap drinks.

'Me? Oh no, please don't let this be a last-minute present for Melissa – I don't think I can squeeze in another thing this side of Christmas.'

'May I come in?'

Bewildered, she stood back and, once he was inside, shut the door. 'Can I get you a cup of tea?' Or perhaps a strong black coffee might be needed.

He declined the offer and righted his footing when he stumbled. 'Lucy, I don't want to speak out of turn.'

Something told her he was going to whether he wanted to or

not and she faced him, arms still crossed from the chill that had crept in with him. 'But...'

'It's about Daniel.' He cleared his throat.

'What about Daniel?' She'd finished the tortoise earlier today and it was sitting at the bottom of the tree, already wrapped and ready to give to him.

'I can tell you two are getting close.' He cleared his throat again. 'Actually, may I have a glass of water, please?'

She filled one at the sink, which gave her time to wonder about what he was here to say. She and Daniel were getting close; tonight she'd thought he was about to kiss her, but maybe he'd been put off by Julian hanging around – another reason she needed Julian to move on and out of her life. Then, finally, she might get to be her own person again.

She handed the water to Harvey and he downed the lot in one as she scooped up Shadow and cuddled him to her chest. 'Your brother and I have become good friends. That's all.'

His look said he thought otherwise. 'There's a lot about our childhood we don't often share, and if we do, it's difficult for others to know what it was really like.' He ran a hand through his hair. 'I'm not doing a very good job of explaining this, am I?'

'Why don't you just come out with it?' She was tired and she wasn't interested in games. She got enough of those with Julian.

'He's bad news, Lucy. You're too good for him.'

'Isn't that for me to decide? And him?' Harvey was a nice guy but surely even he could see he shouldn't be interfering. His brother was a grown man, after all.

'I know you think I'm overstepping, but... well, Melissa told me about your cousin.'

'I don't really see what my cousin has to do with your brother.' Shadow jumped out of her arms as though he suspected trouble and trotted into the kitchen, his crunching of kitty biscuits clearly audible from where they were still standing in the lounge.

'I know your cousin died at the hands of a drunk driver.'

So did she but she didn't need reminding of it. 'Harvey, I'm not sure what any of this has to do with me or with Daniel.'

He was slurring his words the more he spoke as though he'd already used up his quota of well-formed sentences. 'He's been in a lot of trouble is all I'm saying.'

'Harvey...' her voice softened. 'I think perhaps you need to go home, sleep it off.'

He pointed a finger in the air. 'You know what, you're right. And you know something else? I *will* go home, I'll go home on foot, I won't be driving. Because you don't get behind the wheel when you're two sheets to the wind.'

She walked towards him to leave him in no doubt it was time to go, and he retreated. 'I'll see you again another time,' she smiled at him. 'Thanks for stopping by but you don't need to worry. And Melissa will be waiting for you at home by now.'

'Sure, sure...' he stuttered as he headed for the door. But he stopped before he embraced the winter evening once again. 'All I ask is that you think about what I said.'

'I will. Goodnight, Harvey.'

She waited for him to get safely down the steps before she closed the door. And before Shadow could take all of her attention, she messaged Melissa: Harvey was in a bad way and she wasn't sure he'd even make it home across The Street in the state he was in.

But when Melissa didn't reply, she called.

'He's pretty drunk,' Lucy told her. She lay down on the sofa this time. 'He kept running on about my cousin, about how I shouldn't get involved with Daniel, how you shouldn't get behind the wheel when you've been drinking.'

'Oh, God,' came Melissa's reply. 'I'd better make this quick and then see if there's any sign of him coming down the lane.'

Lucy sat up; she didn't like where this was heading.

'I'm not sure it's his place to go telling everyone about Daniel's past. Most people around here know what he did when he lived in the Cove but not many know what happened between then and now.'

'What did happen, Melissa?'

'The trouble continued for Daniel after he left. I don't know the full extent of it and I don't think Carol meant to let it slip that he'd been in trouble with the police. But she did, and now Harvey's even more angry than he was.'

Lucy's insides plummeted and she shut her eyes. It wasn't hard to work out what that trouble was, given Harvey's outburst. But she had to know for sure. And so she asked for any more details Melissa could possibly pass on – third-hand, fourth-hand, she didn't care. She just wanted the truth.

And that was when she found out Daniel had been caught drink driving the same way as the person who killed Joanna had been.

And it was unforgiveable.

There was no way anything could happen between them now, and when she felt tears threaten to come she realised how much she'd been hoping it would.

9

Lucy yelped when a spark from the arc welder jumped onto the skin of her forearm. She hadn't burnt herself in a long while but she was distracted this morning and she hadn't slept well at all last night after Harvey's visit and Melissa's revelation. She'd dreamt about Joanna eating waffles from a truck driven by Daniel, then Joanna's funeral – except instead of flowers on the grave there had been more waffles and sauce and all the toppings. She'd woken in a sweat and the only way she knew how to handle it was to come down here to the workshop.

She had a swig from the water bottle on the desk and then went back to the bird feeder she'd been working on. The wrought-iron bowl was to dangle from three pieces of iron, joined at the top, each with weaving ivy detailing and leaves; the leaves were the last thing for her to join on before it would be ready for the customer. She finished the project, set it aside, worked on the weathervane for another order, replied to customer emails and handed over completed projects to very happy customers.

With such a long to-do list Lucy skipped a proper sit-down lunch, instead grabbing a couple of slices of toast, and she powered through until she knew she'd done enough for the day. She showered and, with no time to stop, turned her attentions to wrapping family Christmas gifts that she wanted to take to her parents' place. She'd be there for the big day itself but she'd been so crazy with work she hadn't visited for a while and, right now, she needed to escape the Cove and get back her equilibrium.

Driving out of the village was like a breath of fresh air for Lucy. She followed country lanes, some still clinging to the frost that had covered the ground in the Cove first thing this morning, deciduous trees bereft of their leaves, evergreens keeping the countryside colour going. Getting away from it all, even if only for a couple of hours, as she made her way to Southwold gave her a huge sense of relief. It was the same feeling she got from keeping busy – it stopped her having to think too much about any of her troubles. And she made her mind up as she drove that she wouldn't be mentioning the new resident of Heritage Cove to her parents, the man who'd done the very thing that had taken a beloved member of their family away.

Lucy was wrapped in hugs when she arrived at her parents'. She admired their tree and, as she did every year, reminisced about some of the decorations they'd kept from her childhood, including the wooden star covered in gold glitter, in the centre of which was a photo of her aged six. She was never sure whether that particular ornament should go to the very back when people came round but she liked seeing it today. Coming home was always grounding and reassuring. Even if you didn't share what was on your mind, just the four walls of the home you grew up in held the power to wash a sense of calm over you. Her mum rambled on about the open-air carol concert she'd persuaded her dad to brave this year three days before Christmas with their good friends the Wallaces, her dad wanted all the little details of what she was working on in her workshop now. He'd come to visit a few weeks ago and sat on the sofa next to the desk taking it all in as she'd worked. Her parents had had their doubts when she shared her career dreams but those doubts had been replaced by a pride she could read in the delight on their faces every time they discussed her projects, old and new.

With every intention of going straight from her parents' to Aubrey House, on the other side of Heritage Cove, for Maud's Christmas gathering, Lucy found herself stopping in the village mid-afternoon when she realised that, with her busyness and her head all over the place from trying to block out thoughts of Daniel, she'd completely forgotten the parcel of Christmas cinnamon-and-ginger cookies she'd ordered from the bakery and the Christmas flowers she'd put on order at the florist for Julian's gran.

She parked at home and used the walk to clear her head, going first to the florist, where she collected the most beautiful bouquet of white lisianthus and Asiatic lilies tied together with branches of white birch and silver-green foliage. She strolled along The Street, ignoring the posters she saw on lamp-posts advertising the opening of the Little Waffle Shack. She didn't want to think about it or Daniel and she'd ignored the text message he sent her earlier saying he hoped she'd be there. More than that, she'd deleted it. She couldn't even bear to see his name there taunting her. He was something she could never have. How could she ever get involved with a man who'd done the same as the person who took Joanna's life? Selfish, that was what it was. And, worse, he'd never told her, which made him a liar. Or at least a liar by omission. Wasn't that the same thing?

'Lucy, you're looking gorgeous,' Celeste grinned when she went into the bakery to collect the cookies.

Lucy laughed, a moment of light relief at being spotted in something other than her work clothes. 'I know, you don't often see me out of dungarees and my old worn coat in the daylight hours, but I've been visiting family.'

'And those flowers... they're like a winter wonderland. Are they for you?'

Lucy had inhaled the floral scents all the way here. 'Unfortunately not, I almost want to keep them though.' Maybe she should get a bouquet to add some cheer to her flat. One of the cupboard doors had come right off in her hand this morning and her mood had almost seen her sling it across the room in frustration.

Jade beamed a hello her way when she emerged from out back with a Christmas cake for another customer. A pair of Christmas-tree earrings dangled from her lobes and swung about as she laughed and chatted.

Celeste found Lucy's box of cookies for her and came around to her side of the counter. 'Who are these for? Same person as the flowers?'

'Another relative.' Strictly speaking, Maud wasn't her relative, of course, but even though most of the people she knew here in the Cove knew about Julian and the divorce, she didn't readily admit she was keeping the truth from an innocent old lady who deserved more. 'It's the season of catching up with people, isn't it?' she added to avoid going into more detail.

'Sure is. My social calendar is nice and full this month, just the way I like it. Thanks for book club last night. Who knows, maybe in the new year we can actually read some books.'

'Maybe,' Lucy laughed. And when another customer came in, Jade and Celeste got back to being busy and Lucy went on her way.

She'd noticed the clock in the bakery and didn't have long before she'd have to leave in order to make it to Aubrey House for five o'clock but as she crossed The Street back to the gate at the front of the path taking her up to her flat, she spotted Daniel waiting at the end of the path leading to the adjacent workshop.

'I can't stop,' she called over, not looking him in the eye.

He didn't waste any time coming towards her and when he reached her side he put a hand on her arm. 'Hey, you don't need to stop but a quick hello would be nice. I'm nervous, about tonight,' he rambled, 'not long to go and either I'll be swamped by customers or nobody will turn up and I'll start to worry it was a huge mistake to come here.'

She held the box of cookies and the bouquet, which she did her best to hide behind. 'Good luck,' she said in a voice that sounded fake even to her.

But he wouldn't let her get away so easily. 'Seriously, Lucy, what's up?' He was tall enough that he'd have to tilt her chin for her to look at him, the way he'd done the other day, but she knew the vibes she was giving off stopped him from doing any such thing. And she missed it. She couldn't help herself. She wanted him to do it. She wanted to be with him, get closer to this man who'd suddenly come here to Heritage Cove, the home she knew she was hooked on and didn't want to leave.

'I'd better go, Daniel. I'm busy, that's all. No big deal.'

'It is a big deal when you can't even look at me.' His hand stopped her again and she just looked at it, his bare skin on the material of her coat yet somehow she could feel his touch as though it were on her bare skin too.

'What's going on?' came a voice behind them and for once Lucy was glad to see Julian make an appearance.

'Daniel, I need to go,' she said more firmly. And her heart broke a little bit more when he held up both hands in defeat and slunk away, shaking his head.

It sickened her to see Julian look triumphant too, like he'd won his trophy in a duel.

'Trouble in paradise?' Julian asked, none too quietly.

But although she wanted to tell him to bugger off, she found herself bursting into tears. With everything she'd discovered in the last twenty-four hours, topped with a lack of sleep and a crazy workload, her emotions picked this moment to boil over. And when he took her in his arms, she didn't have the energy to push him away. So, for once, she let him stand there and hold her.

* * *

Daniel didn't have time to think about Lucy, not even to think about how he'd turned back to see her in Julian's arms as though the confrontation with her ex the other night hadn't happened at all, as though the closeness between them after they'd posed for photographs outside the shack had all been in his imagination.

Right now, Daniel had to put Lucy out of his head. It was time to focus on his launch. This was it, everything he'd worked so hard for, and he wasn't going to let it fail. The Little Waffle Shack was due to open in less than two hours and whatever was going on with Lucy had to take backstage. His extra staff, Brianna and Troy, were ready. He'd been over the workings of the till, everyone knew where things were, the fridge was filled with bowls of batter in different varieties to cater for hundreds of waffles tonight before they'd have to make any more. Toppings were ready, some ingredients were chopped and waiting, everything was in place. And fifteen minutes before he was due to open up the door to the little shack he spotted a crowd had gathered down by the village tree. It sent a whirl of hope right through him that this really could work. His return to the Cove might have been a long time coming, but it felt right and he hoped this was a sign that life would soon settle down.

When there was a knock at the window and he saw Melissa,

he gestured for her to go around the back of the shack. He didn't want people to think he was open yet and so he went out through the kitchen, where there was another door at the far end to take out rubbish and accept deliveries.

'Almost time,' she grinned, gloved hands coming together in front of her in a clap of excitement.

'It sure is,' he beamed.

'Nervous?'

He stepped outside even though he didn't have a coat. He'd been rushing around so much he could do with the blast of air. 'Very. I'd go so far as to say this is the most nervous I've ever been.' He wasn't going to look to see if Harvey was with her. He didn't have to.

'Your mum's down by the tree going on and on about how good these waffles are, she's selling them to the masses.'

'She's my number-one fan,' he smiled. 'She's been a good taste tester for me along the way.' So had someone else but he did his best not to think about the blonde blacksmith right now. He wondered what on earth he could've possibly done to offend her between the last time he saw her and today.

Melissa exhaled into the air, a breath that showed she was getting up the confidence to say something to him. And he didn't have time to tiptoe around. 'Melissa, do you have something on your mind?' Please don't let it be something crazy like Harvey planning to sabotage all this, to put up a protest rather than let opening night run smoothly.

'I need to talk to you about Lucy.'

That was unexpected. 'Lucy? I'm not sure I follow.'

'Harvey went to see her.'

'News to me.'

'Thought it might be.' She hesitated before coming right out with it. 'He kind of hinted that you'd been in trouble with the police for drink driving, and when she asked me, I had to be straight with her.'

Daniel's insides plummeted. He had shared details of everything that had happened to him, his highs and his pathetic lows, and most of all his regrets. He didn't have any need to ask how they'd found out about it. 'Mum told you both.'

'She didn't say much, it kind of slipped out and Harvey prodded, you know what he's like.'

'Oh yeah, I sure do.'

'Don't be angry with your mum.'

'I'm not.' He took a deep breath. 'And I don't want to be rude, but did you really have to lay this on me tonight of all nights?'

'I wanted to tell you before you found out from anyone else that Lucy knew.'

Harvey's actions had a fire igniting in Daniel's belly that he knew he had to dampen and forget about for tonight. But he supposed Melissa's confession did explain Lucy's reluctance to talk to him earlier. It hardly painted him in a good light and now, thanks to Harvey, she probably thought the worst of him. The infuriating thing was, had Harvey kept his mouth shut, Daniel would've told Lucy everything in the end if they'd begun to get closer. He would've told her the truth before she had a chance to hear it embellished with opinions she may or may not have herself.

'I know there are always two sides,' Melissa assured him. 'None of us know what your life was like back then.'

'That's right, you don't,' he snapped.

'And that's on us, but it's also on you.' She'd always been happy to assert herself and Daniel sensed she was good for his brother, who preferred to stew when something bothered him, or talk to the wrong people like he'd done this time. 'I know you and Harvey haven't been in contact for years but it's a big thing you showing up here, and not talking to him has meant he's drawn his own conclusions.'

'Don't you think I've tried talking to him? He goes off at me or doesn't want to know. And now? After what he's done?'

Melissa stepped forwards and enveloped him in a tight hug and refused to let him go until he began to laugh and relax.

'What was that for?'

'You deserve it,' she said. 'You're hurting, Harvey's hurting, and your brother has never been the best at accepting there may be other explanations behind others' actions. I know that from experience. In fact, I did the same thing myself when Harvey didn't follow me to London the day I left here all those years ago. Perhaps it's human nature or a way of protecting ourselves to assume the worst before we're exposed to the truth. I just wanted to come here and let you know that Harvey spoke to Lucy, and for what it's worth, I really am sorry. You both seem keen on each other.

'And now I'm rambling. And you have a busines to open,' she grinned. 'You need to focus, because we need waffles!'

And with a wave, off she went to join friends.

Daniel went back inside, out of the cold. He gathered himself, knowing he had to put thoughts of his past, Lucy and Harvey to the back of his mind for now.

The Little Waffle Shack was about to open and, beneath a sky filled with stars, he had a village to impress.

10

'Are you going to tell me what's got you so upset?' Julian probed as they went in through the front entrance of Aubrey House, the bouquet resting in Lucy's arms.

'Honestly, it's nothing. I'm overtired, that's all.'

In the residents' lounge, Maud waved them over. Lucy couldn't see the rest of Julian's family yet but they'd be sure to pop up at any moment. They'd always loved big gatherings, and if talking were a national sport they'd be top of the league. 'Is there a dining room somewhere?' she asked Julian.

But Julian was already striding towards his gran, telling her how beautiful she looked. And she did. She'd gone to a lot of effort for the occasion and Lucy caught a whiff of the familiar floral perfume she'd used liberally today when she hugged her hello. Maud had picked out a thick-material turquoise dress and pinned on the floral vintage brooch with lavender glass and pink rhinestones that the family had given her when she turned ninety. That day there'd been a grand garden party to celebrate, with helium balloons showing the age Maud said she was proud to reach, and there wasn't a space to be seen on any chair, bench or low wall as family and friends gathered to mark the occasion.

But nobody else was here now. It was just the usual faces Lucy had come to recognise on her visits here. She sighed. Maybe she should be grateful she and Julian had arrived first; she could talk to Maud for a few minutes without being in competition with anyone else, which was exhausting, especially on top of the tiredness she already felt.

'These are beautiful.' Maud held the bouquet Lucy had handed her in her arms and took a long inhale of the blooms, eyes closed to enjoy a simple pleasure. 'And I have the perfect vase in my room too.'

One of the staff came by and offered to put the flowers in water for now but Maud said they could wait. 'I want to look at them right here.' She set them on one of the chairs opposite so they could all see them. 'And they've got a bit of water in the bottom of the cellophane, I can see, so they'll be fine for a little bit while I catch up with you both. Did you choose the flowers, Lucy?'

'I did. You always loved white rather than red.'

'And you always know how to put a smile on my face. It's so good of you to come – I know it's a busy time of the year, and it's dark out there. I wouldn't like to drive in the dark. I don't know how you youngsters do it.'

'Headlights, Gran,' Julian quipped, accepting the offer of tea from the staff member who'd tried to help with the flowers.

'I thought we were going to be late tonight,' Lucy admitted as Maud dismissed her grandson's teasing with a shake of her head.

'You must be busy with work.'

'Always. But it's good, just the way I like it.' She took the box of cookies from her bag. 'I got you these too, they're fresh from the bakery.'

Maud's face lit up. 'They smell divine.' She took the box that brought with it the comforting scents of cinnamon and ginger. It was amazing quite how much of the aroma seeped through a closed lid, but it did, and Lucy almost wished she'd bought some for herself. 'I'll put them beneath this side table. Don't want Percy over there to get wind of me having any sweet treats or they'll be gone before I know it – he's into handing things around. For once I want to be selfish and enjoy them all for myself.'

'I absolutely do not blame you,' Lucy laughed, slotting the box beneath the table for her. She looked around again. 'Where is everyone?'

'I'm not sure I follow,' said Maud, distracted quickly when one of the other residents, clearly a friend of Maud's, came to gush over the flower arrangement. And as Maud's flowers drew a few other residents over and they talked about Christmas foliage and colours, Lucy moved her chair closer to Julian's. 'Julian, where are you parents? Your sisters?'

'Something came up last minute,' he said, unable to look her in the eye.

'For all of them?'

'You know what Bella's like... disorganised is her middle name. And Amelia's the same.'

'And what about your parents?'

'They had another commitment.'

'More important than Maud?' The truth was dawning on her pretty quickly now as Maud relished the attention from the other residents. 'It's just me and you tonight, isn't it?'

'Is that so bad? You like Maud, she loves you. Is it so difficult to spend a bit of time with her at Christmas?'

When he put it that way she felt terrible, but then that's what he was banking on, wasn't it?

She sat fuming but not wanting to make a scene. And as the

others dispersed, leaving Maud to focus on her visitors, Lucy put aside her frustration that Julian had tricked her into being here. Separating had been her idea, the divorce also, and he'd never made it a secret that he would get back together in a heartbeat. Now, he seemed to be trying to get in as much time with her before this ridiculous pretence stopped once and for all. And if that was the case, Lucy was only glad she wouldn't be doing it for much longer.

Over cups of tea Maud told them all about the debacle of the Christmas decorations at Aubrey House, how the tree had been ordered but the delivery date was messed up and when it arrived it stood there for days. She told them how the Christmas lunch menu was exquisite considering this was a place for old people and when she reeled off the list of courses, Lucy suspected it would take most of the day for the residents to get through it all.

'We're having a secret Santa after the Queen's Speech,' Maud confided, before whispering, 'I drew Percy's name out of the hat and when Julian's mum did my shopping for me she managed to find him the same brown cardigan he's wearing now, without holes.'

Lucy discreetly looked over to where the other resident was sitting. 'I can't see any holes.'

'You can when he stands up – all across the bottom, one on the cuff. He's attached to the garment and it's falling apart.'

Lucy kept it to herself but however much Maud complained about Percy and his sharing food around or his clothing malfunctions, Lucy wondered whether she might just have a soft spot for the old man.

'He'd better wear the new one,' Maud rambled on. 'It's the same colour so he doesn't have an excuse.'

Lucy and Julian exchanged a smile. He was obviously wondering whether his gran might like this man too.

'I'm impressed the tree in here is a real one,' said Lucy when a waft of it came her way. They were close enough to see the decorations that had been carefully added to branches, the baubles all silver, the lights a static soft white. 'There's nothing like it... my flat smells beautiful when I wake up.' When Julian threw her a look she realised her slip-up. 'House, I meant house, of course.' She laughed as though she'd made a silly mistake and Maud was off talking about how every Christmas she'd had a tree with roots and planted it in the garden once it was done with for another year.

Lucy hated this. She hated lying – that was Julian's forte. And, it seemed, it was Daniel's too. Tears pricked the back of her eyes at the thought of Daniel and she was so distracted she only caught the tail end of the next thing Maud was telling them.

'...I know it's a bit old-fashioned,' she said, one hand on the brooch against her lapel, 'but it's worth something and one day I'd like to pass it down to my great-grandchild.'

Lucy's discomfort mounted. How had they gone from talking trees to talking babies? She looked to Julian and back to Maud but all she could do was smile. And Julian, wisely for him because Lucy could very well throttle him right now for going along with this charade, made his excuses to use the bathroom, offering to put the flowers in Maud's room first.

'All this talk of wills isn't very cheery,' said Lucy when he'd gone. 'Why don't you try a cookie?' Anything to stop this conversation that was only going to draw her further into the lie by the looks of things.

'Only if you have one too.'

'Go on then, you've persuaded me.' With a grin, Lucy smuggled two from the box and they didn't disappoint.

'If anyone spots them they'll think Patsy brought them over with our cups of tea.'

Maud had been living on her own for years before she came to Aubrey House and much as she'd hesitated about giving up her independence, being here was as though she'd been given a new lease of life. A sociable being, Maud thrived on the company of others. She still had her own room, she could have visitors all through the day and evening and she had the lounge here to mingle with other people whenever she felt the need for conversation and company. It made Lucy feel a little better about shattering the illusion of her grandson's perfect marriage come January.

Lucy finished the cookie and declared she'd have to get some for herself.

'You should,' Maud insisted. 'And don't share them either. Take them back to your flat and keep them for yourself.'

'House, Maud.'

'House?'

'We live in a house, not a flat.'

Maud looked past where Lucy was sitting to see whether Julian was on his way back. 'You're not together any more, you've moved out, you live in Heritage Cove.'

Lucy put down her tea without taking another sip. 'You know?'

'Of course I know. I've still got all my marbles, I'm not daft. And I know Julian was the one who put you up to this, keeping up the pretence.' When Lucy was too gobsmacked to ask how, Maud added, 'He tries to protect me and I can't be angry for that, but I'm not as weak as he thinks I am. I can handle bad news. Lord knows I've had enough in my time – I lost my dad in the Second World War, my best friend emigrated to the other side of the world when I was thirteen and needed her more than ever, I was almost crushed at a civil-rights protest in the sixties, and I've lived through more world health scares than you can imagine. I hardly think the end of a family member's marriage will finish me off.'

'Right.' Lucy had no other words. The truth was out in the open and Maud didn't seem at all bothered by it. Lucy only wished they'd come right out with it and told her sooner.

Maud went on. 'Julian is just like his grandad. He couldn't lie straight in bed either.'

Lucy couldn't help it, she laughed. 'Sorry, I shouldn't find that funny.'

'Laughter is the best medicine. And I should know – since coming here I've laughed more than I had in years.'

'May I ask how long you've known the truth about Julian and me? And how did you know about my new flat?'

'I've known for months. Because unlike his grandad, Julian isn't very good at lying. He likes to think he is but he's slipped up enough times to make me suspicious – believe me, I spent years pulling his grandad up for the fibs he told but in those days you didn't leave a marriage, you put up with it for better or for worse.'

'It was a different time.'

'It was. And he had his good points, it wasn't all bad. We were happy. I found it hard to deal with untruths though and I'm sure you have too. I think my radar is well trained after detecting lies for so many years and I started to get an inkling about you and my grandson. One day I asked Bella to tell me the truth,' Maud told her. 'I pushed until she did. After that, as I do with all members of my family, I kept tabs on you. I did some delving online and could see you'd set up a business in Heritage Cove – a thriving business you should be proud of, I might add.'

'I am proud, I love it.' She gulped. In all the time she'd known Maud she never would've drawn parallels between their lives like this, let alone talked about them so frankly.

Maud reached across and patted her hand. 'I can tell.'

The coast was still clear of Julian. She could pretend he was taking time to arrange those flowers properly but most likely he was sitting in a corridor somewhere scrolling through his phone to catch up on work emails before he came back in here. Maud wouldn't tolerate devices when she was holding court and this wasn't the first time Julian had sneaked off to the toilet and taken forever to return.

'Why didn't you say anything sooner?' Lucy asked now.

Maud hesitated, her hand on her brooch, fingers rubbing the glass. 'Because I didn't want you to stop coming.'

'Julian would never stop, you know that.'

'I didn't want *you* to stop coming.'

Lucy got up and went to sit in the chair next to her. 'The only reason I'd ever be put off coming here is because I don't want Julian to think he's got another chance to pick up where we left off. So, as long as he keeps Sundays or evenings as his visiting times, how about you and I see each other at a different time?'

Maud squeezed her hand, belying the frailty she did her best to hide with confidence and a strong smile. 'That sounds like a good plan to me.'

When Percy came over to say hello, Lucy exchanged a Merry Christmas with him and left Maud chatting away. She'd already offered Percy one of the cookies she was supposedly keeping for herself when Julian sauntered back this way and Lucy caught him at the door before he could get any closer.

She led him back into reception. 'Why did you lie to me about your family coming tonight?' When he opened his mouth, she closed her eyes, took a deep breath and added, 'Don't even think about making something up.'

Unsure of himself, he pushed his hands into his trouser pockets and looked to the floor before he met her gaze once again. 'I want you back, Lucy, simple as that.'

She had no idea what to say.

He reached out and took her hand. 'I knew you were going to pull the pin on all this after New Year and I'm trying to spare Gran any pain.'

'Don't bring your gran into this. This is about us.'

'You don't care about her?'

'Of course I do, so enough with the guilt trip – that's what got us into this mess in the first place. But I'm telling you, Maud is way stronger than you give her credit for. How can you not see that?'

'She won't handle this.' An innocent lock of blond hair at his temple almost hid the frown of frustration forming across his forehead. Maybe his boyish good looks had always been part of the reason he got away with the lies he'd told along the way. 'We don't divorce in this family.'

'Oh, for goodness' sake, you're not the royals.' And before he could say anything else she got in there first. 'She knows. She knows we're divorced and that I live on my own in Heritage Cove. The lie is finished, Julian.'

His face fell and a tiny part of her felt terrible, but then, wasn't that what had kept her with him for so long and then convinced her to keep on pretending for Maud's sake when she knew now that it had really been for his?

But she couldn't let her guilt keep her in this place any longer. The truth was out, the marriage was over once and for all and the dishonesty she couldn't bear could be left right here. She hoped one day Julian would go on to meet someone else, but more than that, she hoped he'd see that a life of untruths wasn't what anyone deserved.

With Julian lost for what to say, shattered his gran might be upset by this news, and clearly wondering what to come up with to persuade Lucy to stay, she kissed him on the cheek. 'Have a merry Christmas, Julian. I'll wave a quick goodbye to your gran and then I'm off.'

'So that's it?' he called after her as she went to the door, leaned into the lounge, got Maud's attention and blew her a kiss. Maud winked back and it gave Lucy even more confidence to walk away at last.

'Be happy,' she told him with a squeeze of his arm as she passed by. And even though he called after her again from the door to Aubrey House, she didn't turn back.

Lucy drove to Heritage Cove with a smile on her face. She felt a sense of freedom that even signing those divorce papers hadn't quite provided. Her happiness only began to fade when she drove into the village and around the bend, past the guesthouse. The Christmas tree was visible from here and crowds were heading in the direction of the Little Waffle Shack for opening night. She tried to be happy for Daniel but couldn't find it in her and so she parked up in the space out front of her workshop and, with a feeling of heaviness inside her yet again, made her way up the steps to her front door. She'd avoid the Little Waffle Shack and all the festive cheer. She needed a soppy movie, some chocolate and Shadow for company. That was all.

'Lucy,' a voice called from behind her and Tilly appeared on the bottom step. 'You coming to the opening?'

'I'm having an early night,' she called down. 'I'm shattered, sorry.'

But it didn't put Tilly off because Tilly was coming up the steps towards her already. 'What's happened?'

'Nothing, honestly.'

'Rubbish.' She nodded to the door. 'It's freezing out here so let's not do this on your doorstep.'

Lucy almost protested but she didn't have the energy. Instead, she let them both inside and offered Tilly a cup of tea.

'No thank you.' Tilly put her hands out to stop Lucy taking off her coat. 'And you can leave that on, you're not missing the opening.'

'Even if I told you Daniel isn't who we think he is? That he's a criminal and I can't even look at him right now?'

Tilly puffed out her cheeks, then let go of Lucy, removed her own coat and sat down. 'I hope you've got wine instead of tea. I think I'm going to need something strong to hear this.'

Lucy poured the wine and Tilly welcomed Shadow jumping onto her lap and happily curling up into a ball. Maybe he sensed Lucy was far too tense to pay him the attention he deserved.

'You're going to have to start from the beginning, Lucy.' Tilly took a gulp of wine, waiting. 'I don't get how you went from being all coy when I mentioned Daniel by name to having this look in your eyes as though he's hurt you all of a sudden. What am I missing?'

And so Lucy started from the beginning. She recounted their first meeting even though Tilly already knew about it. Lucy admitted to Tilly that they'd been getting closer and she could talk to him, she'd felt he was the opposite of Julian with his straightforward attitude and air of honesty. And then she told Tilly what Harvey had said the night he came to the flat and what Melissa had told her on the phone the same night. She explained to Tilly how her own cousin was killed at the hands of a drunk driver and that Daniel had been in trouble with the police for a similar-enough crime.

'All Joanna was doing was walking along a pavement late one evening and a car mounted the kerb and knocked her off her feet.' Lucy's eyes filled with tears. 'She didn't stand a chance. The driver was found to be three times over the legal limit, driving at speeds he never should've been doing in such a quiet neighbourhood.'

Tilly listened, she consoled, she waited. 'I would give you a hug but someone seems to be comfy,' she said, Shadow not showing any signs he was willing to budge.

'It's okay, really, I'm fine.' Lucy dried her eyes. 'But how can I ever treat Daniel the same again? We were getting close, and now...'

'Did Daniel go to prison?'

'I've no idea. Melissa didn't know any more than she told me and what I've now told you.'

'I'm assuming Harvey doesn't know any more details either, then.'

'Carol let the facts slip but she wouldn't elaborate, according to Melissa.'

'And you haven't spoken to Daniel since you found all this out?'

Lucy rested back against the sofa, all of the energy drained from her again as though she was on a roller-coaster, at the highest part when she left Aubrey House free of Julian and now at a big dip that made her stomach lurch as she talked about the man she'd got so wrong. 'He stopped me in The Street earlier today but I couldn't talk to him. He looked hurt, Tilly, and I felt terrible.'

'Why didn't you talk to him and ask for the truth?'

'How can I after what happened to Joanna?'

Tilly laughed when Shadow's purring resulted in dribble landing on her. She ignored the droplets on the lap of her dark brown corduroy dress she'd teamed with black leggings and kept on fussing him. 'When Melissa came back to the Cove after a five-year absence in the summer I was horrible to her. I mean, I was a total bitch.'

'Hard to imagine,' Lucy laughed. Tilly was feisty but never nasty.

'I wasn't nice at all. I was angry at how she'd hurt Barney by running off and never coming back. But what I didn't realise was how much she was hurting too. There were things she didn't share, things Harvey didn't divulge. Honestly, life would be far easier if people just told the truth.'

'Hey, you're preaching to the choir.' Lucy thought about all the messing around Julian had done over the years with his inability to be straight with her. Maud's phrase to describe his grandad who 'couldn't lie straight in bed' fitted perfectly when it came to Lucy's ex-husband. But that wasn't Daniel. She knew it wasn't him deep down. Except for this one lie, he wasn't a man who hid from the truth – he didn't seem to have a problem speaking his own mind. But this one untruth might just be what it took to overshadow anything else about him, the times they'd talked, the waffle-tasting at the shack, seeing him in the pub and wanting to get to know him all the more.

Tilly shifted to set her empty wine glass on the coffee table. 'Remember there are two sides to this, Lucy. It might seem clear-cut with the facts you think you've got from Harvey and Melissa, but doesn't Daniel deserve a chance to tell his side of it?' Her face softened. 'I can tell how much you like him and the feeling appears to be mutual; maybe listen to what he has to say. It might be worth it.'

'I don't know.' But Tilly had already moved Shadow to the cushion on the sofa and was taking away *Lucy's* glass.

'Get your coat back on, let's at least go to the grand opening. And if nothing else, we'll have a big fat waffle to enjoy.'

'I guess I can't argue with that.'

'You could try,' Tilly grinned.

Bundled up in her smart, midnight-blue, wool coat over a teal, tunic top with dark jeans and ankle boots, Lucy was ready to head out to the Little Waffle Shack with Tilly.

Tilly was right; Daniel did deserve a chance to tell his side of the story.

She just wasn't sure she was going to like it when he did.

They set off from the flat, the same crowds Lucy had seen gathering on her return to the Cove a short while ago still lingering. There was an air of festive cheer surrounding them as they passed the village tree, faces illuminated by the lights all the way up the Norway spruce, others lit up by the lights from the shack or by people's phones held in the air snapping shots of one another with smiles all round. Daniel had looped twinkly lights around the roof of the Little Waffle Shack like a beacon across the other side of the green space guiding everyone in the right direction. Lucy stopped when another local asked her about the sign, which had lights wound around it to show it off, and she proudly told them it was indeed her work.

The sweet smell of waffles hung in the air. Everywhere she looked, delight could be seen on the faces of customers with their cardboard containers, waffles topped with all kinds of colourful additions, little wooden forks poised to dig in for another bite. And when she turned again as they drew closer to the shack she saw Daniel handing waffles to three children. He was crouched down on his haunches pointing out the toppings, and when he stood up the parents thanked him and the kids got stuck into the sweet treats at long last.

Before Daniel went inside he turned to survey the crowds and that was when he spotted her. Lucy's heart pounded; she was nervous. Nervous about whether when he talked to her she'd know the horrible truth, or, worse, that she'd listen and want to fall into his arms anyway. It felt like a betrayal of Joanna's memory, but Tilly was right, she should at least give him a chance to tell his side.

Someone was trying to talk to Daniel and he was doing his

best to reply without taking his eyes off Lucy, as though she were an apparition and would disappear if he looked away.

Lucy waved over at him, just to let him know... well, she wasn't sure what she was letting him know, really. Perhaps that she was ready to listen, maybe that she hoped tonight went well, or that he had her friendship if nothing else.

Daniel waved back at her and smiled before letting himself be torn away by customers, tonight being the most important part of establishing the business he'd worked so hard for. Lucy got that.

'He looks pleased to see you,' Tilly whispered, having observed until now without interfering.

Lucy smiled. 'I'm glad you made me come tonight.' If anything, it made her feel better than she would've done hiding out on her own in her flat.

They said a quick hello to Barney and Lois when they emerged from the inside of the shack, where they'd nabbed a table to enjoy savoury parmesan-and-bacon waffles. 'Something different,' Lois announced, 'and this one has far too sweet a tooth already,' she said of Barney, who pretended to be bothered that she was nagging him about long-in-place habits when clearly he loved every moment of it.

'Right, now I'm officially hungry,' Tilly claimed. 'I could get us a menu to look at?'

'No need,' Lucy grinned. 'I'll have the Christmas-gingerbread waffle, please.' She could remember Daniel describing the recipe the night she'd taste-tested waffles with him and she'd been wanting to try them ever since.

Tilly didn't pass comment on her insider knowledge, only agreed to try the same, took out her purse from the deep pocket of her dress, and headed off to brave the queue.

'I saw someone eating the Christmas-gingerbread waffle,' said Barney as Lois looped her arm through his and put her other hand on his upper arm to huddle close. 'Maybe we could order those next time,' he added hopefully.

'We'll see,' smiled Lois before they headed off to chat with other villagers, leaving Lucy waiting near the shack next to a group of kids tucking into the Christmas-tree-shaped waffles that, if her eyes were seeing right in the darkness, were green like a real tree and had what looked like jelly tots for the baubles.

Tilly wasn't anywhere near as long as Lucy thought she'd be and soon returned with the waffles, a wooden fork speared into the surface alongside a toothpick with a tiny flag that had 'the Little Waffle Shack' written in fancy font. The golden delights brought with them the distinct aromas of ginger and cinnamon. A scoop of vanilla-bean ice-cream sat to one side and a generous drizzle of maple syrup zig-zagged across the waffle.

Tilly wasted no time digging in. 'These are to die for,' she said between mouthfuls. 'There are so many flavours and toppings, everything from pumpkin spice, chocolate peppermint and waffles with chocolate bits inside to savoury waffles and waffles shaped like Christmas trees. I can safely say this won't be my last visit here. I'll be back.'

'You sound as though you're on a sugar high already,' Lucy laughed as she got stuck into hers too. She didn't even care that the tips of her fingers were freezing, the taste was well worth the discomfort.

'You'll have to try the red velvet next time,' came Daniel's voice from behind them, taking Lucy by surprise. 'They're red – the colour of Christmas – with a sweet, creamy frosting on top. I put a scoop of the chunky Christmas-cake-crunch ice-cream on the side for good measure.'

Lucy hoped she didn't have anything stuck in her teeth when she managed a smile. 'Maybe we'll try those next time.'

He nodded his approval. Tilly abandoned her fork, shovelled

the last morsel of her own waffle into her mouth and announced she was going to find a bin.

'It's a brilliant turn-out tonight, you must be pretty pleased.' After Tilly's subtle departure she had no idea what to say to someone she needed to have more than a passing chat with in a field when his business was launching at that very moment.

'I am pleased.' He looked directly at her. 'And I'm even more pleased you're here. I didn't think you'd come.'

His attention was snatched away by a holler from the shack. 'I'm sorry, Lucy, I've got to go. That's Brianna. I came out to deliver Celeste and Jade's order but told her to yell if they needed me.'

The veranda of the Little Waffle Shack was buzzing with people going in, coming out, loitering and laughing into the night air. 'No need to explain.'

'Can we talk later on?'

She hesitated. 'It doesn't have to be tonight.' Maybe it would be better for the dust to settle anyway, but Daniel didn't seem to think so.

'It does. Please?'

When she nodded he looked relieved as well as torn between taking her to one side and telling her what he probably should have shared when they first began to get close and honouring his business commitment. But she knew there was no contest. He had to get back to it and make the Little Waffle Shack the success he'd hoped for, the success she hoped for too. Because no matter the truth, she couldn't rid herself of the dream that he was sticking around for good.

With Daniel back inside the shack and Tilly appearing again like an on-stage extra who came and went as required, Lucy assured her she was going to listen to Daniel's story and when she finally let up, they mingled with the crowds, mostly locals but some also who'd come from the neighbouring villages, thrilled that at last they could get proper waffles without having to go to a bigger city. One woman even declared they were as good as the waffles she'd tasted in Europe, and her sister confided in Lucy and Tilly that she'd made her try enough of them that she'd almost not come tonight for fear she'd be as sick of them as she was after that trip. Luckily for Daniel, tonight hadn't had the same effect, as both women declared they'd be back.

Families drifted off home as the evening stretched on and on, crowds thinned, and Lucy had begun to get cold as she hung around waiting to talk to Daniel. She wondered, should she wait inside now tables were becoming free? But she didn't want to look too desperate and he could be hours yet. She supposed she could go and tell him to come to her place when he was done, although she'd rather they talked here as she got the feeling the comfort of his own surroundings might well help him to open up and be totally honest with her. And she really needed him to do that.

'I'm beat,' Tilly declared, reading Lucy's mind. 'And I can't feel my feet. These are my loveable boots – the leather is soft and they're so comfy, but they don't cut it when I'm standing so long and the ground is so cold.'

'Tilly, is this your way of telling me you're going?'

'Yeah, goodnight, Lucy,' she grinned. 'I've got a delivery at the shop coming at six a.m. so if I don't fall into bed soon I'll be letting them in while wearing my pyjamas.'

'No worries, I won't be much longer either. I'm cold too and I'm convinced everyone else here must have had the foresight to wear thermals.'

Tilly enveloped her in a hug. 'I'll try not to think too much about that one, thermals don't really do it for me.'

'Goodnight, Tilly.'

'Don't do anything I wouldn't do,' she winked as she walked away.

Lucy went over to the shack but couldn't get up the steps because there was some kind of altercation at the bottom with a police woman and a girl in a red coat. Lucy waited for them to move on but whatever they were discussing had crowds looking their way and when the girl's profile showed up as the officer moved to one side, Lucy recognised her as the dark-haired girl she'd seen hanging around in The Street almost a week ago. Pretty, with a blunt-cut fringe, she was even more striking in a red wool coat, her baby bump safely tucked away from the winter's night. But she didn't look as though she was having nearly as much of a good time as anyone else at the waffle shack. In one hand she had a wallet and the police woman took it from her before handing it to someone else.

Lucy squeezed past a couple of people to see what the trouble was about and heard the girl insist she was handing the wallet in at the shack after finding it on the ground. 'I promise you, I was,' she told the officer. 'Why is it so hard to believe? Why automatically accuse me of lying?'

Oh dear, perhaps she was protesting too much.

The girl looked at the man who'd been handed the wallet. 'I honestly found it on the ground. I'm not a thief, I'm here visiting, that's all.'

'And so are pickpockets,' answered the police woman, who was having none of it. 'We've had two other complaints already tonight, that's why I'm here to look around. Would you mind turning out your pockets, please?'

'You cannot be serious,' the girl answered, hands on her hips now, nostrils flaring.

'Can you do as I ask, please?' The police woman clearly thought she was onto something and the disagreement had brought Daniel outside onto the veranda by now.

'Everything all right here?' he said, coming down the steps to approach the police woman who was putting a dampener on opening night.

The police woman turned. 'And who might you be?' By the deflated way she spoke she'd obviously had enough for the night, probably fed up with the cold and just wanting to get off shift.

'He's my husband,' piped up the girl before grinning and running straight at Daniel.

Lucy, expecting him to be confused, saw him smile widely at her before she ran into his arms and shouted loudly, 'Hi, honey, I'm home!'

Daniel was laughing by now, the police woman rolled her eyes realising maybe the girl was telling the truth, and Lucy?

Lucy locked eyes with Daniel one more time before she turned and marched away, the foul language and phrases she had going through her mind not anything she'd repeat with a few kids still hanging around.

Why were all men liars?

11

Seeing Lucy's face when Giselle appeared and made her declaration as his wife was something Daniel wished he could put out of his head, and if she hadn't run off so quickly he could've explained it all. But he couldn't do anything now other than plough on at the shack for another half an hour before closing. When you ran your own business the responsibility sat squarely on your shoulders, especially on opening night, and your personal life had to take a back seat.

Giselle had at least quickly cleared things up with the police officer, Daniel had backed her up as a character witness, he supposed, and, better than that, the police officer's colleague had nabbed the pickpockets who'd come to the village with the specific goal of targeting unsuspecting waffle fans. They'd made three arrests and it seemed that was enough to get them off Giselle's back.

When they were at last done for the night, Daniel thanked Brianna and Troy for their hard work and let them out of the shack. They both looked so shattered he bet they hadn't expected to be this exhausted working at an unassuming log cabin when they'd applied for the jobs, but he hoped they'd be back because they'd played a part in making tonight a roaring success. They'd served customers with a smile, neither of them had been flustered at facing a queue – it helped they'd both worked in fast-food joints before – and the feedback from every person who came in had been outright positive.

'Safe to come in this time?' Giselle walked back over to the shack as Daniel swept the veranda.

'I don't know, are you bringing the police this time?' He smiled. It was great to see her. 'Come on in out of the cold. I'm sorry I couldn't talk earlier, it's been crazy.' And all he wanted now was to go and see Lucy and clear things up, properly. To her he must seem like a total liar. It would be hard to persuade her to give him the time to set the record straight, but he had to at least try.

Giselle smiled, taking off her coat and, as he thought he'd noticed earlier, she was pregnant. He nodded to the bump before giving her a huge hug. 'Congratulations, you.' This woman was special to him, always would be. 'When are you due?'

'January twenty-ninth and it can't come soon enough – I feel like a beached whale. Should've seen me trying to get out of the bath this morning... Stu had to haul me out.'

As much as he needed to scarper, he couldn't do it when she'd come here especially. 'I'm pleased for you... not about the bath problems, but a brother or sister for Peter, that's great.'

When he looked at the time yet again she asked, 'Am I keeping you?'

'You are, but it doesn't matter.' She wasn't convinced. 'I can talk for a bit, but I really need to go somewhere so I don't have long.'

'Listen to you... anyone else would want to put their feet up after such a busy time.'

He took two of the upturned chairs off the table and set them down again onto the clean, freshly mopped floor. He'd not heard from Giselle in a while, not seen her in almost a year, until he got a text message out of the blue last week. The lack of contact didn't mean they were no longer good friends, just that their separate lives had taken each of them in a different direction. Daniel had always kept in touch with Peter, her eight-year-old son who'd been in Daniel's life since the day he was born, with cards and the occasional letter. Peter must have passed on the news to his mum that Daniel was going back to Heritage Cove to start a waffle business. Giselle had apparently tried to track him down almost a week ago, and in the end had sent him the text message to say she'd been in the village but hadn't been able to find his place.

'There'll be a sign by the bus stop soon enough and then everyone will know where I am,' he explained, curious as to her persistence to see him all of a sudden. Not that he minded, it was wonderful to catch up.

'I only looked along The Street, then I was so cold I got going, thought perhaps Peter got it wrong. He doesn't let me read his letters any more, says they're private.'

'I don't put anything odd in them, I promise.'

'I know you don't. But it's his thing, you know. He loves you and he misses you. He can't wait to get his own phone, he tells me, so he can message you and send you photos whenever he likes.'

'Well, at least now you've found me.'

'I don't think there's any doubt where the Little Waffle Shack is any more – you're lit up like a Christmas tree and the smell has drifted all the way down to the actual tree on the village green,' she grinned. 'Tell me, how are you and your brother getting on?'

He harrumphed at having to talk about himself but Giselle knew his entire history. She'd been the one to help him turn it around, so it was no surprise she was curious. 'Same old,' he told her, his jaw tensing instantly. He'd scanned the crowds tonight to see if Harvey would show up but he hadn't, at least not to Daniel's knowledge, and he couldn't deny it hurt. His mum had had a word in his ear, told him it was early days, and he hoped she was right. Because as much as they pushed each other away, Daniel could admit to himself that coming back here was with Harvey well and truly in mind. Brothers should at least be on speaking terms, and the pain he saw in his mum's eyes or heard in her voice should be enough to give Harvey the same message.

'I'm sure you'll sort through things eventually. And this place!' She looked around her, unable to stop smiling. 'It's quite something.'

'I'm glad you like it.'

'So, where are you racing off to when I let you out of here? Does it involve a woman?' His face must have given him away. 'I knew it.'

'We are way overdue a chat,' he laughed. She was a lot like Lucy – easy to talk to – but, like Lucy also, she was holding something back, he could tell.

'I know, we've been a bit rubbish at keeping in touch.'

'Lives move on, I get that, no need for either of us to be sorry. It's great to see you now though, I really mean that. Although you could've been a bit less dramatic with your arrival.'

'I can't believe that police woman accused me of pickpocketing of all things,' said Giselle. 'I could've slapped her when she said that, honestly.'

'I'm glad you didn't.'

'You know how I feel about the police.'

'They're not all the same.'

She didn't look convinced. 'Yeah, well, this one asked me to empty my pockets and I'm pretty sure she was close to patting me down to check there was a baby under my clothes and not a whole collection of wallets and other valuables I may have pilfered. Good job you showed up when you did. She was convinced I was a thief – and her face when you stepped in and I said I was your wife!' She laughed with glee, the laugh that reminded him what a good-hearted person she was and always had been. Especially to him.

He shook his head. 'Did you have to say that?' Lucy's face was a picture too, but not a good one. 'It's not true any more. And I have to live here, remember.'

'You know me, always liked to make an entrance. Stu says when we eventually tie the knot I'll be wearing bright red down the aisle as white is way too subtle.'

'He's not wrong there.' Now that he was sitting down he realised how manic today had been. His body was tired, the adrenalin had spiked and his exhaustion was creeping up on him. But not so much he didn't find his manners. 'Sorry, I haven't even offered you a drink. Can I get you something? You've come all the way to see me, it's the least I can do.'

She shook her head. 'No need, I won't keep you too long, and I haven't come that far. I've been staying with Stu's family in Colchester, where we're having Christmas. I was so close I couldn't miss the chance to come here. I wanted to see all this.' She looked around the shack and reached across the table to cover his hands with her own. 'I always knew you'd do great things, I knew you had it in you.'

'I never could've done any of this without you.' There was rock bottom and then there were the depths he'd reached before she'd come into his life. He honestly believed that if it wasn't for her, there was a good chance he wouldn't even be around any more. Surviving on the streets was more than difficult; there were some days when he'd felt he'd be better off putting himself out of his misery. And then, by chance, he'd crossed paths with Giselle and she'd gone from being a friend, to a counsellor, then a wife – even though both of them would readily admit their heads hadn't been in the right place when they'd decided to get married. Now, she remained a firm friend and always would, no matter how often they were in touch. And he'd never turn his back on her. Some people in your life came and went; others, like Giselle, were here to stay.

'Of course you could,' she said firmly. 'You dug deep, pulled yourself out of a hole. Now look at you.' She patted a hand against her chest and pretended to cry happy tears. 'I'm so proud.'

'Stop the dramatics,' he grinned. 'Now, tell me, how's Peter? I haven't spoken to him in a while, we're due a phone call.' Daniel sometimes wondered if he should've made more of staying in touch but part of him knew Giselle had her own life and he didn't want to step on another man's toes when she met someone new. He'd also wondered whether Peter would lose interest in him when someone else became a father figure, so part of him supposed he'd stepped away before he got hurt, just staying in touch enough that he wasn't abandoning him.

'Peter's actually the reason I'm here.'

And this was why he'd tried to distance himself. She was going to ask him to stop writing, stop sending cards. She had someone new now, they were a family and it was too confusing for Peter. 'Giselle, just tell me what you need to say.' He could see she was hesitating, worried about hurting him, perhaps, but he was stronger these days and he'd rather she didn't try to wrap it up in a way that spared him.

'Stu and I are obviously serious.' She patted the baby bump.

'Is he a good man?' That was all he needed to know. 'And good to Peter?'

'He really is. You'd like him.' Her smile faded. 'Peter's not been himself lately. He hasn't been sleeping properly, he's lost his appetite – and you know how much he loves his food – even fish fingers can't tempt him half the time, and he's been messing about at school. He's too early for the teenage angst and moods but I've seen him this way before, a couple of years ago when his grandma moved up to Scotland. He was convinced he'd never see her again. The way he was looking at it, it may as well have been New Zealand.'

Daniel remembered Peter's sensitivity as much as his enthusiasm for Meccano – parts and tools strewn across his bedroom floor as he attempted to put models together, already-accomplished pieces standing proud on the shelves against his walls. Peter was a boy who considered his words before he said them, who picked up on emotions in a room before anyone let on there was a problem. Once, when Daniel had sat nursing a beer after his birthday had passed for another year without word from Harvey and he'd been going on and on about how he could've done things differently as far as his brother was concerned, Peter had overheard him telling Giselle how he wished he'd stayed in the Cove to support Harvey and his mum. The boy had come right on over and hugged Daniel. He'd told him that mistakes were all a part of learning, and it had been the first smile on Daniel's face that whole day. Daniel had ended up smothering Peter in a huge bear hug and when Giselle watched them it was as though she was storing the moment away in her bank full of memories.

'Peter's worried about Stu replacing you,' she blurted out.

'Replacing me? Well, he kind of is. You're marrying him, and you and I are divorced.'

She shook her head. 'He's not worried about a husband being replaced, he's worried about losing you.'

Daniel hadn't realised how much it would hurt to be told he

couldn't be any part of Peter's life until Giselle's words finally told him that wasn't what she wanted after all. He felt relieved, guilty at not having tried more, anxious for Peter.

'In all these years he's never once asked about the guy who is actually his biological father, Daniel, because you were the best role model for him.'

'Some might well argue with that.'

'Only those who don't know the real you. Apart from my dad, you are the only man Peter has known his whole life. And what you did for him that night... neither of us will ever forget it.'

Daniel wouldn't either. That was the night he'd been charged with drink driving, he'd seen the inside of a jail cell for the first time. It was the part of his past formed in a split-second decision and about which his brother, Melissa and, worst of all, Lucy all thought they knew the full story before he was ready to share it and hope they understood his reasons.

'Daniel, Peter is scared stiff you'll fade away now that Stu is in our lives. He loves Stu, he really does, but I think he feels he has to choose.'

Daniel leaned back in his chair, hands behind his head. 'I thought you were going to tell me to keep away.'

'What? Seriously?'

He explained why he'd stepped back a little. 'I didn't want to ever stand in your way.'

'Daniel, you'll always be a part of our lives. You must see that.'

'I do now,' he smiled. This was the Giselle not many people saw. She was outspoken and loved a bit of an entrance and drama, but beneath all that she had such vulnerability – the side you only saw when you knew her really well, the side that came out when she fought for her son.

'Would you bring him here?'

'Peter?'

He grinned. 'I'm thinking Stu wouldn't really be enticed by a day hanging out with me at the waffle shack.'

'Oh, I don't know, he's partial to a good dessert or two.'

'Bring Peter here, it's about time I saw him again.'

She let out a huge sigh. 'Do you mean it?'

'Of course. Leave it a few days, let me settle in or I won't be able to focus, but then I'll have him here in the shack for a few hours.'

'He'd love it, Daniel. I didn't dare tell him I was coming to see you as I knew he'd be torn between jumping in the car and staying put with Stu.'

'Does Stu know why Peter's having a difficult time?'

'He does, and he's told Peter he doesn't have to choose one or the other, but I think Peter needs to hear it from you too.'

'Then it's time for me to step up.' He smiled. 'Did you already get the Christmas present and card I sent for him?'

'I did. And I showed it to Peter, all wrapped up, so he knows you were thinking of him. You know, he did a school project – they had to write a story about someone making a big change in their lives. He wrote a story about a man who started a fish-and-chip shop.'

'Doesn't surprise me.' He had fond memories of sitting next to Peter on the couch, the little boy's glasses in position and reflecting the cartoons they watched as the tang of vinegar coming from the chips and battered fish drifted up from parcels of paper from the local chippy positioned between their laps.

'The story was about a dad who started a fish-and-chip shop and was so busy he couldn't cook at home with his son any more.'

'Shit.'

'He wrote about how he understood there were very important things happening and when he got home one night his dad handed him an apron and told him they could cook whatever he liked.'

'Now I feel really bad.'

'I didn't come here to make you feel that way, I just wanted to tell you and when I was so close by I thought I'd do it in person. And I knew I had to do something before our lives change again with the baby. Peter needs some stability and part of that comes from you.'

'I'm glad you came.'

'Me too. I'm not sure how much time I'll have on my hands to sit around in waffle shacks when the baby comes, and Winchester is far enough away that I know it won't be easy for us to catch up. And besides, I wanted to check this place out and see what all your hard work has brought for you. And thank you, Daniel, for saying Peter can come and hang out here.'

'Least I can do given I'm forever in your debt and I love Peter like he's my own.'

'Hey, I think we've both helped each other enough over the years that we're about even.' She picked up one of the menus. 'Peter's going to love it here. You know, I don't remember ever having made him waffles.'

'Then he's coming to the right place,' he said as she picked up her coat.

He helped her on with it and with a bit of effort she managed to do up the buttons. 'Besides not wanting to turn out my pockets for that police woman, I didn't want her asking me to undo this as I was frightened I'd never manage to do it up again and I'd freeze.'

He locked up for the night and switched off the twinkling lights while she quizzed him about the woman he'd been so desperate to see this evening and he found himself blurting out everything as he walked her back to her car, parked on The Street not too far from Lucy's workshop and flat.

'Talk to her, Daniel.' Giselle hugged him goodbye.

'I will.'

She climbed into the car, waved, and as he waited for her to drive away he turned and noticed the lights were already off in Lucy's place. He'd hoped he'd be able to make out at least one, giving him the go-ahead, but it wasn't to be. He wouldn't get a chance to talk to her tonight but perhaps it would give him an opportunity instead to work out what he was going to say to get everything out in the open once and for all. He just hoped she'd take the time to listen.

He was about to head home when Harvey appeared from the end of the lane that led to Tumbleweed House, which had once been the family home and now belonged to Harvey. Daniel hadn't been back there in years and he doubted he would for a very long time if the look on Harvey's face was anything to go by. He'd realised coming back here was going to be difficult but he hadn't banked on Harvey being so resistant to hearing him out.

'That your wife, was it?' Harvey said without preamble as Giselle's car drove around the bend and she was gone from sight. 'I guess I should say congratulations.'

'Not now, Harvey.'

'Yes, now.' He jolted Daniel's arm to make him spin around and face him.

Daniel put his hands up. 'You want to do this? You want a fight in the street?'

'I don't want a fight. I don't want any trouble, has it not got through to you yet?'

'Then why do you keep insisting on confronting me?'

Harvey's breath curled into the night air as he considered his brother's words. 'I just don't want you upsetting people, that's all.'

'And what makes you the village keeper, looking out for every-one? Let people live their own lives, Harvey. And it might surprise you to know that people can change. Okay, so Dad never did, but that doesn't mean I haven't.' When Harvey said nothing he added, 'Why don't you see that?'

Harvey looked as though he might be considering what his brother was saying until he realised they were outside Lucy's place. 'Don't even think about going to see her.'

'And what's it to you if I do?' He'd wanted to see Lucy; instead he was having a deep-and-meaningful out here in the wintry air and he was already feeling the cold. The shack had been so warm with all the crowds, the cooking, then the clearing up, that he hadn't bothered with his coat when he'd only been walking Giselle to her car. Now he wished he had it. 'Oh, that's right, you've decided it's your duty to tell her what a bastard I am. Is that right?'

'Someone had to let her know the truth.'

'See, that's where you're wrong. *Someone* didn't have to. I did.' Harvey seemed taken aback. But at least it kept him quiet. 'Lucy will get the truth but the only person she needs to get it from is me. You should keep out of it.'

'I'm doing my best to, believe me. I stayed away from the opening tonight but when I was walking the dog I saw Lucy rushing home and she didn't look happy. Somehow I got the feeling you might have played a part in it and when Melissa asked me if I was aware you were married and your wife was in town, I knew you had.' He looked up at Lucy's flat, the windows in darkness. 'Do the right thing for once, Daniel.'

Daniel stared him down. 'You always did this.'

'Did what?'

'Jumped to conclusions, refused to hear people out.'

'It seems pretty clear-cut to me.'

Daniel harrumphed. 'That's your problem, everything always is with you.' He turned to walk away. But he faced his brother one more time from metres away. 'You weren't the only son of Donnie Luddington, you know. You weren't the only one who struggled and looked for an escape route.'

And with nothing else on his mind now apart from his bed, his duvet, and a long sleep before he opened up his business tomorrow, he headed for the cottage he called home.

12

Lucy's eyes felt swollen when she woke, and when she put the tree lights on in the lounge her foot touched the wrapped tortoise still waiting for her to give to Daniel. She supposed she wouldn't be doing that now. Perhaps she'd sell it on her website, or pass it to Tilly for her shop instead. She'd spent hours on it too, the joy at making someone a surprise, a gift that would mean something, never far from her mind.

She fed Shadow, fussed him even though his focus was on crunching his way through the biscuits sprinkled on top of the tinned food in his bowl. Daniel was married, he was expecting a baby. The lies kept mounting up. She'd thought Julian was the biggest liar she'd ever met but it seemed she'd well and truly fallen for whatever charms Daniel had used on her to prevent her from seeing he wasn't much different.

Was it her? Was she a magnet for dishonest men?

She filled a big mug of tea, decided to stop feeling sorry for herself, and went for a shower to wake herself up. Then she'd set to work, use her busyness as a balm for her loneliness and upset. Maybe it would help her regain some semblance of the festive spirit that had well and truly done a bunk last night on her way home.

When her phone pinged it was Tilly, who had no idea how things had panned out last night. Unless, of course, the rumour mill had given her the news, but it didn't seem like it when Tilly asked her if she had time to meet for morning tea at the tea rooms so she could tell her everything that went down last night. 'Don't leave out a single detail', the message had said.

Oh, she wouldn't. But Tilly was in for one hell of a shock.

Lucy got through the morning with her concentration intact, not losing too much of it to the waffle shack and its owner apart from cursing it as a place she probably wouldn't get to enjoy now Daniel was firmly written into her bad books. Maybe she'd focus on the positive side – her waistline would thank her for staying away.

She finished off part of a trellis she'd designed and produced, she put the final touches to a wrought-iron basket a customer wanted to sit by the fireplace, and she took a supply delivery that would keep her going with enough materials for a couple of months. It was great to have all the space in her own workshop. Back when she was living with Julian she'd used the garage to work in but he'd hated it. He said her things were everywhere, which, to be fair, they were, but when you were using tools, some of which created sparks and got incredibly hot, you couldn't do it cramped up. She'd done her best not to irritate him, especially when he kept his road bike and mountain bike in there and paid them so much attention you'd think they were his offspring, but the arrangement had always been strained.

Pausing for a drink break, Lucy couldn't help but take all of this in again – her own space, an organised place for her to work and absorb her love of all things metal. Julian had hated that too. Whereas her parents had eventually come around and seen she was not only serious but reasonably talented, Julian had never grown to like what she loved. It was one of the things he hadn't bothered to lie about either, and somehow that made it worse; he'd lied about everything else but hadn't found it in him to pretend he liked her work or approve of her being a business owner in her own right.

She shook her head and got back to work. It was a wonder she and Julian had lasted so long, really, but it was definitely a learning curve. One she wouldn't ever follow again. And that included with Daniel.

Lucy took any frustrations about the owner of the waffle shack out on pieces of metal that needed an almighty whack with a hammer, others that needed slicing or drilling and yanking into shape. And before she knew it, it was eleven o'clock and she was well due a break.

The little bell tinkled when she went inside the tea rooms and Etna raised a hand in greeting. Etna and Patricia didn't bat an eyelid at Lucy's scruffy work attire – dungarees, stained top beneath, an old coat looped over her arm. Lucy got more looks from the locals when she was dressed up and smart.

She took a seat to wait for Tilly and wound her hair up into a high bun. It might be winter but her workshop had warmed her like a hot-water bottle that held its temperature for quite some time and she didn't really need the coat she'd brought mostly because it felt odd to be out and about without layers when everyone else was bundled up against the cold.

Tilly was one of those people. She tumbled into the tea rooms ten minutes late, apologising as she removed her layers – scarf, gloves, boho burnt-orange coat with tassels fringing the bottom. 'I had a lot of customers this morning.'

Patricia took their order for the morning tea, which came

with their choice of tea blend, a selection of sandwiches and sweet treats.

'I need this break,' Tilly smiled. 'I'm so glad I have Dessie as an assistant, especially with her willing to cover for a whole hour so I could come here.'

'How's Dessie getting on? You must trust her if she's on her own.'

Tilly's bangles shook as she wagged her finger. 'No, no, no, don't even try to get away from the subject of a certain waffle man. I won't be distracted. I want all the gossip. I want to know whether it was a passionate kiss beneath the twinkly lights of the Little Waffle Shack, a smooch over highly indulgent waffles or a trip back to his place.'

'None of the above.' Her smile that had met Tilly upon arrival had gone now. 'Not after someone else showed up.'

'Not Julian again. When's he going to get the message? I'll give him full marks for trying.'

'It wasn't Julian. This time it was Daniel's wife.'

Tilly's mouth fell open. 'You what?'

'Yep. And she's beautiful. Oh, and very pregnant too.'

Tilly was, for once, lost for words.

They paused the conversation when Etna brought the three-tiered cake stand over with a sumptuous-looking morning tea that Lucy was sure she could plough through easily given the work she'd done already today and had Tilly claiming she'd never have room for sandwiches and choux buns let alone the light, buttery scones that sat on the top plate. Lucy ignored Daniel's calls each time her phone display lit up and Tilly didn't miss her annoyance at the last one.

'Has he been doing that all morning?' Tilly asked.

'Yup. He sent me a couple of messages last night too, saying we need to talk.'

'I can't believe he never told you he was married before.'

'I can't either. I mean, I know we're hardly an item, but you'd think the matter of a wife and a baby on the way might have come out somewhere.' Her phone display lit up yet again. 'Honestly, if he doesn't stop calling I'm going to block his number.'

A small smile spread across Tilly's face. 'Why haven't you already done that if you're so sure he's a terrible person?'

'I'll do it now.'

'Are you sure you want to do that?' Tilly lowered her voice when the bell tinkled to indicate someone else coming in behind where they were sitting.

Lucy thought it was obvious, the facts kind of spoke for themselves. 'Give me one reason why I shouldn't block Daniel Luddington's contact forever.'

'I can give you a couple,' came a voice from next to her, and when Lucy looked up she was face to face with Daniel's wife.

Tilly, still chewing on a cucumber sandwich, looked from one woman to the other, clearly putting two and two together with the pregnancy bump protruding from the woman's coat. 'I'll give you two a minute.' She scarpered to talk to Etna at the counter, taking a couple of sandwiches and a cream-filled choux bun with her on a small plate. Clearly she anticipated this taking a lot longer than a minute.

'May I sit down?' In the same red coat that only highlighted her drop-dead gorgeousness all the more, the woman waited for Lucy's consent. 'I'm Giselle, by the way,' she said, taking off her coat and using the laminated menu on the table to waft air at herself. 'Sorry, pregnancy has my internal thermometer all over the place. One minute I'm cold, then I'm too hot.'

Lucy didn't say a word, just sipped her water and wanted more than anything to go and hide out in her workshop. Daniel being married was bad enough but about to become a father? That was unimaginable in his web of lies.

'I must apologise for my sudden appearance last night,' said Giselle, the menu still wafting her ever so slightly until she put it down on the table. 'I've always been one to make an entrance and it seems I managed that – what with the police and then my announcement that I was Daniel's wife.'

Lucy wished she wasn't in ragged dungarees and a T-shirt with more than a couple of oil stains as well as a tear on one sleeve. Her ensemble didn't fill her with confidence next to this woman.

'I'm not, by the way,' Giselle went on. 'I mean, I was... we were. Oh, I'm making a hash of this. Let me get a cold drink and I'll explain.' She went up to the counter and with Tilly on one side gossiping with Etna, Patricia served her with a big glass of iced water.

Back at the table, Giselle gulped most of the water down. 'Wow, I needed that. Right, I'm just going to come right out with it. This,' she said, patting her tummy, 'is not Daniel's baby. And Daniel and I are no longer married, we are divorced. We have been for a long time. We were only ever friends, really, but one thing led to another, both of us were looking for reliability, and we thought getting married was the answer. It was a total mistake on both our parts and we soon realised that, but we've got a past and we've stayed friends.'

'So why announce you were his wife to everyone in the village?' Amongst other things, it was embarrassing to think people might now know how her feelings for Daniel were developing, only for them to be thrown in her face.

Giselle looked as though she felt guilty for doing it and Lucy had to hand it to her for at least trying to set the record straight. 'The police officer had it in for me for some reason. I was furious she'd accused me of stealing a wallet when I was handing it in as a favour. When I saw Daniel, I saw an easy way for him to give me some credibility and get her off my back. I was having a bit of a laugh and it didn't even enter my head that Daniel was from here originally and people may react to the news. I didn't realise, either, that he was keen on someone who was standing right there witnessing it all.'

Lucy supposed that must be her. 'Daniel and I aren't involved.'

'I'm not here to pry.' Giselle gulped more water and Lucy had to wonder what on earth pregnancy did to your body. 'But Daniel did tell me about you.' Lucy wasn't sure how to react to that so staying silent seemed a good option. 'And I have to tell you that as well as this baby not being his and us not being an item, he's a good man. A very good man.' She looked around the tea rooms and at the door. 'He'd also kill me if he knew I was trying to handle this for him.'

When Lucy's phone rang again she declined the call. 'He's been doing that all morning.'

'He wouldn't be doing it if he wasn't keen to set the record straight.'

'I think it may have gone beyond that.' She wasn't about to tell a stranger about Joanna, the loss that made dating someone who could easily have caused similar devastation so intolerable. 'Perhaps I'll keep it polite from now on, no anger or animosity. After all, we both have to live here in the village and run a business.'

Giselle seemed to recognise a strong woman when she saw one and so finished her water and picked up her coat. 'I've said what I needed to, the rest is up to you.' She looked like she was about to be on her way but stopped and said, 'It's not for me to tell you everything about Daniel, I think he'd quite like to do that himself. And in my opinion, it's other people interfering that makes everything so much worse. Please, just listen to what he has to say. Then form an opinion about him. He deserves that much.'

Lucy found herself nodding and, with a smile as she did her coat back up, Giselle left the tea rooms.

Tilly wasted no time racing over. 'That wasn't pistols at dawn so, tell me, what's going on?'

Lucy recounted what Giselle had told her – about the divorce, the friendship, the past that only he had the right to share. 'I don't think I can hear him out just yet, Tilly.' She tried to enjoy a scone from the top tier but after she'd covered it in raspberry jam and then cream, she didn't quite fancy it. 'I was blindsided and Julian did that enough to me over the years, I can't be with someone like that again.'

'So tell him all of that. And ask him for some time. There's no rush. He has a business, you have a business – that's full on. If he's the man I suspect he is, he'll wait for you to be ready.' She had Etna pop the last couple of scones into a paper bag when Lucy refused them. Her appetite had gone for now. 'I have to get back to work. Text me if you need me.'

They hugged goodbye, Tilly turning left for the shop, Lucy turning right for home. But her better mood soon changed when she got closer to the workshop and saw who was waiting for her at the door.

Daniel stood up straight from where he was leaning against the wall as he waited.

'I've got a lot of work on, Daniel, I can't really stop.' Unfortunately her stomach betrayed her with a nervous flip at how handsome he looked standing there. She let herself in and he picked up on the vibe not to follow but when she turned round as she hung her coat on a hook against the wall, he had one arm resting on the door jamb as he watched her.

'I've only nipped out quickly to see you,' he said, 'I can't be long either. But you won't take my phone calls.'

'Maybe take the hint.' Her harsh tone mellowed to a slightly friendlier, if wary, one. 'I will talk to you but right now I've got too much going on and any more drama is way, way down on my list.'

'Who said anything about drama? All I want is a chance to explain.'

'And I promise you I'll listen.' But that might be all she'd do. 'For now, I need to get back to work and finish up so I can enjoy some time off over Christmas.' With only six days to go, she was already very close to wrapping up for the break, but he didn't need to know that. She picked up a long piece of metal to take over to the table.

'Perhaps I should've told Brianna that if I'm not back in half an hour then call the police as I've been murdered.'

Lucy did her best not to grin when he nodded at the piece of steel that she guessed could double as a weapon if she wanted it to. She set it down and turned on the forge to heat up, hoping her actions would see him finally give in. She was making a boot scraper for Hazel from the riding stables to position outside the office and it was to be a practical piece to rid shoes and boots of unwanted dirt and mud, but Lucy would add ornate twisted finials to either side so it was attractive to look at too. She'd finish off by galvanising the boot scraper in a protective coating to prevent it from rusting. Little did Hazel know that she was in for a surprise herself, as her brother had also commissioned Lucy to make her Christmas present from him this year.

Daniel still hadn't left. But with a sigh he announced, 'I'll leave you to it for now, then.' He sounded as though all his energy had been used up last night. 'But for what it's worth, I'm not married and I'm not about to become a father either.'

She didn't make eye contact but stopped still, tongs in one

hand ready to pick up the steel and hold it over the forge. 'I know.'

She stared into the flames, torn between seeing things from his perspective and seeing them from her own, which had to mean protecting herself and keeping her guard up.

She would talk to him, in time. But already she was dreading that whatever he had to say wouldn't change a thing.

And that was what hurt the most.

* * *

Lucy worked some of the longest days she'd ever put in after Daniel came to visit. She turned down the girls' invitations to the pub, she didn't chat with Tilly when she dropped off a set of iron coasters for her to sell in the shop, and the only place she lingered at was the riding stables, when she delivered the finished wine rack to Hazel's brother ready for him to wrap. They'd agreed a time so Hazel would be teaching and when Lucy showed the finished product to Arnold, he was over the moon. Lucy hung around enjoying the space of open fields on one side and the laughter from the kids in Hazel's group in the manège. It was the breathing room Lucy needed out here, with everyone at the stables either seeing to the horses, having lessons or taking care of the land.

Tilly stopped by the workshop soon after Lucy got back to carry on with the boot scraper and picked up the country-style cookbook stand she'd wanted for her assistant Dessie. 'You're a lifesaver, Lucy, thank you so much.'

'It's rather a last-minute Christmas gift.' Lucy took payment with her card reader, a must when people preferred credit these days. It meant she could take advantage in the summer, especially, when people were likely to be strolling by and tempted with impulse buys.

Tilly laughed. 'I knew you weren't listening when I came in here the other day to ask you to make it. I've already got Dessie champagne truffles and a bottle of prosecco but this is a gift for her gran. In the Christmas rush earlier this month I accidentally sold the one I'd meant to put aside for her. She was gutted, she said it didn't matter but I could see that it did. And it matters to me because I promised she could have it.'

'Come to think of it, I do remember you telling me. Sorry, it's a busy time, my head is full of all sorts.'

'Full of all sorts or full of he who shall not be named? And he who we haven't mentioned since we had morning tea the other day?'

'You can say his name.'

'Okay, is your head full of Daniel?'

'Perhaps a little, when I'm not making emergency cookbook stands,' she grinned.

'And have you given any thought to talking to him?'

'Nope.'

'Not even if I said he was asking after you?'

Lucy's head whipped up from where she was filing away her copy of the receipt for the cookbook stand.

'He didn't mention your name exactly but the thought was there, I know it was. I saw his spirits lift when he noticed me and Melissa and then sink again when he realised you weren't with us. You have been most other times, you see.'

'Like I said—'

'This isn't like you, Lucy. You don't hide away from your friends. Do yourself a favour, talk to Daniel, get it out of the way. And then at least you can come for a drink with us.'

'You've got a point, I suppose.'

'Of course I have. And, remember, he wouldn't be trying so hard to get your attention if everything they were saying about him was true. We already know he isn't married or expecting a baby, that's a start.'

'It doesn't matter if the rumours are true, it's more that he didn't say anything.'

'Give the guy a chance, he's only just got back to town. I went out with a guy a few years ago and we were only on our first date when he told me he'd had a drug problem. It was enough to make me back off – not because of the problem, but it was too much to take on board when I had trouble remembering his last name, let alone learning his deepest, darkest secrets.' She had hold of the cookbook stand against her chest. 'Right, lecture over. And thanks again for this. Dessie will be very happy and her gran will be too, I'm sure.'

'My pleasure.'

When Tilly went on her way, Lucy finished up her work on the boot scraper, headed upstairs for a bowl of soup for lunch and took a much-needed shower. But before she had a chance to make a cup of tea, there was a knock at the door.

Melissa, standing on the doorstep, didn't waste time getting to the point. 'I spent a lot of time living a life I thought I was happy with.' Lucy went to interrupt her but she jumped in pretty quickly. 'I told myself I was happy that way, I shut out voices that told me I should find answers before I could be sure moving on was the right thing to do. I'm not here to lecture you, Lucy, but what I do need is your help.'

'Then you'd better come in.' She had no idea where this conversation was going.

'I will, but only for as long as it takes you to get your coat on.'

'I don't understand.'

'It's almost Christmas and as much as Harvey pretends he

wants nothing more than for his brother to bugger off out of the village and leave him in peace, he's being as stubborn as when he and I needed to talk and work through our problems. Which, as you know, could've worked out very differently if Barney and half the village hadn't intervened.'

Lucy rubbed the tops of her arms but Melissa was gesturing for her to get her coat and she found herself doing as she was told. Even if she wasn't willing to give Daniel a chance, something deep inside of her wanted for him to be happy. He'd looked lost when she saw him the other day waiting for her to give him a chance, and she didn't want him to be miserable, no matter what he had or hadn't done. And she'd also been around the brothers enough to realise how unlikely he was to ever feel happy here if he couldn't work it out with Harvey.

'What do you suggest?' Lucy asked as she grabbed her keys and bundled out of the flat.

But Melissa wasn't saying anything. Obviously this wasn't up for debate and all Lucy had to do was obey and follow her friend's lead. They were heading along The Street and then down the lane that led to Tumbleweed House.

'I'm not sure I want to get in the middle of this,' said Lucy as they let themselves into the house and the dog, Winnie, charged at both of them. Lucy had to laugh – she was a bundle of joy, uncomplicated, unable to tell a lie. Maybe she should get a dog instead of looking for anything resembling a human relationship, but she doubted Shadow would be impressed if she did.

'You're in the middle of it whether you like it or not,' Melissa claimed as they sat down in the kitchen at the battered oak table that must've been in the family for years, given the dents in its surface, the scratches here and there, the damaged corner that had been varnished over, all giving it as much character as Tumbleweed House itself, with the wisteria vines on its frontage that come next year would hold vibrant purple blooms. 'And I have to take some kind of action, for Carol. The boys' mum has confided in me a lot over the last few weeks. She's always been aware of the division between her sons but seeing it with her own eyes now they're in such close proximity has made it all the more shocking for her. She's trying not to interfere but doesn't want to take such a step back that she'd be neglecting them when they both need a bit of encouragement to try harder. She's blaming herself and wondering whether she should've stood up to their lowlife dad to help pave their way to a better future.'

Lucy had often wondered what this was like for Carol, whether it was a good thing Daniel was back or not. 'The poor woman.'

'She doesn't deserve any of it; neither do they. But they're both too pig-headed to see it.'

Lucy smiled. 'It seems that way, doesn't it?'

'Carol held it together over the years, pretending she was fine with the way things are, but that's hard to do with Daniel back in the village. The other day, I was having coffee and cake with her and she could barely disguise the tremble in her voice when she spoke about them both. And when Harvey refused to go to the opening of the Little Waffle Shack, any smile she gave or phrase laced with pride couldn't disguise how much it hurt her. If Harvey and Daniel carry on like this, never dealing with what's between them, then they'll regret it. Carol knows it too and her biggest fear is that one day she won't be around and she'll have died with a broken heart.'

'It must be really hard for her. But, Melissa, I still don't understand why I'm here. Is Harvey coming home? Does he want to ask me to talk to Daniel? Because that might be a problem.'

'No, I don't think those two need a go-between,' said Melissa as they sat at the dining table with Winnie contentedly snuggled at Melissa's feet. 'But they do need to be in the same place at the same time and they need to listen. I didn't want to have them forced together but it's the only way I can see it ever working. I thought long and hard about where to do this – the pub is too noisy and crowded, The Street is too public and easy to escape from, the cove itself poses the danger of either one of them drowning the other in the sea – and this way, they'll both be going to a place where they don't expect to see the other.

'I decided that because all of this stems from their childhood, the best place to bring things to a head was right here,' she said, looking around the kitchen, over at the butler's sink that added an olde-worlde touch and was positioned so you could look out at the fields beyond whenever it was light, up at the stars if it was dark.

Lucy knew Harvey must have decorated this place along the way but so many features spoke of the family home it might once have been, or perhaps the home they'd hoped it would be without the trouble their dad had brought their way. A pots-and-pans rack hung above the island and blended in with the house's personality and Lucy suspected Melissa was right to bring the boys here. The trouble had started within these walls and it could end here in whatever way they both decided.

'I almost told Carol I was doing this,' said Melissa, 'but if it doesn't go well, I don't want to break her heart any more than it's broken already.'

'I'll help in any way I can, but I still don't understand why I'm here.'

'Harvey will come home soon. He's driving back from Cambridge after going to talk through plans with a new client for a loft conversion, so that part's easy, but Daniel coming here after closing the Little Waffle Shack for the night is pretty hard to achieve. He won't come if I ask...'

'And you're thinking he will if I do?'

'It's a case of desperate measures. This place might trigger something in the both of them that makes them talk or listen, hopefully both. After that, I've done all that I can. I've been over this with Barney too.'

'What were his thoughts?' Ever-wise Barney, a village favourite, was always on hand with advice when you needed it. He'd had Lucy over for afternoon tea when she first arrived in Heritage Cove and had given her the low-down on the village and its residents whether she wanted it or not. She suspected he could see she'd come to the Cove not in trouble, particularly, but still looking for a place to belong.

'He's worried it'll fire up the anger in both of them. He knows Harvey well, remember. But it's almost Christmas and I know how much this would mean to Carol if there could be a sense of peace for the season. I'm not expecting a miracle – for them to suddenly forget everything and be the closest brothers in the world – just hoping for a little civility, for everyone's sake.'

'So you want me to go over and ask Daniel to come here after hours? Won't that look a bit odd?'

'Tilly tells me he's been calling you and he won't give up trying.'

'He gets full marks for persistence,' she agreed. Something had stopped her fingers from flying over the keys to block his number and she wondered whether it was because that would be final, it would cut him off. 'How do you suggest I persuade him to come over?'

Melissa had it all worked out. Lucy was to call Daniel and say she needed help, that she'd fallen and twisted her ankle, she couldn't get up. She'd then tell him she was in the loft room at Tumbleweed House as Melissa had given her a key while she and Harvey were out for the evening, asking her to put the towel rail she'd made on request and that Melissa intended to give Harvey for Christmas up there out of sight in the wall cupboard.

'And why would I be calling Daniel and not someone else?' Lucy asked.

Melissa grinned. 'Say you meant to call someone else but called him by mistake. Easy enough if he's the most recent contact, given how much he's trying to get hold of you.'

'Plausible, I suppose. But I'd feel terrible lying. Lying is something I just don't do.'

Melissa nudged her. 'You did it the other day.'

'When?'

'When we were in the queue at the bakery and Patricia came in for some croissants and asked us all what we thought to her new hairdo. All I can say is that I'm glad I had a mouth full of mince pie and couldn't answer.'

Lucy began to laugh. 'It's hideous. Why she thought blue hair was a good idea I'll never know. Thank goodness it wasn't permanent and she's back to normal now.' She shuddered at the memory. 'But lying then was different. It was a white lie, told to spare her feelings.'

'And this lie will be to help Carol, to hopefully bring her sons to a point where at least they can be in the same vicinity without wanting to kill each other.'

Lucy guessed, when she put it that way, it wasn't a bad thing to do. 'Fine, I'll do it.'

'You're going to have to act like you're in agony,' Melissa said conspiratorially. 'You need to make him come running.' She took out her phone and pinged off a text. 'Just reminding Harvey to pick up some milk because I dropped the entire carton over the floor earlier.'

'Clumsy.'

Melissa grinned. 'I didn't drop anything, but I need him to

stop at the supermarket to give us a bit longer after closing time at the waffle shack.'

'You've got this all planned.'

'Barney came up with some of it for me.'

Lucy laughed. 'Doesn't surprise me at all after his cunning plan to reunite you and Harvey back in the summer.'

They went up into the loft space. The plan was to get Daniel here, then Melissa would hide before intercepting Harvey's arrival home and sending him up to the loft to turn off the television she'd left running while she saw to the dinner.

'Right, make the call,' said Melissa when they'd discussed the plan and the timing was right. Melissa would keep Winnie behind a closed door when Daniel arrived too in case she tried to scare a newcomer away. Lucy doubted she would, though. Winnie was a big softie and would likely roll over when she saw a stranger rather than bark or anything else.

Knowing the waffle shack would now be shut, Lucy made the call to Daniel. She pretended to cry out in pain and garbled out a story of where she was, that she was stuck at Tumbleweed House with Harvey and Melissa out all evening and couldn't get down the stairs. He didn't ask why she'd called him, he was probably caught up on the fact she'd actually got in touch, and already she felt terrible for manipulating him and at the lift of hope in his voice when he'd answered.

Lucy's wait for Daniel to arrive was laced with guilt. She'd come to care for him far more than she'd admit to anyone.

Less than five minutes later she heard Daniel come in the front door, which had been left unlocked. Lucy, as instructed, was upstairs in the converted loft room. It was a beautiful space at the top of the house, with a yucca plant in the far corner, a slate-grey sofa, a charcoal suede bean-bag sofa and white units running along one wall and around beneath the window. An old-fashioned record player and a collection of vinyl sat on a small cabinet next to the yucca plant and the angles in the roof added to the casual vibe. Lucy wondered how long it would be before that vibe was something else altogether.

Lucy heard Daniel's footsteps on the first flight of stairs as he called out her name.

'I'm here,' she called back, sitting on the carpet with her back against the sofa, legs outstretched. Melissa had told her she might have to keep up the pretence for a while, at least until she sent Lucy a text to say Harvey was home and she could reveal this was a set-up.

When Daniel appeared she said, 'It's not serious. I stumbled, that's all.'

He fussed over her, his breathing ragged at having run to reach her. He smelled sweet, like the waffles he'd surely been cooking before he came here. His sleeves were rolled up to reveal muscular forearms that could definitely handle carrying her home and she found herself almost wishing she was really injured, just to have the closeness she wasn't ready to admit she wanted. He looked so handsome, blue eyes full of concern, and the guilt she had coursing through her made it hard to comprehend how Julian had ever been okay with lying.

'May I?' Daniel indicated her outstretched leg and when she nodded, he pulled up the end of her jeans to inspect the ankle. 'It's not swollen, is it tender?'

'A little.'

'And you've tried to put weight on it?'

She wished Melissa would hurry up and send that text so she could stop fibbing, the very trait she detested. 'I tried, but I couldn't stand.'

'I'll have to help you. I didn't have the car at the shack but I can carry you back to your flat if you'll let me.'

She was staring at him and cleared her throat when he caught her looking as he inspected her ankle yet again as though his touch would be able to fix it all up for her. 'Sure.'

He made a move to help her out but she hadn't got the text yet. 'We should talk first.'

His face broke into a smile that reminded her of the easy chatter they'd had those times in her workshop, at the waffle shack when he'd asked her to help him taste the ice-creams as toppings. 'I've been trying to talk for a long time, does it need to be now? Does it need to be here?' He'd done well to not take anything in but all of a sudden was jolted. 'It's years since I came up to the top of the house and I certainly haven't ever seen it looking anything like this.'

'It's nice what Harvey's done, isn't it?'

He was looking around him now and spotted the old record player in the far corner. 'I never thought he'd keep this, it's a relic.' He was laughing, it was a good sign. 'Harvey nabbed this at a car-boot sale when we were kids, brought it back and kept it hidden in his room away from our dad, who would've probably thrown it out. I think it was made in the 1970s... probably worth something these days.'

'There are some records there,' she said, encouraging the train of thought, the nice memories about his brother rather than the angst. 'It's a decent vinyl collection.'

Daniel flipped through and pulled out an R.E.M. album, another by U2. And all the while the scowl that usually came when either brother was within a hundred metres of the other one was replaced by a peaceful nostalgia. 'We'd play these as loud as they would go when Dad was away, usually at breakfast. Mum would join in too – she knew the tracks better than we did. All three of us would pretend to be in a band, me on guitar, Harvey and Mum on vocals. I'd forgotten all that.'

'It sounds as though you and Harvey have had some good times,' she prompted.

But she'd gone one step too far. He snapped out of the happy thoughts he'd allowed to reel him in. 'Yeah, and plenty not so good. Come on, let's get you home.' He crouched down on his haunches. 'How about you shuffle over to the stairs and go down on your bum? Then I'll carry you once we're safely at the bottom.' He smiled, and when she gave him a look, he said, 'I've been trying to get your attention for days, and now I have it.'

She smiled back at him, her heart pounding at his possible reaction when he found out she was lying. She needed to stall some more.

'Why did you call me of all people?' he wondered, buying her some time without realising it.

'As you said, you've been calling and messaging me and when I picked up my phone you were first in the contacts and I clicked on you. I thought I was clicking on Tilly's contact.'

He looked at her more closely. 'Did you hit your head or anything?'

'No, it was clumsiness, that's all.' At that moment her phone pinged and on the screen she saw a series of hearts from Melissa's number. That was the symbol they'd agreed would alert Lucy to Harvey being home and on his way up here any second. Lucy still couldn't believe Melissa had kept so quiet down there and only now could they hear footsteps.

Daniel looked panicked. 'They're home. I'm not ready for this.'

But he didn't have a chance to run because the footsteps drew closer and closer until Harvey's head appeared at the top of the stairs and he took the last few steps into the same room as his brother and Lucy.

Judging by Harvey's surprise, Lucy and Melissa had done a good job of keeping this from both of the brothers.

Lucy got to her feet. 'You two need to talk. Try not to kill each other.'

'Wait,' said Daniel, watching her get up and move quite easily. 'What's going on? Your ankle's fine.'

'As I said, you two need to talk.' She couldn't meet Daniel's eye. 'Do this once and for all. Do it for each other and do it for your mum.'

Daniel was so gobsmacked he didn't say anything else as Lucy escaped downstairs to where Melissa was sitting in the kitchen, fingers crossed on both hands. She took one look at Lucy and said, 'Pub?'

'You bet,' Lucy replied. This could either be exactly what the boys needed or the worst idea in history.

13

Daniel and Harvey stood looking at one another until Daniel turned his focus to the darkness on the other side of the window instead. Out there in the fields beyond he'd escaped the family home as much as he could. He'd got far, far away from the man who in his opinion should never have been allowed to have children. He'd hidden out in the top of the house enough times too, but of course it was different back then. There hadn't been a cosy room – instead, it had been dust, cobwebs, old and broken toys or household items that had come up here to die keeping him company. Sometimes Harvey had been here too. They'd listened to their dad pacing the floors below, thankfully too lazy to bother chasing them all the way up here.

Beneath the outside light Daniel could see the girls head off away from the front door and turn down the side of the house, making their escape now they'd engineered this. He'd rather be here with Lucy, ankle injury or not, than turn around and face Harvey, but Melissa and Lucy had obviously had other plans and Lucy's words about doing this for their mother rang in his ears. Over the years his mum's feelings had been lurking in his mind, sometimes at the back of it, other times at the forefront when she sounded upset, and, now, he had a feeling that if he and his brother didn't get anywhere tonight then it wasn't going to happen full stop.

He turned at last to find Harvey sitting on the arm of the sofa, forearms rested along his thighs, hands clenched together and head bowed as though he was trying to summon an appropriate emotion. At least he wasn't yelling or throwing accusations his way, that was something.

'You kept the record player,' said Daniel. 'Does it still work?'

'Still works,' said Harvey without looking up.

'Do you use it?'

But Harvey didn't answer the question. Instead, he asked one of his own. 'Did you plan this?'

'You've got your other half to blame for that. Lucy's clearly in on it but I suspect this came from Melissa.'

'Sounds about right. She's been going on at me for ages to talk to you.'

Daniel didn't miss the fact that when Melissa's name was mentioned Harvey's face relaxed into something that was border-line defensive rather than a boiling pot of fury ready to explode. 'Lucy hasn't been going on about anything. She wouldn't talk to me until now.'

'Can you blame her?'

Daniel looked at the collection of vinyl again as a memory surfaced. 'Do you remember when we were boys and had a fight outside the convenience store?' Harvey's look suggested he failed to understand what that had to do with anything, so Daniel ploughed on. 'Barney came along and found us, then he handed me an orange from the bag in his hand. He told us that we clearly had things to say and suggested we try to listen to each other. We could only speak when holding the orange and so with him policing us we passed it back and forth until we got to the bottom of the issue.'

'I remember the orange,' Harvey admitted. 'I don't remember the argument.'

'Me neither. But that wasn't my point. I thought perhaps we need an orange now.'

'We're not kids any more.'

'We're acting like it.' He resisted the urge to say Harvey was acting like it, putting them both at fault instead.

Neither of them spoke and Daniel wondered whether he should just up and leave.

But then he looked around the room for an object to use in place of the orange in a last-ditch attempt. He was about to pick up a paperweight with a pair of field mice etched into the glass when Harvey headed for the record collection and took one of the albums out.

'That's mine,' said Daniel, looking at the INXS cover with its familiar ink stain on the bottom right-hand corner. 'I thought I'd lost it.'

Harvey nodded as a memory seemed to surface. 'That's what the fight was about. I remember now.'

'I accused you of taking it.' It was all coming back to him too. 'You told me I must've loaned it to someone. Barney came along while we were fighting about it, gave us the orange, and eventually we agreed to both look for it together at home.' Funny how something so simple had worked. 'We decided that if it didn't turn up then we'd let the issue go. Brotherhood was too important, Barney told us.' And at the time they'd agreed wholeheartedly that it was.

Harvey grimaced. 'I hid it. I'm sorry. It was after Dad went mental when you lit the fire behind the shed and he found me trying to put it out. He assumed it was me, he said I had no respect for other people's property and he took one of my Transformers and crushed it under his foot. Stamped on it, from what I recall.'

'You should've told him it was me.'

'I could've.' A look passed between them. 'But I wasn't about to drop my brother in it.'

'Might've saved your Transformer's life.'

'Yeah, it probably would've done. Instead, I took the album. I was going to break it into pieces in front of you the same way Dad broke something that mattered to me, but I knew if I did then I'd get into trouble.'

'And so the vicious circle continued,' said Daniel.

'Something like that.'

'See, we *can* hold a civilised conversation. We just did.'

Harvey ran a hand across his jaw. 'You're right. But it's getting late and I'm knackered, so maybe we should get everything else out in the open.' But the open approach narrowed as his brow creased and he handed the record to Daniel to have his turn. 'How's the missus?'

Daniel wondered how much of Melissa's love was behind his brother's sudden willingness to hear him out or whether it was being here in their childhood home at long last, both ready for answers they'd never found up until now. He took the album, stirring memories of putting the music on downstairs and increasing the volume every time their dad was at work or away for a few days giving them the sort of freedom you shouldn't have to crave from a member of your own family.

With the album in his hands he told his brother, 'The missus is my ex-missus. Giselle's announcement on opening night, that she was my wife, was more for her own dramatic effect than anything else. She didn't really think through the repercussions it might have for me. We got married a long time ago, divorced very soon after. I never even told Mum about it until recently. Giselle was back in town to talk to me about her son, Peter, who was born shortly after we met and who's a part of my life.'

Harvey didn't hide his surprise. Daniel guessed that perhaps somewhere along the way his brother had pigeon-holed him into this person he didn't like, this person he'd pushed from his life and tried not to think too much about. Daniel suspected that Harvey had, for a long time, assumed he wasn't a man who took care of anyone else, he was still a boy who couldn't even look after himself.

With a firm hold on the record, Daniel carried on. 'When I left Heritage Cove I was in a world of trouble – not that I need to tell you that. It got worse, and then worse still. I'm ashamed to say I nabbed wallets from back pockets so I could buy myself food, I stole a woman's handbag on the train once, I shoplifted as much as I could without getting caught.' He tried to ignore how his brother's jaw had tensed, but, true to the arrangement, he wasn't interrupting when Daniel had a hold of the record. 'I went down to Winchester with my mate Lionel and he found a place for us to squat. I was with him until he was arrested for crimes I would never want to be involved in. I got away from him after that – even I could see I didn't have a hope hanging around with him. I stayed in Winchester, bummed around, I lived in another squat, but I was homeless pretty quick so my humble abode became a sleeping bag and whatever shelter I could find. My first night sleeping rough was at the back of a church. I'd tried to get in but couldn't, and it seemed one of the safer places to be. Until I realised I needed food, I needed handouts if anyone would take pity, and I wasn't likely to get them from the occupants of the graves I was putting my sleeping bag beside.'

Harvey gestured to take the record for his turn but Daniel shook his head and kept a firm hold of it. 'I migrated to the high street where there was more action, sometimes good when I got a hot drink or food, sometimes awful when people without an ounce of compassion would hurl insults our way, even try to assault us. Lucky I'm tall, have a decent build, and I wasn't scared of them. I'd stand up and they'd scarper. It was the one time I was glad to have a bit of Dad in me.

'I was half asleep in a shop doorway one morning when this businessman was in such a hurry to hail the taxi a heavily pregnant woman was going for that he knocked her flying into a lamp-post without a backwards glance. I could see the woman was hurting, clutching her stomach through her summer dress, and I knew she was in trouble. Nobody was helping her, they were all too busy going about their business to notice, so I went over to ask if she was all right. She didn't say anything, just cried out in so much pain. I led her over to another taxi who'd just dropped off a passenger and I told her to get inside. The cabbie, total arsehole, told me he didn't want her giving birth inside the cab so call an ambulance. Rather than help her out of the back-seat again I got in and refused to move until he took us to the hospital. She asked me what about my things on the street; I ignored the question and told the cabbie to drive.

'That woman was Giselle,' said Daniel, his fingers tracing the stain on the album cover. 'And after I left her at the hospital – I think the cabbie was shitting himself too much to even ask for the fare, or perhaps he thought I'd turn violent, given I didn't exactly look like an upstanding member of society – I went back to my shop front. My things were still there, still in the doorway as though the drama hadn't unfolded at all. A few weeks later Giselle came and found me. I'd moved to a different shop doorway by then, but over she came, pushing a pram as though I was a neighbour and she wanted to show off her baby. Melvin was the other guy in the same doorway and he gave us a look as if to say, mate, if you're with her, why are you even here? I explained after she left that I didn't know her until recently. Giselle had talked to me that day as though we'd been friends for years, she didn't hold back showing Peter off to me, she even blurted out that the father wasn't ready to be a dad and had left her to it. We compared notes on shitty father figures, ended up having a bit of a laugh, and it was the best I'd felt in ages.

'She kept coming back, pretty much every day, to bring me a morning coffee and something hot to eat now that it was autumn. We'd talk, about nothing mostly, anything from the stuck-up shop owner who'd asked me to move along to the stray dog that wandered the streets more than I did. We even had some laughs when she told me about her sister's wedding, where the focus right after the speeches had been whether she should marry the father for the sake of her baby even though she didn't love him. Giselle rolled her eyes at that one, pretended she was so strong, but I could see she wasn't.'

Harvey gestured again for the record and this time Daniel gave it to him. 'I never knew any of this. I assumed you'd left, found your feet and never looked back. Giselle must be very special to you – and, I hear, beautiful... word travels fast.'

Daniel took the record back as though they were those two young boys standing in the street, Barney refereeing between them. 'She is beautiful, inside and out, and she'll always be in my life. She moved things on even more for me by coming one day to ask if I'd help her out with some odd jobs around the house and garden. She said she didn't want to give her family a chance to moan at her and tell her to beg the father to come home; they'd told her enough times she couldn't make it on her own and one thing I quickly learned about Giselle was that she's stubborn. Seems a common trait.' He risked not an accusation but an obser-vation at a Luddington family characteristic Harvey had definitely kept going. 'I went to help, I was never going to say no. I cleaned leaves out of the gutters, fixed a roof tile in place, put a bolt on her back gate for her and fixed a leaky tap. When she asked me to come and jet wash her driveway, I called her out on it. I told her not to feel sorry for me, that I wasn't a charity case. Do you know what she said? You can answer me without holding the record if you like.'

Harvey took the record and propped it up against the edge of the sofa, showing his confidence that they were mature enough to carry on without it.

'She told me that she was the charity case, she looked forward to my company, she enjoyed it more than being with her own family because I didn't come with conditions or constant questions and demands, or criticisms of her parenting. She said that she was a freakishly house-proud person and, yes, she did jet wash her driveway once a year, usually in the summer months, but with Peter's arrival she hadn't bothered. I went and did it, she cooked me a proper meal and it was that day she offered me her spare room in exchange for helping her out around the house. She said I could use her house as an address and get myself a job.'

'She sounds like a really good person.'

'She is. And that was my chance to turn things around. I was well aware it would probably be my only one before I went hurtling towards rock bottom and never found my way back up. I moved in, cleaned myself up, scored some interviews and got work as a maintenance man. It wasn't a job I especially loved but it was a start. It was money coming in to live on and contribute to the household, it was the base for a future I never would've found without Giselle's help.'

'Is that why you guys got married?'

'We were both in totally different situations but one thing we had in common was the strong friendship we'd formed. Getting married seemed logical. I did it to be grounded and because I thought it was what I wanted; Giselle did it for Peter, to give him a dad. We'd grown close spending so much time with each other, but we soon realised friendship was as far as we should've taken it. It sounds ridiculous but there wasn't any kind of spark. There was a strength we had when we were together but it was one that worked when we were friends. So we divorced, I moved out, I got a job with a catering firm somewhere along the line and apart from the odd meet-up and then phone calls, we both got on with our own lives. It's now that Giselle's with her partner Stu and they're expecting a baby that Peter has started to wonder about his own place in the world. And I know what that's like.' He saw Harvey glance his way. 'The kid doesn't know what my role is, what Stu's role is, whether he's supposed to treat us both the same or favour one over the other. Giselle's here because she's worried about him. He's a great kid, he really is, and he deserves to be happy. All kids do. And his own dad sounds a real piece of work, not even interested in his own son. I can relate to that.'

'We both can,' sighed Harvey and, after a beat, added, 'You want a beer?'

Daniel shook his head. 'No, because a beer means this will stop and I think if we don't talk now, that'll be it.'

'It won't be, because I still have plenty to say. You haven't let me get a word in yet.'

Daniel grinned. 'I can't believe you've let me talk. Go on, then, get a couple of beers before round two.'

When Harvey went to get the drinks, at least it gave him a chance to prepare himself for what came next.

'Any sign of Melissa downstairs?' Daniel asked as he thanked his brother for the beer, cold to the touch and a welcome refreshment up here at the top of the house he'd once vowed he'd never set foot in again.

'Nope.' He swigged his beer.

'Do you think she's worried you'll have a go at her?'

Harvey laughed. 'You've forgotten, Melissa can hold her own. The possibility of me having any kind of go at her wouldn't deter her at all.'

'That's a good point. I remember you two as teenagers – you always seemed like equals. I was always jealous of that, you know.'

'Not many people meet their soulmate so young, I'm lucky. Even more lucky she came back.' He swigged his beer. 'Can I ask why you wanted to come back to the Cove all of a sudden?'

'Given how hard you were going to make it for me, you mean?'

Harvey glared at him but not for long before his focus returned to his beer. 'I guess I deserved that.'

'I'd been thinking about it for a long while. I called Mum often and every time I did I could hear in her voice that she was happy I'd turned my life around, but I knew she was breaking inside that her sons hadn't spoken in years and weren't likely to either. I'd found what I was looking for when I moved into the catering arena, and I knew that one day I wanted my own business. It all happened quickly when Mum mentioned the old beach shop had come up for sale. It was almost a sign.'

'You never believed in those,' Harvey harrumphed.

'No, I never did. I thought it was just a way of looking for a reason to do something rather than having the guts to admit it was what you wanted or needed.'

'I wasn't happy when I saw you back here. I didn't even have any warning.'

'Would it have made any difference?'

'Probably not.' Harvey took his beer and went to stand by the window. He had to duck at the section of roof approaching but up close to the glass he was at a point that was high enough to cope with his height. 'I've spent so long being angry at you that I don't remember how not to be.'

'Why are you so angry? I mean, I know I upset a lot of people around here, but as far as I knew, apart from leaving I didn't do anything to you. There was a time we hung out together, had a laugh even.'

Harvey didn't reply straight away and when he did he kept his gaze directed out to the blackness of the night. 'I was just as angry at myself as I was at you. You're my younger brother, I wasn't there when you needed me. I ran to Barney's and found something so good there that I spent every waking moment I could out of this house and with him and Melissa. Mum never minded but I think that was before she realised the damage it was doing to you. To us.'

Harvey was spot on with that. 'I felt as though you didn't care any more,' Daniel admitted. 'And the less I saw of you, the more trouble I got into. I don't know why I did it. It wasn't like I wanted attention; I think I wanted something to change.'

'I wish I'd been around to help more. Or insisted you came to Barney's with me.'

Daniel had a sinking feeling in the pit of his stomach. 'You used to ask me to go.'

'I did.'

He'd forgotten. All this time he'd blocked it out, thinking his brother had turned his back when Harvey had actually tried. He'd just been too pig-headed to let him in. 'Why didn't I go with you?'

'I've no idea. You said no so many times I stopped asking. Maybe I didn't make going to a man's barn to hang out and pick apples sound appealing enough. But I did try.'

'I think I was jealous.'

'Jealous?'

'You came home happy. You didn't have to say anything but even as you washed dishes or did your chores there was something different about you. I wanted that too, but I wanted to find it myself. I guess I was torn between wanting you to help me and wanting to help myself. You were my older brother but I wanted to be like you. I wanted to man up and stand on my own two feet. God knows Dad told me often enough that I never would.'

'He told me I wouldn't either.'

'Bastard.' Daniel swigged his beer.

'I still felt responsible for you. I did back then, I have over the years right up until you came back into town. It wasn't just embarrassment that all the trouble you caused made me look bad, it was that I felt bad. Does that make sense?'

'You shouldn't feel that way. Brothers don't have to oversee each other's lives to the extent they control the other one – even healthy relationships don't work that way. I had my own mind and I had to make my own mistakes. Our biggest fault was not hearing each other out; letting Dad's years of neglect and misery shape our lives rather than fighting back.'

'I don't think I had the energy back then.'

'Me neither.' He looked at Harvey. 'Can I say the unthinkable?'

'You're glad he's gone.'

Daniel tore at the label on his glass bottle, ripped it enough that the brand name was distorted.

'Can I address the other elephant in the room?' Harvey asked.

'The drink-driving charge.' Daniel put his beer bottle down on the floor beside his chair as though it was at odds with what he needed to say. He'd known this question was coming. 'It happened a few years back. I was visiting and cooking up a storm in the kitchen at Giselle's place, treating her to a recipe I'd picked up from a chef friend. She was always a big fan of lobster and, being a single mum, didn't exactly splash out on food so I picked some up on the cheap and showed up to cook it for her. I put Peter to bed, read him one of his favourite stories from his collection of *Thomas the Tank Engine* books, and then Giselle and I sat, ate and enjoyed some wine – a lot of wine in Giselle's case, not quite so much in mine but enough that I wasn't sober.

'We finished eating, carried on drinking and played a few games of cards. We must've been loud and Peter came downstairs to see what was going on – he hated missing out – but he tripped and when he fell he smashed his head on the radiator against the wall at the bottom of the stairs. There was blood everywhere, so much blood, he was screaming, Giselle was screaming. I couldn't get reception on my phone to call an ambulance – Giselle had moved out to a village by then and the coverage was shocking. I ran outside but had no luck with that either and so calling an ambulance was impossible. We tried knocking on a couple of neighbouring doors but couldn't get hold of anyone. Giselle was pressing a tea towel against Peter's head to stop the blood, he was slipping in and out of consciousness and in a split-second decision I found her car keys and got into the car. Giselle wasn't thinking straight either and didn't argue because her mind was on her son and that was it. She sat in the back seat with him, both clinging to each other, and I drove, windows down, all the way to the hospital.

'I must've been speeding – in fact, there's no doubt I was – and the police were tailing me as we approached the hospital. They were flashing at me to pull over but I put my foot down harder when Giselle screamed she couldn't get Peter to wake up. Nothing else mattered apart from him, Harvey.' His eyes welled up, the memory almost too much. He cleared his throat. 'I screeched up outside emergency, Giselle and Peter went in and the police right behind me arrested me for reckless driving. I was breathalysed and drink driving was added to the list of charges.'

Harvey swore and scraped a hand across his chin.

'Yeah, exactly. Not my proudest moment in some ways, but in others? I'd do it again in a heartbeat if it meant saving Peter's life, which we were told is exactly what it did.' Harvey was looking at him as though he couldn't believe his kid brother had taken responsibility, had sacrificed his own self to save a little boy. And then his face changed.

'Did you go to prison?' It was as though he was bracing himself for hearing the worst news possible, wondering whether his guilt trip could take another downturn.

'No, I didn't. I was disqualified from driving for twelve months, I got a hefty fine, but no jail time. I wasn't so far over the limit that they wanted to throw the book at me, and they took my circumstances into account. I'm just grateful they didn't ignore the reason I was behind the wheel in the first place.'

'When I heard you'd been in trouble with the police and Mum couldn't give me any details, I assumed the worst. And I shouldn't have done. I'm an arse. A total arse.'

'No, you're not, Harvey. I had form, lots of it. You stayed in the Cove when I buggered off and I expect you got a bit of flack.'

'Some. Not so much I couldn't handle it.'

'And you had Dad to deal with too. I wouldn't have wanted to swap places with you for anything – even living on the streets was better than wondering what he'd do next. He was never violent, not like some stories you hear, but my biggest dread was that one day he would be. I was a coward and I ran.'

'You're not a coward. If anyone's a coward it's me, for blaming you rather than waking up to myself enough to see you needed my help.'

'You know, we could go round and round in circles about this if we let ourselves. That, or we could let ourselves off the hook from here on in.'

'I guess you're right.'

'I should tell you that getting charged by the police wasn't quite the end of me messing up. I was in a bad way. I could've killed someone on the roads driving like that at those speeds, and even though I knew I'd do it again to save Peter, I couldn't accept that what I'd done might well have had consequences for anyone else on the road. I could've killed a pedestrian – a mother, a child, a father or a brother – and my head couldn't wrap around any of that.

'I dealt with it by spending a lot of time in the pub – went on benders most nights. I nearly lost my job after one too many late arrivals for my shift, and it was Giselle who pulled me out of it yet again. I'd gone to see Peter and she knew what was going on. She pointed right at him and yelled at me that her son was alive because of what I did and that I had to forgive myself. She was crying, almost as upset as the night it happened. She got through to me and not long after that was when we got married. I think our heightened emotions got the better of us and it seemed the next logical step, except it really wasn't.'

'And you didn't tell Mum any of this?'

'Not at the time, not until recently.' He shook his head. 'You know, Giselle hated the police after that. She'd been around enough officers to know that some of them had wanted to ignore any extenuating circumstances, some of them ridiculed me during interviews, threw their weight around. I took it all; she was livid, but all I wanted was to face up to whatever punishment I got and move forward. Her dislike of police officers was why she was so mouthy with the copper at the opening night of the Little Waffle Shack. She was being accused of something she hadn't done and it would've triggered plenty of reminders so that's why she needed me to vouch for her and for added effect announced she was my wife.'

Harvey began to laugh. 'It was a bit dramatic from what I've heard.' The laughter faded. 'Especially for Lucy.'

'Lucy ran off before I had a chance to explain.'

'It seems to be a common way of dealing with things around here.' Harvey let the revelations between him and his brother settle. 'I should've come after you when you left the Cove. I know part of the reason you left was because we'd drifted apart.'

'And what would you have done? Given me my INXS album back and said all was forgiven?'

Harvey put his hand to his forehead and rubbed his fingers against his brow. 'All my life I feel like I've been trying to protect – Mum, you, then Mum again, then Melissa until she was so stifled she had to get away. It's as though I don't know how to do anything else. When you came back here I put up barriers to protect myself as much as anyone and those barriers were built of anger and meant distance. I wanted to avoid you as though I was a little kid and if I closed my eyes long enough the problem would go away. Pathetic, eh?'

'No, not pathetic. I'd probably have done the same thing in your shoes.'

Harvey blew out from between his lips. 'I wanted to come to the grand opening of the Little Waffle Shack. I very nearly talked myself into it, but I couldn't see past all the bad stuff. It's not that I refuse to give second chances, more that I worry that with second chances to do the right thing comes double the possibility of everything going wrong. And I knew that if I saw the success you'd made of yourself, it would hit me full force that I'd had nothing to do with that. Not that I'm jealous, I don't mean that – what I mean is that I should've been a part of your life, even in the background.'

'Hey, maybe it's okay we went our separate ways. Maybe, like Melissa leaving, we needed to do it, be our own men for a while. Heaven forbid if we'd turned out like Dad.'

'Amen to that.' When Daniel lifted his empty bottle to clink it against Harvey's, Harvey offered to make them a strong cup of coffee each.

They drank the coffees wandering around Tumbleweed House. Daniel was impressed with the changes and rather than the nightmares he thought it would bring flooding back, it brought a funny sense of life evolving, moving on to a better place. 'The loft conversion is pretty impressive,' he said when they settled in the kitchen.

'I had to do something. I couldn't keep the loft as it was.'

'You must've needed a skip to shift all that stuff.'

'I did a few trips to the tip.'

'What happened to your old sled?' Amongst the junk up there, that was the item that stood out in his mind.

Harvey put down his coffee. 'I still have it, it's in my shed. I repaired it too.'

'You know, I was always jealous you still had yours. Dad used mine for firewood, do you remember?'

Harvey swore loud enough the dog's ear twitched upwards until she decided she couldn't be bothered to join in with the drama and went back to sleep. 'I'd forgotten. I think half the things he did I've blocked out. Why did he do it again?'

'I bought the wrong newspaper for him when he sent me to the convenience store.'

'That's a crime against humanity, shocking, terrible.'

At least they could laugh about it. Daniel suspected if they didn't, life would err on the side of misery far too often for either of them to be able to manage a normal existence. 'The phrase walking on eggshells doesn't even come close when it comes to our childhood, does it?'

Harvey told him all about the time Donnie came back as though he'd only nipped out for a pint of milk. He'd heard the story from his mum but the way Harvey told it was evocative to the point that he could imagine being a part of it, witnessing their dad hurling insults at their mum, punching Harvey, and Harvey fighting back by pushing him so hard he put him through the glass floor-to-ceiling window in the kitchen.

'I thought about going to the funeral,' Daniel admitted. 'Not for an emotional goodbye but in a way to prove I was still standing, he wasn't. That I'd gone on to sort myself out and he'd remained a pitiful excuse for a man until the day he died.' He realised how venomous he sounded but Harvey took it in his stride.

'He didn't deserve for any of us to be there.'

'I sat at Giselle's place instead,' said Daniel. 'She'd made Peter's favourite spaghetti Bolognese topped with lots of grated cheese and when he got it all over his face by slurping it up, I did the same.'

Harvey started to laugh. 'Dad hated it when we made a mess with food.'

'Kind of why I did it that day.' Daniel wondered if the smirk on Harvey's face meant that he could remember them sitting at dinner when their dad was away and finding it a source of instant amusement whenever anyone had less-than-perfect manners. Their mum had been in on it too, not that she'd encouraged it or said it out loud, but you could just tell by the mischievous look on her face whenever one of them dropped something or accidentally spilt anything on their clothing.

The memories settled around them as they finished their coffees, Daniel venturing to ask, 'How are things with Melissa

these days?' Conversation with his brother was a newfound terri-
tory he didn't mind exploring for once. 'I'm glad you're back with
her. She's good for you.'

'You mean she doesn't let me boss her around?'

'Something like that.'

'I nearly lost her, though.'

'She was engaged, is that right?'

He nodded. 'To Jay, a pilot she once worked with. She always
felt terrible about the way things ended but she found out last
week that he's engaged to an old flame of his own.'

'Melissa was always kind; she wouldn't have been happy
making someone miserable.'

'Talking of women, when are you going to talk with Lucy?'

'Well, I kind of thought I was tonight.'

'I'm sorry I was the one who told her about you getting in
trouble with the police. I'd been to the pub, I had it in my head
that you were causing trouble in the village again like days of old
and I went to see her. I didn't come out with it, something stopped
me, but I was babbling on and she obviously thought I was in no
fit state to get home in one piece so she called Melissa. She
mentioned to Melissa what I'd said to her and Melissa filled in
the missing details she knew.'

'I get it, I caused a lot of trouble around here and this is your
home. You were looking out for Lucy, who has made the village
her home too. But I swear to you, I'm not here to make trouble.
I'm different now.'

'I know.' And something about the way he said it told Daniel
he meant it wholeheartedly. 'Do you know about Lucy's cousin,
Joanna?'

'Her cousin who died? Yeah, she mentioned her. They were
close.' When Harvey nodded he realised why his brother was

bringing this up now. 'She was killed by a drunk driver,' he concluded. No need to ask the question, it made sense now. He swore and apologised to Winnie, who jumped for the second time. 'So now Lucy doesn't know how she can possibly give me the time of day, let alone anything else, when I did the same thing.'

'It wasn't the same thing though, was it?'

'It was. At the end of the day, I was behind the wheel of a car and even though it was to save a life, it could've cost another in the process.'

'I think it was one of those situations where nobody knows what they'd do until they were faced with the same dilemma,' said Harvey. 'And Lucy was here tonight helping Melissa with her plan, that shows she cares.'

'It could be she cares about you and Mum rather than me.'

'You really believe that?'

He didn't know what he believed any more. All he knew was that the way Lucy had looked at him earlier when he'd come to her supposed rescue, she was interested in him. But would she ever give him a chance?

'Do you think you'd be willing to help me set up Melissa in the same way she set us up tonight?' Harvey had the same expression now as he'd had when they were boys and he had suggested they make a supply of snowballs and use the wheelbarrow in the shed to transport them to the laneway near the florist one Sunday morning. The plan was to hide behind the wall and ambush Calvin Trilby when he set out for his paper round. Calvin had been teasing Melissa, calling her carrot top on account of her red hair, and even though she'd promptly told him he was stupid because carrot tops are in fact green, Harvey thought he'd give the dude the message that any more insults Melissa's way and he'd have him to deal with. Calvin hadn't expected them to be lying in wait for him but he got the message loud and clear and left her alone after that.

'Get your own back?' Daniel laughed. 'I like your style. What do you have in mind?'

And no matter what Harvey might tell him, he didn't care. They were talking, they were beginning to repair some of the damage that he'd thought would leave everlasting scars.

It was a start.

14

Once Tilly had finished wrapping a gift and waved goodbye to her customer with a Merry Christmas, she rejoined Lucy at the back of the shop to carry on with their mulled-wine tea and mince-pie meet-up, squeezed into Tilly's working hours because she was still busy. 'Have you heard from Melissa?' she asked.

It was the day before Christmas Eve and Heritage Cove had woken to a light sprinkling of snow on the tarmac of The Street, an intermittent dusting on the parts of roofs it had managed to reach, the odd branch of the village tree if you looked close enough like Lucy had on a walk this morning. Today marked day one of a two-week break from work for Lucy and one of the joys of time off from her business was being able to get out nice and early, bundled up warm, before the rest of the village stirred. Another joy was the absence of Julian's games and at last she was beginning to feel festive and ready for Christmas. The only thing she was a bit confused about was that since she and Melissa had thrown Harvey and Daniel together, she hadn't heard a word about it and according to Melissa's text, she didn't know anything either. Even more weirdly, Daniel hadn't once tried to get in touch with her since. It had all gone mysteriously quiet.

'I haven't spoken to her. She texted but she doesn't know how it went down. It seems Harvey's keeping quiet about it all, which I'm not sure is a good sign.' Melissa and Lucy had filled Tilly in on their antics when they met her in the pub while on exile from Tumbleweed House as Daniel and Harvey finally confronted one another properly.

'You two played a dangerous game.' Tilly managed half a mince pie and a swig of tea before serving another customer, who was after a last-minute gift for her best friend. It seemed Tilly's business would be going right up until the big day itself. 'I was expecting them to come to blows,' she said the second she came back over and resumed her tea break.

'No broken bones, according to Melissa, and from what I hear, people are still getting their waffles so Daniel must be in one piece too.'

'Talking of waffles, aren't you desperate for more?'

'No comment,' she said, gesturing with her hands that she had too much of a mouthful to say anything else. She knew Tilly wasn't referring to waffles at all.

'If you play your cards right you could have that special someone just in time for Christmas.'

Lucy laughed. 'You've been watching too many soppy movies.'

'If I had a Daniel to snuggle up to for Christmas I wouldn't even care what was under the tree.'

'You're terrible,' she laughed, but she hated to admit Tilly might have a point. It wasn't as if she hadn't thought about it, but the drink-driving charge he'd once faced still loomed at the back of her mind, confusing her more and more. And with everything he was bound to still have going on with his brother, perhaps he needed to sort out those differences first.

'Do yourself a favour,' said Tilly after three more customers came in the shop and she finally admitted she'd have to get back to work. 'Don't let this one go. I know we've not been friends for very long but I've seen the way you look at him and the way he looks at you. That kind of connection doesn't come along very often.'

Lucy left her to it and headed off down The Street to Barney's place. Lois was holding a girls-only get-together. They'd all acknowledged there was no time to read a book to discuss so they may as well admit it was more of a Christmas party than anything else.

A sign pinned on the front door at Barney's indicated for Lucy to head in the direction of the barn. She passed by the quaint box garden at the front of the house, went through the archway formed between hardy juniper trees and then on across the courtyard. In the summer she'd been here at the barn for her first Wedding Dress Ball, the charity fundraiser Barney held every year, and the barn looked every bit as special now as she went in through the open door on the right, the other one remaining closed, presumably to keep the heat in. It had been different in the warmer months, with both doors flung open to let the light and warmth filter through.

Lois and Barney were over on the other side of the barn fixing the end of a row of twinkly lights that had been wound around one of the upright beams. Lucy smiled, taking it all in. There was a fresh Christmas tree on the stage loaded up with silver and red baubles, bows in alternating colours tied at intervals on the branches, and a sparkling tree topper. Behind the tree, at the back of the stage, the wall was lined with a row of black-and-white photographs depicting Wedding Dress Ball events over the years. Lucy knew she was in the last one added to the collection, taken by a photographer who'd climbed up on a ladder to get a shot of everyone as they mingled at the Cove's event of the year.

Lois and Barney finished up and Lucy set the bottle of wine she'd brought with her down on the table. 'I wondered why you'd pointed us in this direction,' she beamed, taking in the beauty of the inside of the barn she'd only seen done up for a summer event. Hay bales were still dotted here and there, the old barrels that had been here for the ball were in the same position, one by the door and the other on the far side, and each had an arrangement of a glass bowl half-filled with water and floating candles, the bowl set in another shallow dish of berries, pine cones and snowberries. Twinkly lights had been twisted around plenty of the beams, others had garlands filled with greenery and red berries, three outdoor heaters stood tall, not too close but near enough that they'd warm the group when they sat at the long table covered in a white linen cloth. Places had been set, cutlery gleamed, and where Christmas crackers would usually be were long, shiny silver boxes containing festive bonbonnière, one for each of them, tied up with a snow-coloured bow. Dotted along the middle of the table were mason jars stuffed with bright white lights and decorated with red velvet ribbon and a sprig of greenery and winter berries. 'You did all of this for us girls?'

'It was a good excuse to see what the barn would be like in winter as opposed to summer,' Barney confessed.

'That's right, you're talking about having a winter Wedding Dress Ball too,' Lucy smiled, remembering he'd mentioned it once or twice.

'Not any more,' Lois put in. 'We've talked about it and the one scheduled charity event a year is enough.'

'But,' Barney continued, 'I am thinking of hiring this place out for parties – nothing wild, you understand – or maybe even weddings. It's going to take a lot of planning but Lois is way more clued up than me when it comes to events so it's something we're looking into. This place is big, the barn takes upkeep as does the land, and it makes me sad not to see the barn filled with people who can enjoy it.'

Lucy remembered Melissa's stories of coming to this barn as a kid, how it had been her escape and Harvey's too. And knowing how Barney liked company, how he loved to be in amongst it, holding events here made perfect sense. 'So, we're the winter guinea pigs?' Lucy wondered.

'You are, I'm afraid,' said Lois. 'I wanted to know what difference these heaters made, whether they'll do the job or whether we need something more. And already they seem to be working just fine.' As though to prove her point, she unbuttoned her coat.

Lucy wasn't about to take her own coat off just yet but Lois was right, for heaters that weren't overly large, they did a good job of filling the space with warmth and once they were all inside it would be even cosier with the now-open barn door shut.

'You've got Lois's highly acclaimed beef Wellington for lunch,' Barney announced, 'so that'll warm you up even more.'

When Lois had invited them all here she'd told them not to worry, she wouldn't be making them sit through a traditional Christmas lunch given they'd all be doing that the day after tomorrow.

'And you have to miss out?' asked Lucy.

Lois laughed under her breath. 'You're joking. He's already told me to leave his portion inside.'

'I feel bad you won't be joining us, Barney.'

'Don't feel guilty, I'll be just fine in the house with a bit of peace and quiet.' He squeezed Lois to his side as though he didn't really want to be separated from her at all.

Barney loved company and after he headed over to the house, Lois said she wouldn't mind betting he'd eat his lunch and then go for a walk along The Street to see who was around for a chat. 'He won't be able to help himself,' she whispered to Lucy as she adjusted the cutlery on the place settings even though it all looked pretty perfect already.

'You must like entertaining,' said Lucy when Lois greeted Melissa next. At the door to the barn, her auburn hair caught the light as she stepped inside.

'It's my guilty pleasure,' Lois admitted.

'Hey, anytime you need us,' grinned Melissa, who set down another bottle of wine on the table. 'Barney's always telling everyone how amazing your cooking is. We'll bring the wine every time, just let us know when you next want us.'

With a smile, Lois nodded to the bottles and told them they'd all be checking into rehab if they did these sorts of lunches too many times.

Lottie, who ran the convenience store, joined them, coming inside with Patricia from the tea rooms, who could be away from work for an hour, leaving Etna to manage with the help of a family friend. Tilly would unfortunately miss out today because business was booming so spectacularly. Tracy was next through the doors, apologising for her tardiness after checking in more guests at the Heritage Inn. She laid down her own rule immediately by saying she'd only have one glass of alcohol given she'd have to return to work and, with a personality as bouncy as the curls in her dark-blonde hair, she took herself on a tour around the barn extolling the virtues of the decorations, comparing what they'd done here with what she'd done at the inn.

Braving the cold without coats, Lucy and Lois, with Barney's help, brought food from the oven inside the house to the table in the barn and, cosied up with the barn doors shut, candles lit and lights twinkling away, they toasted to Christmas in Heritage Cove.

According to Lois, the secret to the silky mash served with the beef Wellington was a good dose of cream and a generous amount of butter. Tracy shared her concern that it was going straight to her hips and she'd rather not know the sinful truth, but whatever the recipe secrets, the entire meal went down a treat and Lucy, with a glass of red wine, found herself sitting back and looking around the barn at these smiling faces, these people who'd become so familiar in such a short time. Julian's family had always enjoyed a good get-together and after she ended things with him, Lucy had missed the sociable family so much that at times she'd thought about rejoining it. She never would, of course, but the urge had been there. She'd grown up an only child and when she met Julian, being whisked into a chaotic all-embracing family had been part of the spiral of attraction. She was similar to Barney in that regard; she liked to be around people, and the laugher and chatter now washed over her like it was meant to be.

Lois topped up Lucy's wine. 'You look as though you're away with the fairies,' she whispered, handing the bottle to Tracy next, who quickly passed it on like a pass-the-parcel she was tempted to open but thought she'd better not.

'I'm fine – just daydreaming, that's all.'

'About waffles?' Lois ventured.

She looked so sincere, Lucy began to laugh. 'Why do I get the feeling you're not really talking about sweet treats?'

'It's Christmas, there's a chill on the air, can I help it if I'm wanting a little romance?'

'You've got plenty of that with Barney, I'd say.'

'About time. We waited years; don't do the same.' She patted Lucy's hand before she jostled Tracy out of the barn to help her bring back mince pies, warmed and served with a good dollop of thick cream, from the kitchen for dessert.

Talk turned to the Heritage Inn and the kitchen renovations Tracy had planned for the new year as well as the resurfacing of the parking area out front.

'I'm desperate to redo my kitchen,' said Lucy, 'but I haven't got around to it yet, and then there's the money.'

'You can get decent kitchens from IKEA, you just need someone to fit it,' said Lottie.

'I'll bet you could do it yourself,' Tracy put in. 'You're a practical kind of girl.'

'I can design and make things, but a kitchen?' Lucy turned up her nose. 'I don't think I'd do myself any favours there.'

They chatted about Lucy's work since she came to the Cove and the amazing creations that were making their way around town, from the trellis Lucy was making for the pub, the shoe rack she'd designed and made for Lottie to have at home, to the beautiful candle holders Lois had in her lounge in Ireland. Lois confided in everyone about the copper mugs she'd had Lucy make for Barney for his gift this year.

'We'll drink a hot toddy in them on Christmas night,' said Lois. 'He'll love them. Something made in the Cove is perfect for him, don't you think?'

They all agreed and again Lucy was amused they'd both been thinking along the exact same wavelength when it came to gifts this year and neither had any idea.

'How are you coping with a long-distance relationship, Lois?' Lottie's dimples always made her seem cheeky when she made any remark, but this time the cheekiness seemed to be what she was hoping for.

Lois broke off another piece of mince pie with her spoon, ensuring she got a portion of cream along with it. 'It's not easy but it's a lot of fun with technology. We can talk, message each other, even see each other when we call.'

Melissa was well and truly into the wine, making the most of the long holiday in the Cove and no return to work for a while yet. 'I'm not sure we need the details. I don't want to know about any sexting or nude pics.'

Laughter erupted and Tracy insisted, 'Speak for yourself, I want to know *everything*.'

'Well, I hope you ladies are ready to see a lot more of me in the new year, because I'm selling my house in Ireland and as soon as it's all sorted I'll be moving here to the Cove.'

'Listen to you,' Lucy smiled, '"the Cove" – that means you're local. It didn't take long for me to start saying it either.' She raised a glass and everyone followed suit. 'To Lois and her move to the Cove.'

'To Lois!' they chorused.

They asked all about Lois's life back in Ireland and she told them about the beauty of the country, the unspoiled landscapes she and Barney had explored together, the climate that made it so beautiful and green, the distance that at her age she no longer wanted to tolerate. 'Barney and I spent a long time apart. It's time for us to be closer and I could never take him away from this village.'

'Thank goodness,' said Melissa. 'I had visions of him moving to be with you. Harvey and I talked about it and we would've come to visit, we never would've made him feel guilty for going, but his heart really is here. And now I feel terrible for telling you that, because your heart might be in Ireland.'

'My life currently is in Ireland,' Lois smiled, 'but my children are grown up, they understand, and my heart is with Barney. Coming here makes sense to us both.' When her voice wobbled it was a case of who could hug her first, which made a tear of emotion snake down her cheek at the proper affection she had here already in a community that looked out for each other.

Lucy admired the bonbonnière at her place setting. 'These are wonderful, Lois.' Inside the silver box were eight Father Christmas chocolates and Tracy had already announced she'd be hiding them from Giles, her husband, who loved chocolate more than anyone else in her family.

'I thought it was a nice touch and I didn't want to do crackers.'

'I approve,' said Lottie. 'And chocolate is way better than something made out of plastic that I have to spend hours trying to work out a use for.'

When lunch was over and Lois had reluctantly let the girls help her clear and wash everything up – Barney had predictably taken himself out somewhere – Lucy was more than ready for a long walk to work off the rich meal. 'Anyone else interested in working off Lois's wonderful cooking by going down to the cove for a walk?' She shrugged on her coat after Lois had taken charge of blowing out all the candles. Melissa had switched off the twinkly lights, Tracy unplugged the Christmas-tree lights and they shut the doors to the barn behind them.

Tracy needed to get back to the inn with a full house of guests this year, Lottie had to relieve her friend at the convenience store, and so it was just Melissa, Lois and Lucy who headed away from Barney's, along The Street, and gingerly made their way down, the bracing temperatures already surrounding them, until they reached the cove itself. Lucy caught her breath. The ground on the way down here had been hard-packed but now the sand, damp beneath their feet, held a familiar feeling. This had always been Melissa's favourite thinking spot and it was fast becoming Lucy's. The openness and seclusion from anyone not willing to make the trek on foot and negotiate the uneven path down here was what made it the ideal spot for contemplation.

The salt spray from the water in the wine-glass-shaped bay had brought all three women out of what Melissa described as a food coma by the time they headed back up The Street and parted at the end of the track. Lois made her way to the bakery, Melissa returned to Tumbleweed House and Lucy walked on to the Heritage Inn to drop off Tracy's chocolate bonbonnière she'd left behind in her hurry to get back to work.

After leaving the inn, Lucy crossed over the road to walk beside the village tree and in amongst the crowds. It seemed there didn't have to be a big event planned, this was a drawcard for the village and people still viewed it in awe as though it hadn't been standing since early December and they'd only just noticed its beauty. A teenager stood nearby eating waffles from a cardboard tray and the sweet smell grabbed Lucy, tugged at her insides not through hunger but through the turmoil of not knowing whether to hear Daniel out or whether to put him well out of her head and honour Joanna's memory by never getting involved. She thought about the tortoise she'd made for him, the care and precision as well as the time invested in a gift she knew would mean a lot to the man she cared about. Now, it was beneath her tree, wrapped and waiting.

Lucy had asked herself more than once, what would Joanna do in her situation? They both had similar taste in men, both of them attracted to taller men with cute smiles. Neither of them had ever been bothered about a partner's job – he didn't have to be a high-flyer, and Joanna had often joked that being able to work with your hands was far higher up the criteria than being able to sit at a desk would ever be.

The sky, not yet dark, was the palest of blues with an orange hue, white streaks like stretched-out cotton wool behind a backdrop of trees that looked as though they were in shadow, and the buzz of the village was one you'd expect in the run-up to Christmas. Voices filled the air, laughter, greetings from person to person, and when Lucy caught sight of an angel decoration the women next to her were fawning over having just bought it from Tilly's shop, Lucy thought again of Joanna. She looked up at the shack. Joanna would like Daniel; she'd find him mysterious and enjoy his company, and she'd be very impressed by his occupation. And Joanna would likely push her in his direction and ask why she was hesitating.

Lucy found herself walking closer to the shack. She trudged across the green space as the sign she'd made for Daniel's business swung lightly in the winter wind, generating a faint squeak that made her smile. It made the place feel old somehow, cosy, the markings of a village with history even though the shack itself hadn't been here that long.

People milled on the veranda, a couple sat on the bench that looked over this way, others huddled indoors beyond the windows, away from the cold, in the timber structure. The scent of waffles and all their glorious toppings drifted her way and the twinkly lights Daniel had left up made the shack a beacon people could swarm to. Daniel had got it sussed when it came to location, as well as launching the Little Waffle Shack so close to Christmas.

Lucy stopped. Did she really want to go inside? What was she going to say? She almost wished they'd had longer up in the loft at Tumbleweed House before Harvey came up and the girls left the brothers to it. The atmosphere had been less tense than any other time Daniel had tried to talk to her, and when he'd begun to dig deep and find memories that gave her a glimpse of an innocent young boy whose family had let him down, her heart had gone out to him. The wall she'd built up because of the rumours that had come her way had been torn down a little back in that loft.

With hope that they could have a similar moment, she was about to step up onto the veranda when she did a double take, because Daniel's ex was in there. Giselle was at the counter with her arm around a boy who was hers – no doubt about it with that same thick dark hair, wide innocent eyes and skin that would hold its glow all year round. And all of them were smiling. The boy had an apron on, Daniel was handing him a plate of waffles topped with a generous couple of scoops of ice-cream, and when the boy looked up at him Daniel said something that made him laugh.

'Penny for them.' It was Etna behind her.

Lucy smiled. Sometimes it was odd to see her without her apron on and standing behind the counter at the tea rooms. 'I wasn't expecting to see you out and about. Patricia told us how busy you've been, shame you couldn't make the lunch.'

Etna dismissed the concern. 'Lois had a get-together already for us oldies, and someone had to man the tea rooms. It's Patricia's turn, I'm escaping. Time off for good behaviour. Are you coming in?' She nodded towards the shack. 'I'm trying a savoury waffle this time, something different. And I'm going to treat myself by bringing it out here to eat while I look at the stunning village tree. My husband never got to see it, you know. He's been gone twenty-five long years and the tradition began the December after his passing. But I know he'd have loved it, and he would've approved of this waffle shack. Waffles were his favourite sweet treat – second to my lemon drizzle, of course.'

'Of course,' Lucy grinned. She'd tried the cake a few times and Etna had a point.

'Are you coming in?' she prompted again, in case Lucy hadn't heard her the first time. 'I could order two portions – Daniel, as an apology for mistakes in the past, has given me free waffles until the new year. I'm making the most of it.'

Lucy looked again at the scene beyond the window: Daniel the father figure, tall, handsome, caring, so many qualities she admired. There was only one lingering problem and right now she couldn't seem to get past it. Not with Giselle and her son, not to mention Etna, showing up here. It needed to be just the two of them and until then, she'd have to let it be.

15

It was Christmas Eve and Daniel was in full swing for another day at the Little Waffle Shack. He'd already collected more tubs of ice-cream from Zara at the ice-creamery this morning since the Christmas flavours were still popular despite the dipping temperatures, he'd mixed batches of batter that were now housed in the kitchen fridge, he'd ensured the till had enough change for the rush he was sure to have with the carol concert by the village tree tonight at nine p.m. when the sky would be dark and villagers in the highest of Christmas spirits. And Brianna and Troy had done a great job of preparing the front of house for opening time. They were all in for a long shift today, open from late morning until ten p.m. to make the most of the jolly holiday crowds.

Harvey was the first to show his face when Daniel opened up the front door to the shack ready to welcome customers. Since they'd had a long talk and been in cahoots with Harvey's plan the atmosphere between them had gone from strained to tentative most of the time, but when both off guard, something resembling relaxed. They had a lot still to talk about, years of resentment and frustration to air, both about each other and their mess of a family. But there also existed an unspoken understanding that they didn't have to solve all their woes overnight.

'You're a lifesaver.' Daniel gladly took the takeaway coffee his brother had brought him. 'I need this to wake me up.'

'Late finish last night?'

'No different to any other night and business is booming so can't complain.' He had no doubt that the Cove had been the perfect place to launch his business as well as face his demons. 'I hope it lasts well into the new year.'

Harvey had his own coffee and came in upon Daniel's invite, greeting Troy and Brianna, who'd taken up positions at the back of the room like a waiter and waitress in a fine-dining restaurant ready to tend to their customers the moment they were needed.

'At ease, soldiers,' Harvey whispered to his brother. 'They look tense.'

Daniel kept his voice low. 'They're superstars, the both of them.' He nodded in their direction, told them he'd be in the kitchen and to holler when customers began arriving. 'They've only been with me five minutes but I've given them both a Christmas bonus.'

'You're just hoping they don't leave you to manage all this on your own.'

'That's exactly what I'm scared of,' Daniel laughed as they headed through to the kitchen.

'I stopped by to make sure we're all set for tonight and tomorrow.'

'Yep, all set.' Daniel added red food colouring to a batch of batter for the red-velvet choice that was particularly popular right now. He was doing his best not to think too much about tonight; their plan partly to set up Melissa but also involving Lucy so he could get her on her own to talk. He had a horrible feeling she'd tell him once and for all to leave her alone, making

Christmas Eve memorable for all the wrong reasons. But there was something about the looming Christmas festivities that made him want to do it now more than ever, his impatience winning over common sense, he suspected. But that was the way he was programmed: he didn't want to wait – it was always the same, whether he was eating his toast before it had much colour to it, drinking his coffee when it was still scalding hot or feeling the frustration when he went on a run and got stuck behind slow walkers.

'You all wrapped up with work?' Daniel asked as he finished stirring the batter, now its rightful red colour.

'Yep, that's me done for Christmas.' Harvey unzipped his coat and took it off in the heat of the kitchen. 'I'm looking forward to some quality time with Melissa until both of us have to go back to the real world in the new year.' Perched on the high bar stool in one corner of the room where Daniel usually sat to make notes for reordering stock, he asked, 'How did it go yesterday?'

Daniel slotted the bowl of batter into the fridge. He appreciated his brother remembering what had been on the agenda for him. 'Peter loved it here. I knew he would, and it was a good place for him to relax and then have a talk. He put on an apron, Giselle left him here for a couple of hours and she was pretty relieved to see how happy he was when she came to pick him up. He wouldn't stop going on about how he'd been allowed to make any shapes of waffle he wanted and come up with any recipe to put on top.'

'He sounds like a great kid.'

'He really is. And now I think he knows his place in my world and realises that doesn't have to change.' Peter had cried when he first showed up and saw Daniel, as though the separation for so long had balled up his emotions and this release had been a long time coming. After he'd had some fun at the shack Daniel had waited for a quieter moment and taken him out to the kitchen, where they talked. Daniel had assured Peter he didn't have to make a choice between him and Stu. He'd apologised to the little boy who'd come to see him as a dad for letting the ending of his relationship with Giselle and him moving on with his own life overshadow the importance of making time for those he loved. Daniel had, of course, been talking about his relationship with Peter, but the same could be said about Harvey, about his mum. If he'd invested time in the both of them then maybe they wouldn't all have ended up in quite the mess they were trying to find a way out of now. Harvey had said much the same thing during their time over the last two days, not in a deep-and-meaningful as such, but instead as a gradual process with little grievances or frustrations airing themselves now and again. They'd dealt with each as it arose, and rather than slinging all the mud in one direction at a single target, it was a smattering here and there and far easier to clean up along the way.

'I'd like to meet him,' said Harvey, surprising Daniel. 'He's been in your life more recently than I have,' he shrugged, another little tug to unveil the cracks in their relationship that weren't irreparable. 'I'd like to spend time with him and hear about my brother.'

Daniel finished washing the whisk he'd used for the batter and set it onto the draining board. Harvey wanting to know Peter suggested his brother needed to somehow piece together the Daniel who had left the Cove and the Daniel who had become a business owner. Peter would perhaps show a side to Daniel that Harvey had no other way of seeing. The facts spoke for themselves – he was a mess when he left the Cove at eighteen and now he wasn't, but maybe Harvey needed a way to marry up the two versions.

'I'm sure he'll be back,' said Daniel. 'Giselle's happy to bring him and I think it'll be good for him when the baby comes too, so I'll let you know.'

Brianna called through to the kitchen that they had their first customers of the day and a tiny part of Daniel did a jump of relief. They'd been crazy busy, had more custom than he'd predicted when he planned to launch his waffle place in this village, but there was always that moment when the doors were locked and you asked yourself, could this be the day nobody shows up and you'll have to stand there and call for customers to please come up and buy something? Daniel wondered if that feeling would ever pass.

Harvey went on his way. The takeaway coffees had no doubt been a pretext to come here without feeling overly awkward, forging their sibling relationship carefully, one step at a time.

And, for now, Daniel threw himself into the busyness of his own life, because later on they had plans he hoped would work out exactly the way they both wanted.

* * *

Daniel and Harvey had both known all along that Melissa and Lucy were planning Christmas Eve carols followed by a few drinks at the pub tonight. Harvey had been invited as Melissa's other half but he'd told Melissa he was spending the evening with his brother talking things through, which he and Daniel knew was a foolproof alibi she wouldn't challenge when she wanted them to get back to being the brothers they'd once been.

And, now, here the men were, in the barn at Barney's place – the phrase had a nice ring to it – and they were almost ready for the next phase of the plan. Harvey was all kinds of nervous. Daniel could see it in the way he kept fiddling with his collar, pacing the floor inside, muttering to himself. The other night, when he'd suggested they turn the tables and set the girls up the way they'd done to them, the truth had come tumbling out. Harvey had been wanting to ask Melissa to marry him since the day they got back together in the summer but things hadn't felt right then. She'd only just broken off an engagement and she felt guilty about it for months. But recently, after she'd heard on her work grapevine that her ex, Jay, was happily together with someone else, it was as though a weight had lifted from her mind, which meant Harvey was ready to go ahead with his plans.

'You're up, Daniel,' Harvey told him. They'd been waiting until Barney and Lois were home from the village carol concert and hidden indoors and the girls would be over at the pub enjoying a drink. Barney and Lois were, of course, in on this plan. They loved it, and when Barney had let the boys into the barn earlier before bustling off to the carol concert with Lois, he'd told Daniel more details of how he'd helped to get his brother and Melissa back together when she showed up in the village after five long years away. The old man loved the drama, he was full of mischief, and a pang of jealousy that Harvey had had him in his life when Daniel hadn't gave way to Daniel's acknowledgement that he'd been the one to stop himself being a part of all that. He'd been asked often enough by Harvey, some of those times he'd forgotten until recently. This morning as he'd eaten his breakfast he'd remembered Harvey whispering to him when he was yelled at as a kid one time for spilling porridge on the floor, telling him to come and pick apples with him. 'We can make juice', he'd said to his younger brother, but Daniel had gone off over the fields that day instead and met up with the boys from his school who hung out by a row of derelict garages on the outskirts of the Cove, smoking, doing dope, some of them drinking. He'd not joined in with any of it, but he'd felt a part of something that was his own and that he could control. He was slowly beginning to realise, now he was back in the Cove, that it hadn't only been Harvey's fault he was left out, a lot of it he'd brought on himself. And he'd readily admit that he definitely had the Luddington stubborn streak Harvey had too.

Daniel headed off to the Copper Plough, not quite as nervous as his brother with such a monumental question to ask, but anxious all the same.

When he got there the place was packed and it took a while to squeeze through the crowds and find the girls. The idea was that he would tell Melissa he and Harvey had had a huge fight and Harvey was her problem now, he was over at the barn licking his wounds. Then, when she left, he'd walk Lucy home and finally get to talk with her properly.

But things didn't quite go according to plan. Melissa, her concern immediately with Harvey, as expected, ran off out of the pub, but Lucy went with her.

'I'm not letting her deal with this on her own,' Lucy told him, and so he followed them both down the street, moving so fast to keep up with them that the cold didn't matter.

When they filed in through Barney's gate, past the windows at the front of the house, through the archway of trees and into the courtyard, Daniel put a hand to Lucy's arm and stopped her before she could follow Melissa into the barn. 'Let them do this on their own.'

'Do what?'

'You'll see,' he grinned, because no matter what happened with Lucy, this was his brother's moment.

Barney and Lois must have been spying on them and crept out of the house, confusing Lucy all the more. 'Come on,' said Lois, ushering Lucy towards the barn as the men followed. 'I don't want to miss it.'

'You're all crazy – miss what?' Lucy asked, confused as ever.

But they all filed over, Barney shushing them as they drew closer.

The door was ajar; Harvey must've closed it most of the way to keep the heat in. Harvey had told him the only place he could imagine proposing to Melissa was here and it had to be a surprise. He'd said he'd only ever do this the once and he wanted it to be done properly.

With all of them peeking through the crack in the barn door to see the scene unfolding, they heard Melissa's voice first.

'What's going on, Harvey?' Melissa asked. She was looking around her. 'What happened with your brother? He said you were in a bad way.'

'I'm still in one piece.'

'What happened?'

'Nothing bad, I promise. I asked Daniel to tell you differently because I wanted to get you here without ruining the surprise.'

The twinkly lights gave a romantic atmosphere, the heaters offered comfort, the low-playing music in the background set the mood. Lois had already had a practice run by using the barn for a lunch with the girls yesterday, she'd said, and knew this setting would be everything Harvey had wanted.

Lucy suddenly realised what must surely be happening beyond the doors and her eyes lit up. Even in the darkness Daniel didn't miss the spark. She was close, her body almost pressed against his and threatening to buckle him at the knees, but all of them were hooked on the story unfolding inside the barn.

Harvey had taken Melissa's coat and put it on the back of a chair and she was looking as confused as when she'd first arrived, but when he took hold of her hands something clicked. Daniel had seen a lot of emotions play out on his brother's face lately, but adoration for Melissa hadn't been one of them. He'd not seen them together enough to realise how strong their bond was, how much this moment meant to Harvey, how long his brother had been wanting and waiting to do this.

Harvey's voice was strong, it didn't waver. He was keeping it together as always. 'Melissa, I wanted to do this here because this is the place that reminds me the most of you. Down at the cove is another, but it's here we first kissed, here we first danced together, it's here I realised I wanted to spend the rest of my days with you at my side.'

A gasp from Lois almost revealed their presence and they all held their breath in case either Melissa or Harvey turned around.

They couldn't see whether Melissa was crying but Daniel wouldn't mind betting her eyes were filled with tears. He could tell by the flush on her cheeks, the way her voice wobbled as she said his brother's name.

It was then that Harvey got down on one knee. After their separation for so many years and her almost having a life with someone else, Daniel wasn't surprised at the emotion inside the barn. His fingers were freezing as he steadied himself against the barn door so he wouldn't topple into Lucy even more. The only thing keeping him warm was her being so close.

'Melissa Drew,' came Harvey's voice, 'love of my life, would you please do me the honour of becoming my wife? Will you live out your days here with me in Heritage Cove, at Tumbleweed House with Winnie and maybe even a whole bunch of kids one day?'

'Yes, yes, yes... a thousand times yes!' Melissa flung her arms around him.

Lois sniffed, Daniel was sure Barney did too, and when Lucy looked up at him with a smile, their eyes locked. He guessed it was hard not to be happy when something like this played out so close to you between people who were important in your life.

'There's no ring,' Lois whispered to Barney as they watched Harvey twirl Melissa around in his arms.

'Oh, there's a ring,' said Daniel. He and Harvey had talked about it over the last couple of days. Their grandma had left a vintage ornate floral-design ring with bead-set diamonds to their mum and she'd never got around to resizing it to wear herself. Instead, she'd kept it for either son if an engagement was ever on the horizon. Harvey had managed to have the ring resized for Melissa, having Tilly ask Melissa to help her decide which dress rings to sell in her shop, giving them the size to work with. She'd fed the information to Harvey, who had pushed on with his plan. The only stumbling block he'd had was asking Daniel if he could use the ring that was always there for either brother. Daniel had appreciated the concern but laughed that he was so way off getting married that if Melissa didn't use it there was a danger of it never living out its full potential. He'd also had to find a jeweller who was willing to do a last-minute alteration and Daniel suspected it had been done so fast the jeweller must surely be someone well and truly caught up in the romance of a Christmas proposal.

And now, beyond the barn doors, Harvey was pushing the ring onto Melissa's finger, their bodies pressed up as close as they could be for it to still be possible. When Harvey kissed Melissa, Lois sighed a romantic sigh that had Barney rolling his eyes and Lucy giggling, her breath creating little puffs of white air Daniel wanted to kiss away.

'You can come in, you lot,' Harvey called out, his eyes not leaving his bride-to-be.

Lucy opened up first and ran to Melissa, to see the ring, to throw her arms around her. Daniel shook hands with his brother, Lois embraced the both of them and so did Barney. These two were special to him and Daniel didn't mind one bit.

'We saw the entire thing,' Lois admitted.

'We know,' Melissa laughed. 'You weren't exactly discreet about it.'

Barney had already turned the volume up on the iPod speaker. He and Lois were obviously on the same wavelength and, her with one hand on his shoulder and the other nestled in his hand, they began to dance. Melissa did the same with Harvey, dancing as though they were the only two people in the barn and hadn't had an audience witness the proposal at all.

Daniel, heart pounding against his chest beneath his coat, looked at Lucy. In jeans and boots, her coat buttoned up to the wine-coloured scarf to keep the chill from her neck, blonde hair curled into big sexy waves and a hint of the cold creating a redness on her cheeks, she looked more beautiful than ever.

'Come on, you two,' Barney encouraged, 'you can't be in here if you're not dancing.' But he was an intuitive man and instead of forcing them together, he came over to take Lucy's coat and put it on the stage before taking her hand to dance. Lois did the same for Daniel and soon they were dancing too, then he danced with Melissa, then it was back to their original partners as though the two warm-up dances had been put on by the others for his and Lucy's benefit. Daniel had never been to one of the Wedding Dress Balls that Barney held. He'd seen people heading in this direction for the village event of the year, and until now he hadn't understood the hype. But he could see it tonight. Even without any crowds the barn held a magical atmosphere. Or perhaps it was him being swept up in the moment, wishful thinking as he looked at Lucy.

Both on the sidelines as the others danced once again, he braved stepping closer to her. 'I don't bite, you know.' For a moment he thought she was going to refuse but, instead, she let him take her hand.

Holding Lucy in his arms was something he'd wanted for a long time but having her so close was going to make it even worse if she wasn't willing to give him a chance. He was supposed to be back at the pub right now offering to walk Lucy home, talking to her with nobody else around. But the plan hadn't unfolded as expected and he was kind of glad it hadn't. He wouldn't have wanted to miss Harvey's big moment and he definitely wouldn't have wanted to miss this dance.

'Can we go somewhere?' he whispered into Lucy's hair as the tune shifted to the next track, a throaty laugh escaping when he realised what his request sounded like. 'I mean to talk.'

She nodded and they quietly grabbed their coats. With Barney and Lois happily dancing and Melissa and Harvey doing the same, they doubted they'd be missed.

'Do you think it'll snow soon?' Lucy asked the minute they were outside the barn. She was nervous, he could tell. And somehow it made him calmer to know he wasn't the only one.

'It's on the forecast tonight. The village is pretty spectacular covered in white, it snowed a couple of Christmases when I was younger.'

'I've seen pictures,' she smiled as she finished buttoning her coat and they passed through the archway and out of Barney's front gate to the road that would lead up and around to The Street.

'What did you think to the proposal?' Bereft of anything else to talk about apart from the serious things weighing on his mind and hanging between the two of them, he went for the easy option.

'It was special, he really took Melissa by surprise. Lois had us girls over for lunch yesterday. The barn was all decorated and Barney said they were trying to envisage what it would be like for winter parties or events. Melissa really had no idea this was on the cards.'

'As far as I know, all that is true. Lois had Harvey put some of the lights on the upper beams days ago. I think that's when the idea started churning around in his head, given how much Barney's place means to both him and Melissa.'

'I think it's a moment she'll remember forever.'

He explained how his brother had been waiting for the right time when Melissa still felt guilty about the man she'd left behind after realising she was still in love with Harvey. 'He was holding out for the perfect moment and I guess tonight he found it.' He gulped. There wasn't going to be any perfect moment for the conversation they needed to have.

So he just had to come out with it.

'I should've been honest with you from the start, Lucy,' he said as they rounded the bend, the pub opposite pumping out a jolly beat for everyone still cosied up inside. The convenience store and Tilly's Bits 'n' Pieces were shut for the night, the tea rooms and bakery up ahead had closed their doors for the last time until after Boxing Day.

She made a sound much like an agreement but he wasn't sure and they kept walking on, past the chapel and its nativity out front, past the track that led down to the water's edge, past the ice-creamery.

He stopped her before they could reach her place. If he didn't say all of this now, he'd chicken out, and perhaps a bit of Harvey's bravery tonight might well be rubbing off on him. 'Lucy, I'm sorry I didn't tell you everything about me when we met. I'm sorry I didn't tell you about how much trouble I got in, the risks I took and the life I'd led after I left the village.'

'If you had, I'd have run a mile,' she smiled.

He hadn't expected that and appreciated her trying to make

him feel better. 'Maybe. But I should've talked to you when we started to become friends, there's no excuse for that.'

'Do you remember that day in my workshop when you saw a picture of Julian and me?'

'The one in the snow globe? I do.'

'I told you he was my ex-husband, so why didn't you tell me then about Giselle? It would've been the perfect time.'

'I honestly – and I'm not lying when I say this – I didn't think about it. We were talking about you and the pretence you had to go along with, that was all I had in my head. I guess over time I've blocked out talking about any of my past and maybe subconsciously I didn't want to tell you and trigger more questions about my life before I'd come back to Heritage Cove.'

She waited a while to let his explanation settle. 'You seem to be getting somewhere with Harvey.'

'After you set us up, you mean? We've both said and done things we regret, and those actions and behaviours were ingrained in us for so long that we never moved past it. We're doing all right at the moment – a long way to go, but it's a start.'

'I'm pleased for you. And I'm pleased for your mum too. You're not angry with Melissa and me?'

He stopped her as they reached her place, his hand on her arm. 'Lucy, I could never be angry with you. And both of us should be thanking you – we weren't managing to get anywhere on our own. If you hadn't stepped in then we might well have gone on for months, forever even, without either one of us backing down.'

'Harvey is known for being stubborn.'

'It runs in the family.'

She pulled a face. 'Can we please keep walking? It's freezing out here, and I left my gloves at home. Knew I'd lose them at the pub otherwise.'

Not only did she want to keep on walking rather than run up to her flat or flee into her workshop, she was talking to him. He hadn't realised how tense he'd become until now.

They stood by the tree a moment, close enough to admire the decorations and the feel of the pine needles Lucy couldn't resist touching, and they made their way up to the shack, all closed for the night.

They sat on the bench he'd put on the veranda for the lucky customers who got there first with their hot waffles to sit and admire the tree that everyone in the village was sure to miss when it came down in the new year.

'This is a wonderful location.' Lucy finally looked as though she was relaxing in his company. He hoped so, at least. 'Melissa tells me that although the beach shop was good when she was a kid, this waffle shack is way better.'

'I'm hoping locals stay as enthusiastic even when the new-year diets kick in.'

She laughed. 'You must have some healthier versions. Okay, maybe not too many. And if I was coming here I'd want to have exactly what I fancied, as sinful as it might be.'

'You're planning on coming here again?'

After an awkward silence she told him she'd come here last night. 'You were really busy, I didn't come in.'

'It's been getting busier and busier since opening.' And then it dawned on him. 'You saw Giselle here,' he said. 'You realise we're not together, don't you?'

'I do, but whoever that little boy is, I don't want to be the one to break his heart.'

He rubbed his hands together to keep them warm. He hadn't thought to bring gloves either. That was the problem with rushing here, there and everywhere – you forgot the simple things. 'You won't break his heart, Lucy. Peter isn't my child, but I have been in his life since he was born. He's important to me, but my relationship with Giselle is only friendship.

'This is all so hard to explain. Probably why I shied away from doing it when we first met.' He wasn't sure where to start. There was so much to say. Did he start with Giselle and Peter? Did he start with how his life spiralled out of control?

Her voice came out softly. 'People keep telling me I should hear you out and give you a chance to tell your side of the story.'

He leaned back against the wood of the shack. 'I like how people help around here but sometimes I'd like to block them out so that all that matters are the people actually involved in a situation.'

'Yeah, and how did that work out for you and Harvey?'

'Good point.' He stood up. It was time to get to the enormous elephant not in the room but doing a dance all around him outside the Little Waffle Shack. He couldn't look at Lucy when he said half of this so with her on the bench, him leaning against the rail of the veranda looking at the Christmas tree full of light, cheer and hope, he started at the beginning.

Daniel recalled details of his childhood, the dad who was a bully and who didn't show a whole lot of love to his sons, the way he'd rebelled whenever he could, cocooning himself in his own world and not letting anyone, including his brother, in. He told her how he'd left the Cove in the end, unable to stand it any longer. It had been better to have nowhere to live than stay under the same roof as a man he detested and resented. He told Lucy about some of the petty crimes he was ashamed of, the apologies he'd been making since he came back to the village, and he explained how he'd helped Giselle one day and she'd literally taken him in and given him more than anyone else had in years.

'She and Peter will always be in my life, but please believe me when I say it's friendship with Giselle.'

'I believe you,' she said.

He sat down again and this time he recounted the same story he'd told Harvey. He spoke about Peter's fall and his injury, how they couldn't get help, how he'd got in the car to drive Peter to the hospital and the police chase had him put his foot down even more, the charges that had been brought on him. 'That night I couldn't see or hear anything other than Giselle in the rear-view mirror screaming that Peter had stopped breathing. The blue lights flashing through the interior of the car made me feel as though we were in another universe and I knew I had to keep going. I screeched around corners, I was double the speed limit in most places, but all I had in my head was getting to the hospital. It was an end goal I couldn't miss.'

He explained his court appearance, the punishment that had taken his circumstances into account. 'I got off lightly in many ways but I was irresponsible that night and it plagued me for a long time. I was in a bad way – the guilt that I could've caused the loss of an innocent life.' He couldn't look at her now, he knew she'd be thinking about her cousin. This was make-or-break time for them. She'd either give him a chance or walk away for good.

'Lucy, I never told you any of this because I didn't know how to, and I was ashamed. That was the worst thing I'd done out of everything. I had nightmares for a long time after, of people dying at my hands because of a decision I'd made. Giselle forced me to look at Peter and realise that he might not be with us any more if I hadn't got behind the wheel. And I had to pull myself together for him and for her. After what she'd done to save me from the streets and from myself I owed her everything. The guilt still eats at me if I let it, thinking about what could've been.

'Harvey told me about your cousin and how she died,' he said when silence was the only thing between them. He turned to look at her and her tears gave her eyes such a sheen of sadness that he had to turn away again. 'Is that why you couldn't look at me or talk to me, when you found out what I'd done?' She didn't answer. 'I guess I didn't make it easy for myself – I didn't give anyone any details and so the gossip that spread and found you was only one side of the story.'

A group of twenty-somethings staggered over full of Christmas cheer and asked if the waffle shack was open. When they declared they had the munchies Daniel suspected they may well have had more than booze. Part of him wanted to shake them and tell them they only got one chance to live a good life, but then again, maybe they had more than he'd had at home at that age and that was the winning formula. Love and support from the right people could dilute the mistakes you made or the dramas that came your way, maybe that was what enabled you to keep on standing.

'Lucy, please say something,' he said when the revellers had gone on their way. 'Yell at me, tell me you hate me and never want to see me again, I don't care what you do, just please talk to me.'

She took a deep breath as the laughter coming from the group faded into the distance. And then she took something from her pocket that was wrapped in white-and-silver Christmas paper and she handed it to him. 'I didn't think I'd see you tonight but I was going to leave this here at the shack for you.' Her voice held steady. 'Open it.'

'It's not a grenade, is it?' he said of the baseball-shaped item he could feel through the wrapping with something akin to a pin at one end.

Lucy's laughter made him want to be as close as they'd been back there in the barn, dancing. 'No, it's not a grenade,' she told him.

He undid the bow, pulled back the paper and when his eyes fell on the cast-iron tortoise he was the one lost for words.

She reached across and turned it over to reveal the secret compartment to hide a spare key. 'You know, in case you lock yourself out. Leave this in the flowerbed or something and—'

But he didn't let her say anything else. He'd put his arm around her, a hand to the back of her hair, and pulled her to him, kissing her the way he'd wanted to for a long time. And if she was going to tell him she didn't want anything to do with him because of his past then he'd save this away in his memory bank and that would have to be enough.

Lucy said nothing when they pulled apart, when his thumb rubbed along her jawbone towards her bottom lip. And this time it was her who moved to kiss him. It took him by surprise, took his breath away, and when she climbed onto his lap he began to laugh. 'Is this your way of letting me know I have a chance?'

Her lips twisted as she pretended to think. 'There is a condition.'

He didn't want to sound desperate but right now he'd do anything to get back to kissing her. 'Whatever you want, name your price.'

'Make me some waffles, I'm bloody starving.'

He put his hands around her waist and with her legs still wrapped around him, he lifted her up to take her inside the shack.

And it wasn't only waffles on the menu for Christmas Eve.

16

Lucy picked up Shadow as she came out of the bathroom on Christmas morning. It was light already and she'd had a welcome sleep-in after such a late finish. She and Daniel had kissed like a couple of teenagers at the waffle shack and then back here after he walked her home. In the end she'd had to tell him to go home or she'd never get up today ready to head to her parents' for Christmas lunch.

She fed Shadow, cursing as usual when the wonky shelf inside the cupboard where she kept the tinned foods wobbled and stopped the cupboard door from shutting properly. With the cat happy, she put on the tree lights and picked up Tilly's text in reply to the one she'd sent late last night telling her about Daniel. She smiled at the GIF of a kissing couple Tilly had sent along with a request for 'all the juicy gossip' when they met up tomorrow for Boxing Day drinks at the pub.

Lucy opened up the curtains and although last night had been tantalisingly cold with the hint of a white Christmas, she was pretty sure nobody in the Cove had expected it to happen. The forecast had said there was an eighty-per-cent chance of snow but nobody had quite believed it. They would now. The rooftops of the bakery and tea rooms and the bushes at the end of the lane that led behind and down to countryside were covered and it looked just like those photographs she'd seen from years gone by. Daniel had already texted to say Merry Christmas and she took a picture of the snow on The Street before pinging it his way. He responded with a phone call and when he asked whether she could still drive to her parents' today, she told him she'd call him right back. She hadn't even thought about that, her mind filled with Daniel and how it felt to kiss the man she knew her cousin Joanna would love.

She called her parents and the resounding message was do not go on the roads today. There was a possibility if the snow melted over the next few hours that she might make it, but it was thickly layered out there and a quick glance out of the window revealed flakes were still falling down from the heavens above. When her dad fussed that she'd be on her own she reassured him she'd be fine. She wasn't quite ready to share anything about the new man in her life just yet but she told them she'd find somewhere to go and, if no friends were available, there was always the pub.

'Honestly, you've had Benjamin's food, Dad,' she said. 'You know he's talented and I won't go hungry. Why don't you go to the Wallaces' for Christmas lunch, you said they invite you every year?'

'I'm sure they'd welcome us, but I don't want to miss Christmas with our favourite daughter.'

'Dad, I'm your only daughter,' she laughed. 'And the weather means we won't be together so get in touch with them, and have a wonderful time.'

Lucy could hear muffled sounds and she knew her mum was taking the phone from her dad, usually done mid-conversation when her mum felt the exchange wasn't going the way it should. It was always funny, and it was just their way; a bit like how some couples finished sentences for each other, her mum finished phone calls.

'Lucy, are you still there?' her mum chimed down the phone.

You could always rely on her to say that too, as though Lucy might have lost interest and gone off somewhere else. 'Yes, still here, Mum.'

'This snow has taken us all by surprise, are you sure you'll be all right on your own?'

'I won't be on my own, I promise.'

'You could see Tilly, she seems nice. Or that Melissa you talk about. Or—'

'Mum, I can organise myself. Now, you get on the phone to the Wallaces and tell them Christmas-with-the-neighbours is a go.'

'What about your presents? We always open them together.'

'Then we'll do it another day. Let's have a second Christmas. It's a good excuse.' Maybe she'd even take Daniel along and introduce him. The thought of doing that was exciting, a new beginning. They never asked about her love life. They knew she'd had her fill with Julian, but they'd be happy, she was sure of it. Her dad would get out that age-old bottle of scotch he only gave to select visitors, her mum would fuss over him and feed him until he said stop.

'Let me know as soon as you have plans,' her mum insisted. 'And we'll talk again after lunch, I shall want to know whether you've had a proper Christmas meal. This isn't right.'

'Stop worrying.' With the snow falling outside the window, as much as she loved being at her parents' and her mum's delicious roast potatoes cooked in duck fat with just the right ratio of fluffy inside to crunchy outside, she had a sneaky suspicion someone in the Cove might be very happy she was hanging around.

The second she ended the call she phoned Daniel to tell him the news and he didn't even hesitate, he invited her over to the Little Waffle Shack as soon as she was ready.

'We're eating Christmas lunch here?' she asked when he let her in. She'd made her way slowly over, enjoying the bite of cold as snowflakes fell on her cheeks when she looked upwards, the crunch of snow beneath her feet as she trudged across the grass to the shack.

'Call this the pre-lunch gathering,' he said. 'The main event is at Tumbleweed House.' She was already in his arms, neither of them able to keep apart. 'And don't worry, I've got you on the guest list – Melissa and Harvey have enough food to feed most of the village, by the sounds of it.'

In the far corner of the shack Daniel had put a tree decorated in soft white lights with silver baubles and bows on the branches. A table had been pulled into the middle of the main area and low lighting, as well as white lights looped across the windows and the door, gave the whole waffle shack a cosy ambience. In the centre of the table sat a rustic arrangement of snow-dusted greenery and berries displayed in a hessian bag, white square plates were at each setting along with napkins tied off with red-and-white-candy-cane-striped ribbon. 'You look prepared,' Lucy smiled. 'Who's coming here today?'

'Mum, Harvey and Melissa.'

'Is this the first time—'

'That we've been together properly? Yes. It's been a work in the making. After you and Melissa meddled and got Harvey and me together, my brother and I did a little messing of our own, starting with Harvey's proposal last night. I was supposed to get you talking. Which' – he dipped his head to kiss her on the lips – 'incidentally' – he kissed her again – 'worked out very well.'

'What's the plan for today?' she asked when she caught her breath.

'This is the final part of operation pull-the-Luddingtons-back-together and after that I'm about done.'

Lucy kissed him firmly on the lips. 'I'm glad it's happening. And hearing you talk about your brother is nice too.'

It transpired that Carol was under the impression she was to have waffles here with Daniel and then she'd be going on to lunch at Harvey's before returning here in the evening. The poor woman probably had no idea whether she was coming or going with those arrangements and two sons supposedly still at odds with one another. But Lucy hoped this would be an end to the family angst and it would make her Christmas pretty much perfect.

They were all camped out in the kitchen, where Daniel had a good batch of chocolate-peppermint batter on standby to serve their mum her favourite kind of waffles, when Carol arrived and Daniel had to break away from debating what shape they should cook them in and go out to welcome her. Lucy could hear their voices and made a thumbs-up to Harvey that their plan was intact. She heard Daniel offer to pour Carol a glass of champagne, they talked about the magic of the snow, and it was when she asked about the place settings at the table that he told her he and his brother had talked.

Lucy heard the wobble in Carol's voice. They'd agreed they'd wait in the kitchen to give the poor woman some time to get her head around this, her emotions probably on a roller-coaster ride that might take a while to come to a standstill. Harvey was out next and Melissa dried her eyes when she heard tears from her soon-to-be mother-in-law. And when Harvey finally called them through and the girls came out from hiding, Daniel put his arm around Lucy.

'Mum, I have more news. Lucy and I are together.'

'Well, I can see that,' she said, drying her eyes. 'And it's about time – any fool could see you two were keen on one another.' She hugged Daniel and whispered something in his ear before giving Lucy a hug. 'I'm pleased for you both.' And she gripped both of Lucy's hands in a gesture that said she was happy Lucy was in her son's life.

'There's something else,' said Harvey.

'I don't think I can take many more surprises today,' Carol laughed. 'Do I need more champagne for this?'

Melissa and Harvey were sandwiched together, Melissa with her left hand splayed against Harvey's chest until finally Carol noticed the gleaming diamond ring and realised what it meant.

'She said yes.' Harvey's pride was mainly for Melissa but a tiny bit had been reserved for the reunion with his brother when he looked across at him and they exchanged a nod of approval. Quite what it was about Lucy wasn't sure, but they needed these little moments between them. They had a rocky foundation but in time there was no reason it couldn't be smoothed over.

Lucy headed out to the kitchen to give the family some time to come to grips with their emotions. She was busy thinking which shape of waffles she'd go for when Daniel came to join her.

'Why are you hiding?' He stood behind her and wrapped his arms around her waist.

She was going to enjoy this just-in-a-relationship phase where they couldn't keep their hands off one another. She hoped it lasted a long while. 'I'm not hiding, I'm giving your mum some time with her boys, some time to adjust.'

'After we put her through the mill, you mean.'

'Something like that.'

'She's fine, she's on her second glass of champagne so it's calming her nerves,' he smiled. 'I have something for you.'

'You do?'

With a grin he reached into the drawer beside the fridge and took out an envelope. 'Open it.'

And when she did, she laughed. It was a photograph of him with a toolbelt and no top on, the muscle definition something she was pretty sure she'd get to see for herself soon enough. 'I know you've got a nice body but this is a bit I-love-myself, don't you think?'

'My gift to you – because I got no warning we were exchanging presents this year, given you weren't speaking to me – is me and my toolbelt. I've got plenty of contacts, I'll get you a good deal and my present is to fit a new kitchen for you whenever you're ready. I've got a few hidden talents to show you yet.'

She put her arms around his neck and kissed him. 'As long as I get to see you in this toolbelt for real, looking exactly like you do in this picture, then you've got yourself a deal.'

Melissa called through asking when they could have the waffles, Carol declared they had to be heart-shaped and Harvey shouted to his brother to ask if he wanted a beer instead of champagne.

Daniel put the waffle maker on to warm up, Lucy got the batter from the fridge and Melissa came through to get the chocolate curls and whipped cream to set on the side of them.

As a family put back together with some extras added on, all five of them sat inside the Little Waffle Shack, the snow falling once again beyond the windows and cocooning them in their own winter wonderland for now. Lucy sent Fred Gilbertson, previous owner of the blacksmith's, a Merry Christmas message. She'd sent him a card of course but this was another thank you because he'd given her more than a new business to take over, he'd given her a completely different life.

When Melissa, Harvey and Carol made their way to Tumbleweed House to get things organised for the big Christmas lunch today, Daniel and Lucy hung back for some alone time they were both craving, under the guise of double-checking everything was as it should be at the waffle shack before they left.

They sat outside on the bench in each other's arms, Lucy's head resting on Daniel's shoulder. 'I'm glad you told me everything,' she said.

'I'm glad you're giving me a chance to prove myself to you.'

She looked up at him. 'There's no need to prove yourself – at least, no need to try. Just be yourself, that's all I ask.'

'Ditto.'

Her hand on his chest, she remembered something that had happened after Carol arrived at the shack and they'd told her they were together. 'I meant to ask, what did your mum whisper in your ear earlier?'

'She told me to have a shave before I meet my in-laws. I assume I'll get to meet them someday.'

'You certainly will. But do me a favour? Don't shave.' She reached a hand out to trace the stubble on his jaw. 'That look is beyond sexy on you, I don't ever want you to change.'

'I wouldn't want you to change either, Lucy.'

And when he kissed her this time before they made their way from the Little Waffle Shack down past the village Christmas tree, their footprints in the snow going in one direction before a fresh layer could erase all evidence, she knew her future was well and truly here in Heritage Cove.

And it was set to be the best Christmas Lucy had had in a long while.

ACKNOWLEDGMENTS

Firstly I'd like to say a huge thank you to the entire team at Boldwood for offering me a book deal to write new books and bring some of my backlist to even more readers in even more formats. In particular I would like to thank Nia Beynon for the initial chat regarding Boldwood as a publisher and Tara Loder for many lengthy conversations about my series books and next steps. It took a while to work out a way forwards and I'm so pleased to be working with you all.

A very big thank you to Jessica Redland, an amazing author and friend who has found a home with Boldwood and introduced me to the team. Jessica is always generous with her time and her advice and I'm so glad to be a part of the writing tribe known as The Write Romantics who are there for each other along the way. Social media keeps us close and the constant support and encouragement is something I could never imagine being without.

My thanks goes to Katharine Walkden for being a whizz with editing, grammar, and punctuation, as well as spotting potential plot holes. Her care and precision are second to none and she is a pleasure to work with every time. I'd also like to thank Emily Reader for giving the story a final polish to make it sparkle.

Thank you to my husband for encouraging me when I have doubts, for cooking delicious meals during the week, for managing my website and being there as my sounding board when I need to work out plot problems or issues with my characters. I love my job as an author and I know how incredibly lucky I am to have his unwavering support.

And finally, to my readers... an enormous thank you for buying this book. I hope it was a pleasure to read and that you continue to enjoy the series!

MORE FROM HELEN ROLFE

We hope you enjoyed reading *Christmas at the Little Waffle Shack*. If you did, please leave a review.

If you'd like to gift a copy, this book is also available as an ebook, digital audio download and audiobook CD.

Sign up to Helen Rolfe's mailing list for news, competitions and updates on future books.

https://bit.ly/HelenRolfeNews

Summer at the Twist and Turn Bakery, the next in the Heritage Cove series, is available to order now.

ABOUT THE AUTHOR

Helen Rolfe is the author of many bestselling contemporary women's fiction titles, set in different locations from the Cotswolds to New York. She lives in Hertfordshire with her husband and children.

Follow Helen on social media:

 twitter.com/hjrolfe

facebook.com/helenjrolfewriter

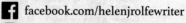 instagram.com/helen_j_rolfe

Boldwood

Boldwood Books is an award-winning fiction publishing company seeking out the best stories from around the world.

Find out more at www.boldwoodbooks.com

Join our reader community for brilliant books, competitions and offers!

Follow us
@BoldwoodBooks
@BookandTonic

Sign up to our weekly deals newsletter

https://bit.ly/BoldwoodBNewsletter